In him was life, and that life was the light of all mankind.
The light shines in the darkness, and
the darkness has not overcome it.

—John 1:4–5 (NIV)

MYSTERIES OF COBBLE HILL FARM

Digging Up Secrets
Hide and Seek
Into Thin Air
Three Dog Knight
Show Stopper
A Little Bird Told Me
The Christmas Camel Caper

MYSTERIES OF COBBLE HILL FARM

The Christmas Camel Caper

JANE WILLAN

Guideposts

Mysteries of Cobble Hill Farm is a trademark of Guideposts.

Published by Guideposts
100 Reserve Road, Suite E200, Danbury, CT 06810
Guideposts.org

Cover and interior design by Müllerhaus
Cover illustration by Bob Kayganich at Illustration Online LLC.
Typeset by Aptara, Inc.

ISBN 978-1-961251-94-6 (hardcover)
ISBN 978-1-961251-95-3 (softcover)
ISBN 978-1-961251-96-0 (epub)

Printed and bound in the United States of America
10 9 8 7 6 5 4 3 2 1

MYSTERIES OF COBBLE HILL FARM

The Christmas Camel Caper

GLOSSARY OF UK TERMS

biscuit • cookie

Bob's your uncle • "and there it is" or "there you have it" or "it's done"

cheery-bye • goodbye

croft • a small farm

crofter • a farmer of a small farm

cuppa • cup of a hot beverage, usually tea

jumper • sweater, usually a pullover

knackered • exhausted, tired

mucking about • messing around

peckish • hungry

ramble • a walk or hike

wellies • Wellington boots

wireless • radio

CHAPTER ONE

There was little Dr. Harriet Bailey loved more than a challenge.

With her medical bag in one hand and a still-warm cranberry pie in the other, she hurried down the cobblestone street toward the White Church Christmas Fair. She was ready to assume her role as the on-duty vet for the live Nativity. The following day was the first Sunday of Advent, the usual weekend for White Church to host the annual event.

Although it wasn't the most direct route, she wound through the village on her way to the church so she could soak in the enchanting atmosphere of White Church Bay at Christmas. Twinkling lights adorned each shop window. Festive music floated from overhead speakers, and the inviting aroma of hot chocolate wafted from the Happy Cup Tearoom and Bakery. She felt as if she had stepped into a scene from Charles Dickens's *A Christmas Carol*.

The church steeple poked up from the far edge of the village with the bay sprawling beyond. She smiled, thinking about the upcoming live Nativity, which promised to be something special. Along with the customary sheep and donkeys, this year's animal selection showcased a new celebrity, a camel named Calvin.

She was glad for the long walk to the church. It gave her time to review her knowledge of camels, which she'd never treated before.

They could drink salt water, their humps stored fat, and their nostrils sealed to prevent sand from flying up their noses. Despite their lumbering appearance, camels could zip along at up to forty miles per hour in short bursts. They also had a sweet tooth. Perhaps a sweet yet healthy Christmas snack would appeal to Calvin. Her dad would get a kick out of her brainstorming produce to share with a camel.

She had said goodbye to her parents the day before, and she already missed them. They flew in from Connecticut to spend Thanksgiving with her at Cobble Hill Farm, the property she'd inherited from her late grandfather. It had been a wonderful time together, but now, all the holiday lights and Christmas cheer made her wish they'd been able to stay.

She paused at the window of Tales and Treasures, a corner shop that sold books and even toys, to collect herself. Amid holiday cookbooks and Advent calendars, a children's book lay open, its pages displaying a radiant star. The inscription beneath read: THE STAR THEY HAD SEEN IN THE EAST GUIDED THEM TO THE PLACE WHERE THE CHILD WAS.

As she admired the artist's depiction of the brilliant star against the night sky, she experienced a moment of clarity. God's light would guide her as it had guided the magi. Resolved to find the spirit and joy of Christmas in White Church Bay despite her parents' absence, she took a deep breath and continued down the street. Time to concentrate on her work.

The live Nativity hummed with activity. Church members, clad in makeshift biblical attire of bathrobes, sandals, and thick socks, were stationed around the stable. A miniature donkey shared the scene with three goats, two sheep, and a beautiful Belgian hare. The baby Jesus gurgled with happiness from the manger under the watchful eyes of Mary and Joseph.

Calvin the camel stood apart from it all, his tall, elegant frame towering over the Bethlehem tableau. Harriet immediately loved his velvety muzzle and large, expressive eyes. He seemed to observe everything with a mixture of curiosity and apprehension. "Hello, you beautiful boy," she greeted him, patting his shaggy neck in an attempt to soothe any nerves he might feel.

Ethan Grimshaw, a skilled farrier she'd met since moving to Yorkshire, approached her with his lanky gait. His tall frame and broad shoulders were complemented by a warm smile that lit his ruggedly handsome face. His sandy-brown hair was worn longer than most men in the village chose to go, giving him a tousled yet charming appearance.

Ethan ran a mobile business from his van, equipped with every tool needed for his trade, offering his services across the region. Though new to the area, he was establishing Yorkshire as his home and business hub. He had reached out to Harriet for client leads, and he was integrating himself into the community's daily life.

Harriet had checked his references and then recommended him to a horse owner nearby. Ethan had soon shown that he was talented and hardworking, and he had already proved a useful connection for Harriet as well. Just last week, he'd crafted special shoes for a Shetland pony with a condition that made it hard to walk, and a few days later, its owner had sent Harriet a video of the pony trotting joyfully around the barnyard.

"How's the big guy doing?" Ethan asked Harriet with a nod to Calvin. Ethan's cheerful voice matched his welcoming smile and warm brown eyes. He immediately came off as approachable, someone to chat with over a cup of coffee or rely on in a pinch. She could see why her clients liked him.

Harriet reached up to scratch behind Calvin's ear. "He's fine, Ethan." She placed a stethoscope against the camel's chest and listened. "His heart rate's a little fast, but nothing to worry about." She coiled the stethoscope and slid it into her bag. "As an equine specialist, are you as intrigued by camels as I am?"

"Not really." Ethan shrugged. "Camels and horses have very little in common, despite being used for the same kinds of tasks in different parts of the world. Besides, since they don't wear shoes, I never work with them."

"Of course," she said. "But they have a similar nobility, don't you think?"

He grinned at her. "Is there any animal in which you don't find a certain nobility?"

"Probably not. I even adore Dottie, Lloyd Throckmorton's armadillo who's been coming to Cobble Hill for a long time."

He laughed. "That's what makes you such a good vet. You can even find beauty in an elderly armadillo." He glanced at his cell phone. "I'm off for an appointment with Lord Miltshire. His chestnut mare threw a shoe, and he wants me to tend to her straightaway."

"Take a piece of my cranberry pie. You'll need something for the drive."

"Thanks for the offer, but I don't have time. Best of luck with the manger menagerie, though."

She watched him navigate through the Nativity crowd, heading for his brightly painted van parked by the parish graveyard entrance.

Emblazoned on the side was Ethan's logo, a stylized anvil and horseshoe alongside the name of his business, Gallop & Forge Farriery Services in bold letters.

Calvin stamped his front feet, as if demanding Harriet's attention.

"Calm down, my friend," she told him. "It's going to be a long day. Save your energy."

She checked his water and hay then stood with him until he relaxed, the camel's eyes with their long, curled lashes almost closing in the morning sun.

Harriet checked on the other animals then meandered through the churchyard, chatting with an angel who had paired a set of sparkly wings with sneakers, and the actor playing Joseph, who had left the stable to stretch his legs and enjoy a cup of tea.

In the everyday world, "Joseph" was better known as Mark Butler, a local dentist who also directed the White Church youth group. "What do you think of our Bethlehem star?" He pointed to the roof of the manger. The star, a concoction of glitter and sturdy pasteboard, appeared pieced together with an abundance of glue. "Eloise Pennington helped the kids make it," Mark said. "You've met her, haven't you? She's one of White Church Bay's resident artists. She seemed to have a lot of fun making the star and the other decorations with the kids."

"It's very artistic," Harriet replied with a smile. "I've never seen pasteboard quite so resplendent."

The sight of the star with all its glitter reminded her of her grandad's tales of another star—one made of pure silver and encrusted with sapphires. At the beginning of the twentieth century, an anonymous benefactor had gifted it to the village. It was meant to be a symbol of God's light shining in the darkness. Since 1919, villagers had gathered for the midnight Christmas Eve service at White Church, where they watched the star be placed atop the church tree. This year, she would finally witness the tradition herself.

A bellow reverberated through the quiet air, and the tranquil scene exploded. Calvin plunged through the gate of his pen, charged across the churchyard, and paused for a moment in the middle of the road past the church. Nativity participants scattered, a car screeched to a sudden stop, and pedestrians froze, staring. Calvin sniffed the air then swung around and galloped off toward the village center, his padded feet thudding on the cobblestones.

Shouts erupted from the crowd as Calvin raced out of sight, easily outpacing anyone who chased him. He even bumped into a caroler as he passed, sending the man's sheet music flying.

Harriet dashed after him, Pastor Fitzwilliam "Will" Knight on her heels. When they finally caught up with the runaway camel, Calvin stood in Miss Jane Birtwhistle's winter cabbages, his nose buried in a large wicker basket among the frosty cruciferous leaves. He lifted his majestic head to gaze at them as if wondering what all the fuss was about.

She caught a whiff of sweetness in the air, and her eyes landed on the sticky substance at the basket's bottom, the same stuff that coated Calvin's lips. "Figs," she said, grabbing Calvin's halter. "He picked up their scent all the way from the church."

"That's quite the sense of smell you've got there," Will said to Calvin. "It must be your superpower." The pastor of White Church was always quick to smile, an honest expression that said he was genuinely glad to see his parishioners. He was easily one of the kindest people Harriet had ever met, a man who walked the walk of his faith and went far beyond simply preaching it from the pulpit.

"Camels have a keen sense of smell and can sniff out food from great distances. It's an ability that helps them survive in the desert." She led Calvin out of the cabbages. "It's natural that he likes figs, as camels often enjoy sweets."

"Not just figs," Will said. He picked up the basket and peered inside. "Figgy pudding."

"How do you know?"

"Because I know a good figgy pudding when I meet one, even if it's been half devoured by a greedy camel. And I believe your aunt Jinny's award-winning figgy pudding went missing this morning from the Christmas fair."

Harriet's aunt, Dr. Jinny Garrett, lived in the dower cottage at Cobble Hill Farm. Getting to be so close to her was one of Harriet's favorite things about her move to Yorkshire.

"How would Aunt Jinny's figgy pudding end up in a basket in Jane Birtwhistle's cabbages?"

Will shrugged. "Stranger things have happened at the Christmas fair."

"Like what?" They fell into step as they headed back to the live Nativity, Calvin in tow.

"Well, there was the great glitter bomb incident a few years ago, and who could forget the eggnog fountain fiasco the year before that?"

She laughed. "So what will future generations call today's excitement?"

"How about 'The Christmas Camel Caper'?"

As she laughed with him, it hit her again how much she really liked Will. He was funny, genuinely kind, and so easy to talk to. Sharing a laugh with him felt like the most natural thing in the world. And she had to admit he was attractive. Feeling her cheeks warm, she focused on adjusting Calvin's halter to hide her blush. She didn't know what Will felt for her—if anything. And she wasn't ready to show her feelings yet, especially since they were so new.

When they returned to the church with the wayward camel in tow, Will headed off to check in with other participants of the fair. She guided Calvin back into his pen, reflecting that he was probably ready for a long nap after his adventure and snack.

Once she had him settled, she checked the gate. The latch hadn't been broken. Calvin must have bumped it just right with his substantial nose. She secured the latch then wrapped it with several layers of medical tape from her bag to prevent Calvin from escaping again. She left him dozing then checked the other animals again.

A sharp cry of alarm sliced the air. Will stood rooted to the spot on the front steps of the church. "It's gone!" he shouted. "The silver Christmas star is gone!"

CHAPTER TWO

Will's alarm silenced the lively chatter, drawing all eyes to him. Detective Constable Van Worthington sprinted toward the church, his blue bathrobe flapping.

Harriet checked on her four-legged charges to make sure they hadn't been too disturbed by the commotion then raced after Van. She took the church steps two at a time and hurried through the front door and down the long hall to the library, drawn by the voices she heard within.

Will and Van huddled in the center of the room, surrounded by bookshelves and tables with reading lamps.

Harriet scanned the room, surprised to see it in disarray. A lamp knocked over, books scattered across the floor, dirt spilled from a toppled potted plant. But what caught her eye was the small antique safe sitting on a shelf with the door open. Empty.

"Harriet, thank goodness you're here," Will said.

"What can I do?" she asked, surprised by the relief on his face at her appearance.

"Could you search for Cocoa?" he asked. "I brought her into the church so she'd have more room to roam while I was busy with the fair. I thought she'd be too lonely in the parsonage, but I also didn't think about how people might be going in and out of the church. I worry that she got out, and she's an indoor cat. I'd search for her myself, but Van needs me here."

Will was cat-sitting for a friend from seminary who had moved to a Whitby parish. Once the friend got his new place sorted, he would retrieve Cocoa, a Havana Brown female with a rich mahogany coat and bright green eyes.

"No problem." Cocoa had likely either hidden or fled when the intruder broke in, alarmed by the noisy stranger. Or she might have slipped out through a door someone opened without realizing she was there. "I'll call Aunt Jinny to help. We'll check inside the church first to make sure she's not hiding somewhere."

"Sounds good," Will said. "Thank you so much."

"Of course." Harriet left the library, her phone already to her ear.

Aunt Jinny met her inside the front door a few moments later, and together they searched every corner, closet, and cupboard of the church's three floors. But they found no cat, so they headed back to the library.

"No sign of Cocoa yet," she told Will.

Will ran a hand through his brown hair, his jaw tight. "This is all bad enough without losing my friend's cat."

"We'll find her," she assured him. "I'll put out some fragrant canned cat food. She'll be home before teatime."

He nodded, but the tension around his eyes didn't ease.

"You kept that safe locked, right?" Van asked from where he crouched on the floor, examining the rug.

"Always." Will's hazel eyes, usually warm and laughing, were clouded with worry. "What a disaster. The Christmas star is one of a kind—handcrafted silver, embedded with sapphires. It's over a century old."

"Tomorrow is already the first of December," Aunt Jinny added. "Which means that Christmas Eve is mere weeks away. I can't imagine the candlelight service without the silver star."

"Me neither. We'll find it." But Will's tone wasn't as confident as he probably wished.

"When was the last time you saw it?" Van asked.

"This morning. I took it out to polish it."

"Why this morning?"

"Why not this morning?" Will caught himself and took a breath. "Sorry. I didn't want to leave it till the last minute. Last year I remembered that it had to be polished about an hour before the Christmas Eve service, which added more stress to an already stressful evening. The fair today made me think of it."

"And you're sure you locked the safe when you put it back?"

Will's face tightened, as if he was holding in a storm of frustration. "Yes. I locked it."

Van slowly rose to his feet. "Who knows the combination to the safe?"

"Other than me?" Will asked. "Only Claire Marshall, who works in the church office."

"I'd like to talk to her," Van replied, plucking a pen from a nearby table and scribbling on a bulletin from last week's service. Apparently, he didn't have his usual police gear on him in his shepherd's costume.

"She's on holiday with Russell and the children. Been gone all week," Harriet told Van. Claire had gone to the Peak District, a family friendly winter destination near Yorkshire. Over the past few months, Harriet and Claire had become friends, and Harriet had helped plan the trip while sipping tea at Claire's kitchen table.

"Does she keep the combination somewhere that you know of? Like in her desk?" Van asked.

"Yes," Will replied. "Follow me."

They trailed Will to Claire's office and watched him drop to his hands and knees and crawl under her desk—a tight fit for the six-foot pastor, but he managed. A moment later, he scooted back out and got to his feet. "Here you go." He handed a slip of paper to Van. "She taped it underneath the middle drawer."

"Well, Bob's your uncle," Van said. He held the page up to the light.

"Who else knew it was under the desk drawer besides Claire?" Harriet asked.

"No one," Will said. He hesitated then added, as if to himself, "Absolutely no one."

"Except for you," she pointed out.

"Goodness, Harriet, you can't think Will had anything to do with this," Aunt Jinny scolded.

"Of course not," she replied. "No one could ever think that of Will. I'm simply stating facts."

"She's right," Will said. "It's like that old quote from Sherlock Holmes says. 'Once you eliminate the impossible, whatever remains, no matter how improbable, must be the truth.' We have to examine what we know and weed out the impossible until we figure out what happened."

"Exactly," Harriet agreed. "But I would hope we can eliminate you and Claire right from the get-go."

"I would hope so too," Will said. "Claire is as honest as the day is long. Plus, as you just said, she's out of town."

"Who else has access to her office?" Van asked.

"Just about everyone in the congregation. The knitting circle, the board of deacons, the youth leader. The youth group had an overnight event at the church a few days ago. They probably explored every room."

"You don't lock the office?" Harriet was forever amazed by the trusting nature of the residents of White Church Bay.

"Well, no." Will appeared startled, as if the idea had never occurred to him. "What if someone needs to get in for something?"

"What would they need?" Van asked.

Will shrugged. "Could be anything—an extra hymnal, a Bible study book. The youth group stashes their bocce balls here." He gestured to the pile in a corner of the room.

"Have you found any other clues?" Harriet asked.

"Not yet," Van said. "And nothing else seems to be missing, other than the star."

"And Cocoa," she added.

"Indeed." Van tucked the bulletin he'd made notes on into his pants pocket under his robe. "I need to get to the station so I can make a report and bring my superiors in on the case." As small as White Church Bay was, Van didn't have the resources to handle major crimes alone. He often had to bring in colleagues from county headquarters.

"That's it?" Will asked, surprise in his voice.

"I'll be back. Don't fret." The door closed behind him. Without the detective constable's solid presence, the room felt cold and strangely empty. The sweet notes of "Brightest and Best" drifted down from the carillon in the steeple.

"That's the hymn we sing when we put the silver star on top of the church tree," Aunt Jinny murmured. "Every Christmas Eve."

"So it is," Will replied, his voice flat.

Harriet met Will's gaze then Aunt Jinny's. "Don't lose hope. We'll find both of them—Cocoa and the Christmas star."

CHAPTER THREE

"You look knackered," Aunt Jinny said. She stood at the table, pouring steaming herbal chai tea into festive red-and-green mugs. The sun had sunk toward the horizon, and with twilight came a wintry chill.

"I am." Harriet shrugged off her parka and hung it on a peg by the door. She stepped out of her wellies, as the locals called Wellington boots, feeling the warmth of being back indoors. Aunt Jinny's kitchen always wrapped her in an instant cloak of comfort. Wooden beams crisscrossed the ceiling, copper pots hung on the walls, and a low fire burned in the grate. She could still detect a figgy pudding cinnamon-and-nutmeg aroma from the morning's baking. She smiled to herself, remembering the fate of that pudding—in a camel's stomach.

"Did something else happen after I left?" her aunt asked.

"Not at the fair. But right after we closed down the live Nativity and coaxed Calvin into his trailer for the ride home, I got an emergency call for the clinic." She slid into a chair at the kitchen table. "Darcy Callaghan's ginger cat had some gastrointestinal distress and was drooling a lot."

"What happened?"

Harriet always enjoyed the exchange of medical insights with Aunt Jinny. Especially since they came from both sides of the animal kingdom—two-legged and four. "Holiday hazard. The cat snacked on Darcy's fresh poinsettia from the Christmas fair."

"Will she be all right?"

"Definitely. Poinsettia leaves aren't a cat's best friend but neither are they deadly." She made a mental note to draft a handout for her waiting room on pet-proofing during the holidays. Poinsettias, holly berries, and mistletoe were frequent yuletide decorations and could present problems for pets if ingested.

"A runaway camel, a disappearing church heirloom, a missing pet, and then a veterinary emergency—you've had quite the day. You need tea and biscuits. Doctor's orders." Aunt Jinny slid a plate toward her. "All I had to deal with was an impressive hot chocolate spill in the parish hall."

Harriet grinned. "I didn't hear about a hot chocolate disaster on this evening's news." She still found it odd to call cookies "biscuits," particularly when it came to Aunt Jinny's Viennese whirls. They were light, buttery sandwich cookies filled with jam and cream. She took a bite and hummed as it melted in her mouth.

"I'm surprised. It took most of the kitchen crew to clean it up," Aunt Jinny replied, selecting a biscuit for herself. "No matter how many years we do the Christmas fair, it never seems to go as planned. Which I suppose shouldn't be a surprise at this point, especially when we added a live Nativity menagerie. Animals always add an element of the unexpected, though I never would have guessed how much."

"Imagine if we hadn't recaptured Calvin." A camel galloping wild across the Yorkshire moors was a terrifying thought. Next to it, the image of a cat on the lam seemed almost trivial. They had searched for Cocoa for hours, until Harriet was able to convince Will that even indoor cats knew how to take care of themselves, and he would more than likely find Cocoa on the doorstep in the morning.

"Any clue how he escaped?"

"Camels are super smart. He might have mastered the art of unlatching his own gate or even done it by accident," Harriet suggested.

"Do you think he could smell the figgy pudding?"

"I'm certain that's what drew him down the street. Probably what made him break free and head to Jane's in the first place."

"But how on earth did my pudding end up in her kitchen garden?"

"I can only think of one way. Someone put it there." She took a sip of tea. "On purpose."

"What purpose?"

"To lure Calvin away. Anyone who knows camels also knows they love sweets."

Aunt Jinny raised an eyebrow at her. "You don't think that's a bit of a leap?"

"It sounds crazy to me too, but can you come up with a better explanation? It's not as if your figgy pudding could have gotten up and walked there on its own." Harriet bit into another Viennese whirl, savoring its buttery sweetness.

"And Jane knew nothing about it?"

"She said she was in the parish hall since early morning setting up for the fair. And to quote her, 'I've no time for gallivanting around and planting figgy puddings in my garden.'"

Aunt Jinny laughed. "So, Calvin sniffs out a basket of figgy pudding, opens his pen, and runs to it. Then, while half the village chases after him, the Christmas star disappears?"

"Quite a coincidence, don't you think?"

"I don't believe in coincidence."

"Me neither." She sat for a moment, thinking. "We're both scientists, right? So, let's be scientific. The convergence of events, with applied logic and reason, points to one conclusion."

"Which is?" Aunt Jinny poured more tea into their Christmas mugs.

"That the pudding was put there deliberately by a person with a plan, who has a working knowledge of camels, their preferences, and their abilities. This person is also familiar with the church and knew where the combination was hidden."

"That can't be a wide pool of people," Aunt Jinny mused. "And yet, for the life of me, I can't think of anyone who fits all those criteria."

"Neither can I," Harriet admitted. "But I am sad about the star. From what Grandad told me, I know how much it means to the church and the village."

"Every Christmas Eve, for as long as I can remember, the whole family packed into a pew at White Church to see the Christmas star placed on the tree," Aunt Jinny murmured. "That star is a tradition that has endured since 1919—until maybe this Christmas. It would break your grandad's heart."

"I've always wanted to experience the star placement for myself."

"The star represents light overcoming darkness, and hope in the midst of despair," Aunt Jinny said. "The people of White Church Bay have taken inspiration from it for years."

"Maybe Van will find the thief."

"Van Worthington is a first-rate lad, and a good detective. But even a professional like him might need a little help."

Harriet ignored her aunt's implication. She had been drawn into several mysteries since her move to White Church Bay, but she intended to sit this one out. She changed the subject. "I feel for Will. It's a terrible loss to the church."

"You seem to have made a fast friend in Pastor Will Knight." Aunt Jinny peered at her over her mug.

Harriet should have known better than to mention the pastor to her would-be matchmaker of an aunt. "Of course. Will's a great guy."

Her cell phone buzzed, and she scooped it up, grateful for the distraction. It was a text from a client, asking about Harriet's upcoming rabbit care workshop. She also had a message from a pet store in Whitby, asking her advice on a shipment of tropical fish that had arrived looking "droopy." She needed to call the pet store owner. Slipping her phone into her pocket, she finished her tea and then stood. "I'm sorry, but I have to get going."

"Why don't you team up with him?" Aunt Jinny asked, her tone light.

Harriet had forgotten what they'd been discussing, her mind already churning with possible fish problems. "Team up with who?"

"Will."

"For what?" She shrugged into her parka, mentally reviewing the location of her grandfather's cache of veterinary books on fish.

"To find the star, of course." Her aunt's voice had taken on an expectant, upbeat tone. "You talk to half the village with your vet work, and as a pastor, Will talks with the other half. The two of you would be unstoppable. Together you could figure out who stole the star and get it back in time for Christmas Eve."

Harriet massaged her temples. "The clinic's swamped, and I haven't even started my Christmas shopping." She shoved her feet into her wellies. "Taking on a hunt for the Christmas star? It's hard to see how I could fit that in, especially when I've never actually seen it to know what I'm searching for. I'd rather leave it to the professionals."

"Do it for your grandad."

The weight of her grandfather's legacy already pressed on her shoulders. Taking over his vet practice was both a dream come true and a daunting challenge. She struggled daily with the responsibility.

"Listen, Aunt Jinny, I get why the star matters to the church and the village. I do. But—"

"It's not just the village. It matters to us, the Baileys. That star is part of our family's story." Aunt Jinny crossed the room to a small cabinet. When she returned, she held a slender leather-bound book, its cover worn with age. "I want you to read this." She handed it to Harriet.

The leather cover had seen better days. Scuffed at the edges and faded, it had a tarnished brass lock on the front. A tiny key dangled at the end of a delicate chain attached to the book's spine. Engraved in the leather at the bottom right corner were the initials *LJB*. It looked like something found in a cozy secondhand shop. She glanced up. "Who is LJB?"

"Letitia Joy Bailey, née Baxter. She's your great-grandmother. My dad's mother. This is a journal she started when she was nine years old, back in 1919." She paused, as if choosing her words carefully. "But there's one important thing you need to understand before you read it. The information in here is a secret. No one else in the village knows about it, and it must stay that way. This story is ours and ours alone."

"Ours?"

"You'll understand when you read it."

The journal lay in her lap.

Snuggled into thick woolen socks and an old fisherman-knit sweater, Harriet was curled up in the reading nook of Grandad's study. The clock on the mantel chimed a late hour, and bright moonlight cast an ethereal glow on the garden outside the window. What a long day it had been with Calvin, the star, and Aunt Jinny's challenge, among other things.

She had left Aunt Jinny's cottage determined to go home and straight to bed. But the journal had called to her. Picking up the leather-bound volume, its cover smooth in her hands, she inhaled the scent of old paper and ink. An electronic tablet was fine, but nothing compared to the tangible magic of an actual book.

She opened to the first page and began to read.

CHAPTER FOUR

White Church Bay
December 1919

Letty pulled her thick scarf tighter around her neck to ward off the chilly breeze. She wore a matching hat, knitted by her mother in her favorite shade of rich purple. It reminded her of summer heather on the moors. She tugged the ends of her blond braids free of the scarf and tossed them over her shoulders. The late afternoon sun cast a weak light across the sweeping landscape. Usually, the moors were a source of joy for Letty, the gently rolling hills her playground. But today she didn't feel like playing.

From where she stood on top of a small rise, she could see the cottage on her family's croft. Smoke trailed from the chimney, always a welcoming invitation of warmth in the chilly air. But today, there was nothing warm or welcoming in that small house. Her younger brother, Albie—named after King Albert—lay in his bed, fighting influenza. It was too much for Letty. She had fled the cottage, racing across the meadow and onto the moor.

Albie, with his mischievous blue eyes and blond curls, was Letty's world. He was six years old to her nine, but they shared an unbreakable bond. She had taken on the role of Albie's protector while her mother tended to their growing family. She had taught Albie to count, sing the alphabet, and play hopscotch, using a stick to scratch a pattern of squares in the packed dirt of the farmyard. Albie's laughter and shouts while jumping from square to square echoed in Letty's mind.

But a week ago, his laughter had stopped. Influenza had gripped him with a suddenness that terrified her. Overnight, Albie had gone from running on the moor to shivering uncontrollably with fever. He lay, still and pale, moving in and out of consciousness.

The worst part was that she couldn't be with him. Every day, she begged to visit him, but only her mother was allowed in his room. The thought of him missing her as much as she missed him filled her with anxiety.

She walked across the moor, lost in her thoughts, when her boot nudged something and a flash of color caught her eye. She bent, brushed away the snow, and discovered a group of turkey tail mushrooms. They spread out in fan shapes, their stripes darker in the middle and growing lighter toward the edges.

Letty imagined taking these to Albie, how his eyes would light up when he saw them. Despite the cold, a warm feeling filled her. She carefully picked a few and made her way home.

"For Albie," she told her mother, holding up the mushrooms.

"Get your tea," her mother replied. "You're cold through."

"I want to give them to him. He loves hunting for these."

"No, love. I'm sorry." Her mother brushed back a strand of hair.

Letty saw the dark circles under her mother's eyes and the slump to her shoulders. "I'll stand in the doorway. He misses me. I know he does. I can feel it."

Her mother shook her head. "It's too much of a risk."

"How long until he's better?" Letty's voice trembled.

Her mother wiped away tears and moved to Albie's bedroom without replying. Letty heard the click of the handle as the door closed.

She sank into a chair at the kitchen table. Her mother's silence had told her too much. Albie would never run across the moor with her again. Never play hopscotch or tag or cat's cradle. Never go with her to their secret place.

Albie was going to die.

Covering her face with her hands, she sobbed into the stillness of the room.

Letty trudged alone across the moor, her wool coat buttoned tightly against the chill. She couldn't believe Albie was gone forever. She thought once that she heard his laugh ringing out across the heather. Another time she thought she saw him standing in the tall grass ahead. But he wasn't there. He never would be again.

A week after the funeral at White Church, her house was still so quiet. Her parents moved more slowly, and it seemed like everything made them more and more unhappy. During the service the pastor had looked as sad as Letty felt. She overheard her mother whisper that he had recently buried his father. When he gave his sermon, his voice cracked with emotion while recalling the village children claimed by influenza. Christmas was only ten days away, and Letty didn't know how they could celebrate it. Finally, feeling she just had to get out of all the sadness, she pulled on her winter coat and headed out to the moor.

As she walked, the cold air nipping at her face, memories flooded back of playing with Albie in these fields just two weeks before, when her world seemed so much simpler. They ran wild, playing hide-and-seek in the tall grass or tag under the wide, open sky. Yet, among all the adventures and games they had on the moor, away from their parents' watchful eyes, the most special were their visits to the secret place.

She crested a sloping hill, and the familiar circle of trees appeared. Tears welled up in her eyes, and she blinked them back. This was her first time coming to the secret place without Albie.

They had stumbled upon it by accident, a hidden opening in a mound of dirt, overgrown with brambles and grass. The cramped space was a tight squeeze for the two of them, even crawling. In the dim light, there was barely enough room for them to kneel without hitting their heads on the low ceiling. The tiny den smelled of damp earth and roots. It was too small to be a proper cave. Albie thought it must be a badger's den. She remembered how excited he had been, with cobwebs clinging to his hair and his eyes bright with their discovery of a secret hideaway.

The real surprise was still to come. Tucked away at the very back of the dark burrow, they found a wooden box. They dragged it outside and brushed it off. The box must have been ancient. It had deep, elaborate carvings on its surface, like something out of a fairy tale. They opened it and found a bundle of faded flannel inside. Letty lifted it out, curious at its heaviness, and slowly unwrapped it.

A brilliant silver star was revealed, perhaps an ornament meant for a Christmas tree. A deep blue stone, bluer than anything she had ever seen, shimmered in its center, with smaller, matching stones sprinkled around the rest of the star.

Letty gently rotated it and spotted a faint engraving on the back, an angel with outstretched wings. She traced the lines of the angel, feeling the texture under her fingers. Even though the day was overcast and gray, the star caught the little bit of sun and scattered points of light around their hiding place. The blue stone in the middle didn't send light out the same way. Instead, it seemed to pull light in, becoming deeper and richer in color.

They rewrapped the star in the flannel, put it back in the box, and returned it to its hiding place. Then they placed the brambles and vines over the burrow's opening again. In the weeks and months to come, they went to the secret place as often as they could. With the star as their silent confidant, they made up stories of kings and queens, of knights going on quests under its magic power, of fairies who danced in its glow. The star was theirs and theirs alone.

She heard the wind whisper as she stood at the opening to the secret place. After pushing aside the brambles, she crawled inside and retrieved the box once more. Sitting on the dried, brown grass in the copse of trees, she opened it, imagining Albie there beside her. She took out the star and hefted its weight in her hands. Through the darkness of Albie's illness and passing, the star's buried light had called to her. In her heart, she knew that the light wasn't meant for her alone.

She knew where it should be.

On Christmas Eve morning, on her way to run an errand in the village for her mother, Letty visited the secret place again. She tucked a note into the wooden box then slid it into her knapsack and walked to White Church Bay, her breath visible in the chilly air.

When she reached the church, she placed the box on the back stoop where she knew Pastor Freeman would discover it. As she left, she whispered a prayer for Albie.

White Church never looked so lovely as on Christmas Eve. It was as if Letty had entered a whole new world—warm, cozy, and filled with the comforting smell of pine and candles.

Sitting beside her was her mother, a reassuring anchor. Farther down the pew, her father and sister shared a whispered conversation.

The space on the other side of her was empty. Albie had always sat next to her in church so she could keep him from fidgeting. If he got too restless, she would entertain him with a tiny doll that she'd made by folding a handkerchief. Tucking her hand into the pocket of her pinafore, she squeezed the doll and blinked back tears. The glittering tree captivated her gaze beside the altar.

But there was no star. Hadn't the pastor found it?

Pastor Freeman stepped into the pulpit. He opened the Bible and read the words that always made her shiver.

"'In the beginning was the Word, and the Word was with God, and the Word was God. The same was in the beginning with God. All things were made by him; and without him, was not anything made that was made. In him was life; and the life was the light of men. And the light shineth in darkness; and the darkness comprehended it not.'"

The dim candlelight made Pastor Freeman's face glow and his brown eyes more intense. He scanned the pews, taking in the farmers, shopkeepers, teachers, children, parents, and grandparents.

"A blessed Christmas to you all," he said, his voice clear and firm. "Tonight is…" He stopped, as if unable to speak. He looked down at the Bible. When he looked up again, his voice had regained its strength. "Tonight is a dark Christmas for many of us in White Church Bay." His gaze rested for a

moment on the empty spot next to Letty, and he gave her the slightest nod.

"I ask you to listen well to a story we all know but that holds special meaning as we face each new day." He read the story of Gabriel appearing to the virgin Mary, announcing that she was to bear a child, the Savior. He told how Joseph had not cast her aside and how they had traveled to Bethlehem for the census.

Letty drank in the words. She loved Pastor Freeman's resonant voice and the beautiful story.

Finally, the pastor closed the Bible. "And upon their arrival in Bethlehem, they found the town filled with travelers. They had no place to stay, as the inns were full. A kind innkeeper, seeing Mary's condition, offered them a humble space in a stable. It was there, amidst the hay and the animals, that Mary gave birth to Jesus. She wrapped Him in swaddling clothes and laid Him in a manger because there was no crib for Him."

A hush fell over the room, as if the congregation waited on the edge of their seats.

"A star, brighter and more resplendent than any other, appeared as night fell. It hovered above the stable, casting a radiant glow over the humble scene. This star was a sign from God, signaling the birth of the Savior, the Light of the world."

He stepped down from the pulpit, his footsteps echoing softly as he crossed to the Christmas tree.

Letty caught her breath as he took a familiar wooden box from under the tree.

He slowly opened it and lifted the star, the flannel cloth falling away. The silver star caught the flicker of nearby candles, just as it had caught the sunlight on the moor. In its center, the deep blue stone shimmered.

"Mercy," her mother whispered. "Sapphires."

The pastor continued, his voice ringing out. "Far away, wise men saw this star and journeyed toward it, guided by its light, bringing with them gifts of gold, frankincense, and myrrh." He lowered the star. "The star led them to the very place where the young child lay, and there they paid homage to Jesus, the King of Kings."

He gazed at his flock. "This very morning, a mysterious box was left on the back stoop of the church. And in that box was this star. Whoever left the star also left a note. It said, 'The light shineth in darkness; and the darkness comprehended it not.'"

It had been the Sunday school lesson the week before. Her teacher said it meant finding hope in hard times. She told the children that no matter what darkness they faced, God's love would always shine through like a star to guide them. Letty had taken those words to heart.

The pastor climbed onto a small stepladder and placed the star atop the Christmas tree. The candlelight struck the silver, and she was certain that the star was as bright as the one that had guided the wise men.

Pastor Freeman secured the star and then stepped down. "Let us stand united and lift our voices in the hymn 'Brightest and Best.' As you sing, recall how a star led the wise men to where our Savior lay and how His light continues to guide us every day of our lives."

The congregation rose as one, and as the organ's music resounded across the pews, their voices lifted in harmony to the ancient hymn.

Letty held the hymnal open but kept her eyes on the star. Albie was gone, and that would never change. But she had shared their star and, with it, the light and warmth of Christmas.

The clock on the mantel struck midnight, its chimes echoing through the room.

Harriet raised her head, surprised. Engrossed in Letty's story, she hadn't noticed the time. Gently closing the journal, her finger lingered on the embossed initials on the worn cover. Her family had kept Letty's secret. The star belonged to the village because of her great-grandmother's selfless act, given as a child grieving for her beloved younger brother.

Her gaze shifted to the photo on the mantel. Her grandparents, young and laughing with their arms wrapped around each other, stood in front of White Church. For the Bailey family, the star exemplified the love and courage that lived within her great-grandmother, as it did the church and village. The star was the cornerstone of Christmas, the light shining in the darkness.

She glanced at the calendar on her phone. December first. Less than four weeks to Christmas. Rising to her feet, she made a promise. She would find the star in time for Christmas Eve—for herself and for Letty.

CHAPTER FIVE

Harriet stepped into the Happy Cup Tearoom and Bakery, the bell over the door chiming a welcome. She desperately needed coffee to kick-start her Monday, almost as much as she needed this conversation with Will. Although they had seen each other at church the day before, they hadn't had a chance for a real talk. They'd made plans to meet up in the morning.

Will sat at a table beside a window, with a steaming cup of tea, absorbed in a thick book. Sunlight streamed in, casting a warm glow on his brown hair with its sprinkling of gray. She liked how he combined a tab collar with a black jacket, jeans, and sneakers.

"Good morning," she said, walking over.

Will stood and held out a chair for her. "Good morning to you."

She shrugged off her coat then slid into the chair, setting her purse on the floor. "How are you?"

"I'm worried." He frowned, and then his face relaxed a bit. "But at least I don't have to worry about Cocoa anymore."

"I was so glad to get your text yesterday. How did you find her?"

He grinned as he resumed his seat. "I was out in the garden right after the service calling her name, and I heard yowling from inside the shed. I opened the door, and there she was. The shed is always tightly shut, so I hadn't even checked it."

"Was she okay?"

"Healthy and happy." Will ran a hand over his face. "Thank goodness. I can't imagine having to tell Justin his cat disappeared. He's collecting her next week."

"Poor Cocoa, shut away without food or heat all night."

"That's the weird part. Whoever put her in the shed left a bowl of water and some kibble. They even made a bed out of a couple of blankets."

"No way." She gaped at him, trying to wrap her head around what he'd said. "Who locks up a cat and then treats it like a guest?"

"A thief with a conscience." Will held up the teapot and raised his eyebrows in a silent question.

"No thanks. I'm holding out for coffee. Late night." She paused for a moment, thinking. "If I had just committed a felony and wanted to get away fast, I wouldn't bother making a cat comfortable."

"Maybe they returned later with the blankets and everything? After everyone had cleared out?"

"But why stick the cat in there in the first place?"

"Cocoa is a house cat," Will said. "To someone who loves cats, there's nothing scarier than a house cat wandering outdoors. That could mean lots of things, but it might mean that the thief is an animal lover. Or at least someone who loves cats."

Harriet continued the theory. "Perhaps Cocoa got out as they were entering, or leaving with the star, and they couldn't put her back in the house without getting caught, so they grabbed her and put her in the shed for safety."

"And then they returned to care for her," Will concluded.

"If it's true, that does give us a better picture of the thief," Harriet mused.

Will waved to a bright-eyed young woman with pink-streaked hair. She wore a vibrant green T-shirt and torn jeans, which made quite the contrast to her navy-blue waitress apron.

"Keri Stone," Will said to Harriet, "is the church's brilliant webmaster. Keri, meet Dr. Harriet Bailey, our brilliant village vet."

"Nice to meet you!" Keri chirped, fishing her cell phone out of her apron pocket. "Fancy a photo for the church website?"

"Sure," Harriet agreed.

Keri framed Will and Harriet in the shot. "Smile! Splendid! Posting now," she said, tapping her phone's screen.

"Thanks to Keri, the church's online presence has tripled," Will said.

"Not a big deal." Keri exchanged her cell phone for her notepad. "I'm trying to convince Pastor Will here to join me for a video. That would really boost online traffic."

"I'll stick to the videos of my sermons on our website," he said with a wry smile.

"And I'll let you. For now." Keri turned to Harriet. "What can I get you?"

"A large dark roast coffee with cream. And a bear claw, to remind me of home."

"Coming right up." Keri bustled away, darting between tables and chatting with customers.

"She has over ten thousand followers," Will said. "Our local internet star."

"Wow. I have a couple dozen, most of them family and friends from the States. Speaking of stars, any news?"

He sobered. "I have a dreadful feeling that it's gone."

"We don't know that. It's been less than forty-eight hours," Harriet reminded him. "Anything from Van?"

"Not a word. I'm sure he's working hard on the case."

"Have you gotten in touch with Claire? Did she mention how someone might know where she hid the combination?"

"I did, and she has no idea."

Keri slid Harriet's coffee and pastry onto the table. "There you go, love," she said. "Pastor Will, more tea?" She placed a small ceramic pot in front of him and scooped up the other one. "Anything else? Maybe a pastry?"

"The bear claw Harriet has looks delicious. I'll take one as well, please."

"No problem." Keri darted away, returned with Will's bear claw, and then was off again.

"I've noticed Keri at church events snapping photos. Where did you find her?" Harriet took a long sip of coffee, and life seemed to flow back into her weary bones.

"She came into the service one Sunday with a camera and a pitch about promoting the church on social media. Next thing I knew, she was our digital evangelist."

"She reminds me of Polly—a wizard with websites and social media." Polly Thatcher was Harriet's assistant at the clinic and, more importantly, she'd become Harriet's closest friend in White Church Bay. Harriet would always be grateful that her grandfather's twentysomething assistant had decided to stay on when Harriet had taken the clinic reins.

Feeling fortified by the coffee and bear claw, Harriet decided to say what was on her mind. "Aunt Jinny thinks you and I should work together to find the star."

"Seriously?"

"Seriously. She thinks that since you know the village through the church and I know it through everyone's pets, we're the perfect ones to search."

"Do you want to search for it?" Will asked.

"I do, but I have my own reasons for that. And I don't want you to feel like you have to do it with me just because my aunt wants you to."

"It's an interesting idea," he mused. "And it's not like Scotland Yard can rush in from London to help us." He stirred his tea and grinned at her. "Why not? I mean, what do we have to lose? May I ask your reasons for investigating?"

"Yes, but first I need you to promise to keep it confidential." She had realized after reading the journal that if she and Will were to work together, she wanted him to know about Letty and Albie. She had asked Aunt Jinny, who agreed. If anyone could keep a secret, Will could.

He nodded. "Confidentiality means everything to me. It's part of being a pastor. You can tell me anything."

"Okay then, here it is." She lowered her voice and told him the whole story. She appreciated how Will listened, giving her his full attention, as if she were the only person in the room. "So, my great-grandmother and her little brother found the star on the moor," she concluded. "And now I feel an obligation to find it. An obligation to my great-grandmother, to Albie, and to Grandad. I can't sit back and do nothing."

"Well, I have my own connection to the star because of its history with White Church. I can't sit back and do nothing either."

"All right then. We're a team."

They clinked their cups together as if in a toast.

She dug through her purse for a notepad and the special pen she had brought. It was a sterling silver fountain pen with a gold nib, a parting gift from her dad when she left for Yorkshire. They both loved fine pens, so using this one made her feel close to him.

She flipped to a fresh page in her notepad. "I say we start with Calvin. Whoever let him out likely either stole the star or was involved. First, how did he escape? The enclosure was secure, the gate latched. Someone must have let him out."

"I thought he lifted the latch with his nose," Will said.

"That was my first suspicion, but I did some research, and it's unlikely. And even if he did, that doesn't explain how the figgy pudding ended up in Jane Birtwhistle's cabbages. I think the most likely scenario is that someone put it there, then let Calvin out."

"Because when he took off, everyone would scatter."

"And no one would notice what might be going on at the church." She pinched off a bit of the bear claw and popped it into her mouth then jotted down what they were thinking. "The church wasn't locked that day, was it?"

"No. Church members needed to be able to go in and out for the fair."

She loved that Will was so trusting and that he always thought about the needs of his parishioners, even if it meant leaving the door unlocked.

Glancing out the window, she saw Miss Jane Birtwhistle herself stroll by, her silver hair neatly pulled into a bun and glasses perched on her nose. A cat lover and longtime client at the clinic, Jane was a familiar sight in the neighborhood.

Harriet refocused on the task at hand. "So we agree that the star was probably stolen during the time Calvin was out."

"Were you near him when he escaped?"

"Not right next to him. I was checking on the other animals."

"So Calvin breaks free and takes off running, causing a commotion. Everyone chases him. We find him enjoying a figgy pudding from a basket in Jane's cabbage patch."

Harriet nodded along, scribbling it down.

"The Christmas-star thief relocated the pudding to lure Calvin away from the Nativity and unlatched the gate of his pen. While we all went on a wild-camel chase, the thief then made off with the star." Will tapped his fingers on the tabletop. "Not to mention the house-cat hotel in the shed. Now that is what I call premeditated."

"Which means that somehow the person knew the location of the safe's combination as well as the star."

"Not to mention the layout of the church," Will added. "In addition to at least a guess that it would be unlocked during the fair."

Harriet felt a chill. "Are we looking at an inside job?"

"You mean by a member of my parish?"

"We can't rule anyone out. We need to examine every angle with no assumptions. For example, what about the custodian? He has knowledge of the church, and since he cleans that room, he might know that the combination was under the desk."

"Amos Charlton?" Will clarified. "It can't be him. He twisted his ankle pruning the fruit tree in his garden. He's barely hobbling around, so he's certainly not stealing stars and locking up cats." Will's face eased into a smile as he glanced at her over his teacup.

"What?"

"A pastor and a vet solving a mystery sounds like a detective series. You be Vera. I'll be Tom Barnaby."

To her consternation, Harriet felt her eyes fill with tears.

"Did I say something wrong?" Will asked.

She made herself smile. "No, of course not. I'm just a little homesick. It's my first Christmas away from my folks, and my mom always binges *Midsomer Murders* while she wraps presents."

He laid a gentle hand over hers. "Being away from home is never easy, and it's especially hard during the holidays."

"That's true. Thanks for understanding. Where's your family?"

"My dad's in Shetland, Scotland. Specifically, an island called Muckle Roe."

Harriet chuckled. "I love that name. Is that where you grew up?"

"No. My mom and dad moved from there to White Church Bay before I was born. I grew up in a cottage on the moors. My dad decided to move back closer to his family after my mum passed."

"What's the population?"

"A booming one hundred and thirty people. Comparatively, White Church Bay is a metropolis." He refilled his teacup from the pot. "Dad's a crofter."

"A what?"

"Crofter. He works a small farm. He loves it there, but it's lonely for him since Mum passed." Will glanced out the window.

"I'm sorry."

He met her gaze, his eyes soft. "Thank you. This will be our tenth Christmas without her."

"You'll be visiting your dad for Christmas then?" She realized once again how lucky she was to still have both parents. She needed to remember that not everyone was so fortunate.

"That's right. I'll leave first thing Christmas morning. Will you be all right?"

"Of course. It's not as if I'm alone. I have Aunt Jinny and her clan. But seeing Mom and Dad over Thanksgiving makes me miss them more now that they've gone back home."

"I know what you mean," he said, his voice kind.

Just then Jane Birtwhistle came into the tearoom and promptly made her way to Will and Harriet's table.

"Jane, how are you?" Harriet asked.

"I'm fine. But Margaret Thatcher is poorly."

Will frowned in confusion.

"Jane has named her last five cats after former prime ministers," Harriet told him.

"Of course." He smiled into his teacup.

"Margaret Thatcher is a new cat, meant to be a companion for Winston Churchill," Jane said. "Though he's yet to warm up to her."

"That may not be a match made in heaven," Will said, his voice serious even as his lips quirked up at the corners.

Harriet looked up at her. "Is Margaret Thatcher showing signs of ear mites again?"

"No, that was Antonia Blair," Jane corrected.

Will choked on his tea. "Antonia?"

"And the ointment you prescribed did the trick, Dr. Bailey. Cleared it up in no time."

"Glad to hear it," she said, and then addressed Will. "Tony Blair turned out to be female. Hence, Antonia. That's one of the reasons Grandad named all his cats Charlie no matter the gender. He said it kept things simple."

"Margaret Thatcher is a lovely calico with the most brilliant green eyes," Jane said to him. "And believe it or not, she fetches like a dog."

"Why don't I come to your place, since I'm already in town?" Harriet suggested. There had been a light dusting of snow, and she thought it might be better to make a quick house call rather than make the elderly woman navigate her way to the clinic.

"I was going to bring Margaret Thatcher to you," Jane said.

"Don't worry about it," Harriet assured her. "I can easily stop by and check on her at your house. It'll save you the trip. Next time, we can see about getting her into the clinic."

"Thank you. I'll have the kettle on. Cheery-bye!" Jane headed toward a table of women Harriet recognized as church ladies.

"That was generous," Will said.

"Well, who wants to be on Margaret Thatcher's bad side?"

He laughed, and she enjoyed the pleasant sound.

"Where were we?" She skimmed the notes she'd made and picked up the fountain pen again. "Let's make a list."

"I love lists. They give the illusion of control."

"I'll take even the illusion of control right now." She meant it. Between the busy clinic, the preparations for the holidays, and the need to find the Christmas star, she was beginning to feel overwhelmed. "Suspects," she said, writing the word at the top of a new page in her notepad. "Let's start with the church crowd, agreed?"

"Reluctantly." Will frowned. "I don't like to suspect any member of my congregation. But there's no denying that they all had means and opportunity, if not motive." He sat back. "There were choir members, hot chocolate servers, Nativity actors, and all the people running booths in the parish hall." As he spoke, he ticked the groups off on his fingers.

"How many altogether?"

"At least fifty. Not to mention all the people from the village who came to the fair."

"Yikes. That's a lot of potential suspects." She wrote quickly then skimmed the list. "Too many. We need another angle to narrow it down."

He finished his tea. "Isn't this the part where Barnaby and Vera revisit the crime scene?"

She glanced at the calendar on her phone. The day was filling up with appointments—a Rouen duck with a foot infection, three annual checkups and vaccinations, a dog with a chronic cough, and now, Jane Birtwhistle's cat. "All right, but I can't be too long."

CHAPTER SIX

"I'm just wondering," she said, standing in the middle of the church library.

"Wondering what?" Will asked.

"I'm wondering if we need to look at this differently." She circled the room, thinking. "Maybe it wasn't just one person who stole the star."

"What makes you say that?"

She pointed to the small green plant that had tipped over and spilled dirt on the floor. "Where was that?"

"On that end table by the lamp."

"And the lamp was also knocked over. Why would that happen if the thief was alone? It wasn't dark—it was the middle of the day. Plenty of light in here to see your way around. Do you think maybe there were two of them and they had some kind of altercation? Maybe they were fighting over the star."

"Or someone came in while the thief was opening the safe and tried to stop him." Will shook his head. "No, that couldn't be right. If that had happened, the person would have come forward and told Van about it."

From there, they made their way down the narrow hallway to the secretary's office. The crowded room smelled of coffee and the faintly musty scent of old documents.

The disorganization struck her immediately. Claire, like Polly, was always impeccably organized, which made the chaos all the more jarring. Papers were scattered across the desk and items knocked askew. Had a thief rummaged through the office, searching for the combination? Or did they know exactly where to check but got interrupted? Maybe Cocoa had been startled by the intruder and bounded around the room, causing havoc. Whatever the case, it was clear something had happened here, throwing off the usual precision of the place.

"Is this window usually locked?" she asked. The window faced out onto the busy road.

"I don't know if Claire keeps it locked or not," Will said. "She might, being more careful about security than I am."

"Do you think the thief could have entered through that window?"

"I doubt it. It faces the road, which was very active the day of the fair, and the thief would have risked being spotted."

They walked back to the library. She circled slowly around the room, touching nothing and reflecting. Will stood in the doorway and watched her, waiting.

Stopping at a window, she glanced down at the flower garden below, which had been prepped for winter. She was about to move on when something caught her eye. The week of the Christmas fair had been mild, so the soil had been soft on Saturday. Several distinct shoe prints were visible in the mud, their unique pattern clear even from where she stood. "Will, did you see this?"

He joined her at the window and followed her pointing finger. "Could Van have missed that?"

"I'd be really surprised if he did. It's more likely he just didn't tell us about it."

They made their way out to the flower bed for a closer look. The footprints were unmistakable, frozen solid from the overnight drop in temperature. A clue as distinct and preserved as a fossil in amber.

She snapped photos with her phone, zooming in on the tread—a series of ridges and grooves. "Do you recognize that pattern?"

"I might. Wait here." He hurried into the church, reappearing minutes later with a single work boot. He flipped it over. "Like this?"

"Wow. Hold it for a sec." She snapped several more photos. "This feels more helpful than a basket of figgy pudding in a cabbage patch."

"Except that this is my boot. Half of Yorkshire wears boots like this."

"That's true." She stepped away from the building and stared at the prints. "The question is, why go out the window when the door is right there?"

"This window leads to this garden, which is more private. The door opens onto the road."

"But they already had privacy. They staged the whole thing when everyone was off chasing Calvin."

"But the thief couldn't be sure that everybody would go after Calvin. This was more of a safe bet." Will looked down at her feet, and his eyes widened. "Will you look at that."

"What?" Harriet followed his gaze to a set of paw prints right behind her. "Cocoa?"

"Now we know how she got out," Will said. "She saw her chance and took it."

Harriet met his gaze. "I'm glad we've recovered one escape artist from this debacle. Now we have to find the other one."

CHAPTER SEVEN

Jane Birtwhistle poured peppermint tea into delicate teacups etched with blue flowers. "Thank you for coming, dear."

Harriet had left Will at the church and headed straight to Jane's cottage, her mind racing with the discovery of the boot prints. She had texted Polly that she would be rushing in for her first appointment. If Margaret Thatcher's medical problems were straightforward, Harriet would make it to the clinic in the nick of time.

The front parlor, its wallpaper aged to a yellowed hue with flowered vines, held framed family photos. The soothing scent of lavender hung in the air. In one corner stood a substantial cat tree, where several felines sprawled contentedly. A grandfather clock chimed the hour, and a huge hand-embroidered sampler was framed on one wall.

"You're welcome," Harriet said. "I'll look Margaret Thatcher over, and maybe we can determine the problem. But first, can you describe her symptoms?"

"Her meow is feeble," Jane said. "She doesn't seem to like her new cat food, but she also turns up her nose at her old cat food. Plus, her coat is usually nice and glossy, but lately it's a bit dull."

"I better take a look."

"I'll go get her." Jane disappeared into the bedroom. Moments later, she returned with the cat in question. "Do you see what I mean?

Lethargic and possibly depressed." She set the cat on an upholstered chair beside Harriet.

Harriet took out her stethoscope and thermometer as Margaret Thatcher curled up and licked her paws. After her examination, she said, "I don't think there's anything truly wrong with her. She might simply be feeling a bit under the weather. But keep an eye on her, and let me know if she doesn't start eating again in the next day or so. I'm glad you told me as soon as you did." Jane was the kind of pet owner Harriet especially loved working with—one who noticed as soon as an animal started showing symptoms, and addressed the issue at once.

Jane's face brightened, but when Harriet stood to leave, the older woman put a hand on her arm. "Wait a minute, dear. I have to tell you something about the Christmas star."

Harriet felt her pulse quicken. "Did you see someone or something?"

"No." Jane paused, her voice carrying a sense of urgency. "But there's something I think you should know. Gerald Plum, White Church choir director. You've met him, right?"

"Yes," Harriet replied.

"Well, he was suspected of theft at White Church a few years ago." Jane's tone was reluctant, as if she didn't like to say such things. "Nothing came of it, but people still talk."

Harriet knew Gerald as a friendly, upbeat person and a skilled choir director. But where had he been during the camel chase? She thought the choir had been on break at the time. Could it be a coincidence? On the other hand, if Gerald had merely been suspected of a previous theft, that didn't necessarily mean anything.

"Was he proven guilty?" Harriet stood and put on her parka.

"No, but soon after they dropped the charges, he moved into a big, fancy house on Cedar Lane." She glanced around as if sharing a deep secret.

"Perhaps he inherited money or saved up?"

"Gerald's always broke. He owes money all over the village. And that beautiful house? They say it's almost empty because he's had to sell off the furniture."

The grandfather clock chimed again, so Harriet said her good-byes. "Thanks for the tea. Keep me updated on Margaret Thatcher."

She hurried out the door and down the flagstone path, her mind already plotting how to approach Gerald for a candid talk.

Harriet rushed back from Jane's house and flung herself into a packed schedule of appointments. When she finally finished with her last patient, she stepped into the clinic's reception area, welcomed by the melodic hum of the antique radiator and the soothing aroma of chamomile tea.

Polly was busy at her desk, which was a masterpiece of organization. Manila folders of medical records she was updating were arranged in tidy stacks around her. A desk organizer of neatly sorted writing utensils, paper clips, and other office necessities stood in arm's reach. A row of vintage cat figurines lined a shelf over her computer. Her desk reflected her orderly, efficient personality and her love for the animals she served.

"What's up with Mrs. Bentley's rabbit?" Polly asked, glancing at the file that Harriet had passed to her.

"Fur plucking." She slumped into the chair opposite Polly. It had been an action-packed morning.

"Why would a rabbit pluck out its own fur?"

"Boredom, stress, loneliness. Rabbits are sensitive creatures. They require plenty of enrichment."

"So what did you prescribe?" Polly leaned in, focused on her computer screen as she scrolled. "A spa day?"

Harriet grinned. "Not quite. More like extra toys and more human interaction."

Polly appraised Harriet. Since the two had become close friends, few people could read her better than Polly at this point. "To be honest, you seem like you could use a spa day."

"Thank you for not suggesting I need more toys."

"They couldn't hurt if they bring you joy. Seriously, you need to get out more. And I don't mean tea with your aunt Jinny or vaccinating someone's herd."

"Agreed. I'll do my best. And speaking of socializing, did you happen to see Van this weekend?" Polly had been dating the detective constable steadily for a few months.

Polly's cheeks colored to a soft pink, her eyes sparkling. "We went to the Christmas cookie decorating contest at his grandmother's care center. Our cookies didn't win, but they definitely should have." Polly's expression grew solemn. "Van told me what happened at the fair. I can't believe the silver star was stolen."

"I know. I told Aunt Jinny I'd help look for it."

"With Will?" Polly asked, a playful note in her voice.

"Yes. Why do you ask?" Harriet felt a flush of warmth at the mention of his name.

"Just curious," Polly replied with a mischievous grin.

Harriet was suddenly eager to steer the conversation elsewhere. "I'm glad you had fun with Van. I didn't know he was so creative."

Polly laughed. "He's not. That's what made it so brilliant."

Harriet glanced at her phone. "I should get back to work. Can you check a client's file for me?"

"No problem. What's the name?"

"Gerald Plum." Harriet had no idea whether Gerald had pets or if he brought them to her clinic or someone else's, but it was worth finding out.

Polly tapped on a few keys then nodded. "Two corgis with ear problems." She squinted at the screen. "His account is way overdue. Three notices and a phone call. He keeps saying he'll pay 'soon.'"

"Any clue why he's behind on his bill? Dissatisfied?"

"Nope. He loves us. His dogs practically waddle with joy when they walk in."

"Then do we know why he hasn't paid?"

Polly hesitated. "Word around the village is that Gerald isn't great with money, but it could be just gossip."

"Thanks." She grabbed her phone and texted Will. WHAT DO YOU KNOW ABOUT GERALD PLUM?

His reply only increased her curiosity. MEET ME ON THE BEACH FIRST THING TOMORROW.

CHAPTER EIGHT

"Gerald's not a bad sort," Will explained as the sun rose the next morning.

"I'm not saying he is," she replied.

The shore unfolded before them as they walked, heads down and into the wind. She loved the labyrinth of tidal pools and jagged rocks, the thick mist that clung to her parka. This beach lacked the sandy expanses of Connecticut beaches, but its craggy personality fascinated her. They had decided they needed privacy to discuss what Jane had told her. And in White Church Bay, nothing was more private than the beach in December.

"He's very talented," Will said. "Maybe a bit highbrow sometimes, but it seems to drive his passion for excellence, which, as you know, benefits the choir. Why do you ask about him?"

"Jane Birtwhistle told me he was once accused of stealing from White Church."

Will halted, the sea breeze tousling his hair and tossing his scarf. "Not this again."

"What do you mean?"

"Jane is a lovely person. But this is a bit of village gossip I thought had been laid to rest long ago."

"So he didn't steal from the church?" She adjusted her knitted hat lower over her ears.

"Gerald was completely innocent. That was an ugly rumor—nothing more." He began walking again, and she kept pace with him. "The accusations were thoroughly investigated, and he was cleared without doubt. I wasn't the pastor when it happened, but it's important to me that these rumors don't resurface."

"I'm glad to hear that, and I won't spread anything about him. He seems like a nice person."

"He is. But..." Will trailed off.

"But what?"

"Well, we don't know his whereabouts during the theft, which technically makes him a suspect like everyone else whose alibi we don't have," Will said. "It's also common knowledge that he's been struggling financially, but that's not the reason I think we should look into his possible involvement. If Jane is wondering if he stole the star, then it's likely that others are wondering the same thing. So if we can prove he's not involved, it would clear his name once and for all. Not just about the star, but it might also put to rest any lingering doubts from those past accusations—for good this time."

"What happened last time that made people suspect him?"

"It was a misunderstanding. Gerald was the church treasurer, and one of our wealthier members claimed he'd donated a large amount to the church but didn't get a receipt. By the time he found where he'd misplaced the check, the damage had been done. People were already whispering about Gerald having a secret bank account in the Caymens or wherever it is those things are."

"And the financial troubles?" she ventured.

"He's been facing some hard times, yes. It's a sensitive issue. I wouldn't want this to stir up unnecessary trouble for him." He glanced at her. "Can we keep this between us?"

"Of course," she said, admiring Will's commitment to confidentiality and ethical conduct. As they walked back toward the village, she asked, "Did Gerald have a key to the office?"

"Yes. He's a trusted member of the church, a dedicated volunteer. He has access because I trust him completely."

"But he still has a key," she pointed out. "He could slip in, day or night, unnoticed. Free to rummage through every nook and cranny of the office."

Will paused, his gaze fixed on her. He sighed. "Yes. Including under the desk."

The next day, she headed out early to chat with Gerald. The thought struck her suddenly—it was already December fourth, and that meant three weeks until Christmas. She needed to think of a gift for Will, but so far she was stumped.

As she stood on Gerald's front doorstep, she wished she had waited for Will to join her. He was at a memorial service at the church, and they had agreed she would go ahead without him, taking advantage of a break in her own schedule.

At first glance, Gerald's house was grand, fronted by a sweeping garden and surrounded by an ivy-covered wrought iron fence. But that was from the street. As she walked up the stone path, she noticed its unkempt state. The windows and carvings showed some age, and the garden was wild with weeds. Shrubs encroached on the path, and the porch paint was flaking off.

She rang the doorbell and immediately heard wild barking followed by heavy footsteps. The door swung open.

Gerald's appearance startled her. Mussed hair, untucked shirt, and tattered slippers replaced his meticulous Sunday best. And though normally animated and smiling, his face now bore signs of stress and weariness. He frowned over her shoulder as if he'd expected someone else.

"Good morning," she said cheerfully. "I don't know if you remember me, but I'm Dr. Harriet Bailey. I took over my grandfather's veterinary practice out at Cobble Hill Farm." She realized she hadn't decided yet how to ask about his alibi. She could hardly lead with, "Where were you Saturday when the church's Christmas star was stolen?"

Frantic barks resounded from the depths of the house. Knowing how Gerald doted on his dogs, she pounced on the topic. "I couldn't help but wonder how Bert and Ernie are doing?"

"They're fine. Why?" Gerald had still not invited her inside.

"I stopped by to see how they're doing with their latest ear treatments," Harriet said, remembering that Polly had mentioned their ear problems.

"Well, you can hear them, so you should be able to tell they're fine." He folded his arms across his chest. "If this is about the money I owe, I'll pay you. I need a little time."

"That's not why I'm here."

"Well, I'm good for it."

"I know you are," she assured him.

Gerald's demeanor softened a bit. "It's kind of you to stop by. But the dogs are sorted, so if you don't mind..."

"Wait. I was actually hoping to discuss something else." Her mind spun until she blurted, "The church choir."

Gerald raised an eyebrow, clearly nonplussed. "What about it?"

"I'd, uh, like to join." The last time she'd sung in a choir was the glee club at Windsor Middle School. Her final performance had concluded with the director gently suggesting that she switch to the theatre club or possibly intramural basketball.

Gerald's face bloomed with a smile. "Delightful. I'm always on the lookout for new choir members. Which part do you sing—alto or soprano?"

"Probably alto."

"Splendid. Lots of sopranos out there, but very few altos. Practice is tonight, seven o'clock sharp." He started to close the door.

"Actually, I would love to talk more about choir, singing, and sacred music." She leaned over, speaking through the narrowing gap before he shut the door in her face. "If you have time, that is."

He hesitated, peering over her shoulder again. Was he expecting someone? Someone who might pick up the silver star and leave piles of cash? Although, as Will had said, such money was most likely transferred digitally to an offshore account.

"I suppose I can spare a moment to talk about music if you like." He opened the door wide and gestured for her to come in.

She entered a vestibule with a marble floor and high ceilings. A wide hallway led into the living room. Closed drapes kept out the sun, while light from scattered lamps gave the room a soft feel. A grand stone fireplace anchored one end of the room, and a rich tapestry covered the opposite wall. In one corner sat a magnificent baby grand piano.

But like the exterior of the house, the living room held an air of neglect. Piles of sheet music and scores were strewn across the floor. Choir folders, a tuning fork, and a small ukulele were perched precariously on an oversized upholstered chair. Oddly empty spaces hinted at missing furniture. Had Gerald sold the furniture to try to settle his debts as Jane claimed, or had he never had enough money to furnish the room in the first place?

"Excuse the clutter. My housekeeper is no longer—is on holiday." He shot a glance at the back of the house, toward the source of barking and scratching. "Excuse me." He hurried down the marble hall.

She took advantage of his absence to scan the room. No sign of the star, but she could hardly expect him to display it front and center.

Two tan-and-white corgis raced to her as fast as their short legs would carry them. Their entire bodies wiggled with joy as they sniffed her hands.

She crouched to greet the dogs and quickly peeked into their ears. "You were right. They're the absolute picture of health." One of the dogs placed his front paws on her knee and licked her chin. She chuckled. "Thank you, sweet boy."

Gerald stood in the doorway, twisting his hands. "I would make us a cup of tea, but—"

"I'll only stay a minute." She took a breath. What was she thinking, interrogating a suspect? She was a veterinarian, not a detective. "Um, the choir was spectacular at the live Nativity."

"Well, I don't know about spectacular." Pushing a pile of clothes to the floor, he settled into the chair across from her.

"I thought they were great."

"You didn't notice?" He raised an eyebrow. "Oh, that's right, you were off chasing that camel." His voice held a hint of derision. "You and half the town ran after that beast while I was trying to deal with one of the worst choir crises I've ever experienced."

"Oh dear. What happened?"

He sniffed. "A deplorable lack of commitment. At every major Christmas concert, we conclude with 'O Holy Night,' which requires a talented tenor. But rather than readying himself to sing, my tenor was busy answering his mobile."

She made a mental note to silence her cell phone at choir practice.

"And do you know what the call was about? His wife had gone into *labor*." He said it as if it was the least considerate thing he could think of. "And do you know what he did?"

"He left for home?" Harriet guessed.

"Exactly! And without the slightest apology."

"What else could he do?" Harriet asked, not unreasonably, she thought.

Gerald snorted. "He could have stayed long enough to do his solo. Think about it. Women can be in labor for hours. What was the rush?"

She decided to skip her defense of fathers being present during labor and birth. "What did you do without your tenor?"

"I gathered the choir downstairs in the choir room, and after some discussion, we substituted with a soprano, which is not at all the same as a tenor. By the time I got everybody back outside, you had returned with that ridiculous camel."

"So you were in the choir room the whole time we chased the camel," Harriet clarified. "And all the choir members saw you?"

"Of course they saw me. We were all together, trying to solve the soloist crisis."

"Right. That's what I meant."

Gerald paused and studied her with a raised eyebrow. "I heard you're investigating the theft of the silver star."

"I'm asking around."

"That star means everything to this village." He walked out of the room.

She jumped up and followed him to the entryway, along with Bert and Ernie, their toenails clicking on the marble floor.

"It means a lot to my family too, especially my grandad."

They stopped at the front door, and Gerald actually gave her a small smile. "Your grandad was a splendid chap. Always had a kind word. I miss him."

"I do too." She stepped onto the spacious front porch.

"Don't be late for choir practice at seven tonight," he reminded her. "I detest tardiness."

She waved and headed down the stone walk. "I'm a big fan of punctuality myself," she called over her shoulder.

"I'm pretty sure Gerald is not our thief," she said, settling into a comfortable armchair across from Will. "In the Bleak Midwinter" was still stuck in her head from the previous night's choir practice. She had seen patients at the clinic all morning and finally had a moment to meet with Will—just in time for tea. "His alibi checked out."

She liked Will's cozy study at the church. Warm light from a table lamp filled the room. Myriads of books, family photos, and a collection of model train cars crammed the floor-to-ceiling shelves. Stacks of board games stood in a corner. A cushioned love seat, hand-knitted blanket, and a soft rug completed the room. Comfortable and welcoming, not unlike Will himself.

"How did you check his alibi?" he asked, pouring each of them a cup of tea.

"Choir practice."

He set a plate of crumpets next to the teapot. Crumpets had become one of her favorite treats at White Church Bay. They were perfect with a dab of butter and a dollop of strawberry jam.

"Did you bake these?" Harriet asked as she selected one.

"No. Doreen keeps me well-stocked with pastries and the like."

"That's why they're so good," Harriet said. Her neighbor, Doreen Danby, was a passionate and talented baker. "Anyway, Gerald was definitely with the choir at the time of the theft."

"You're sure?"

"Positive. I asked at choir practice right before he arrived. They all said he was in the choir room during the entire camel chase."

Will eyed her with a grin. "You walked into choir practice and started interrogating people about their director's whereabouts?"

"Give me some credit. I was subtle."

"And no one questioned why you were there?"

"Actually, I fit right in," Harriet informed him.

"How so?"

She leaned back in the overstuffed chair. "Because you're looking at White Church choir's newest alto, of course."

CHAPTER NINE

The woodstove in the corner filled Aunt Jinny's kitchen with a warmth that modern heaters couldn't replicate. Harriet breathed in, savoring the aroma of freshly baked peach scones. She hoped to catch Aunt Jinny up on her investigation into the star.

Following her visit with Will, she had spent some time on the wooden floor of a very cold attic. Mrs. Whiskers, a young calico, had delivered kittens under the eaves of a terraced cottage. Her choice of birthing bed offered lots of privacy for the new feline family but very little space for the veterinarian. The chill set in as she crouched beside Mrs. Whiskers, barely moving until the final kitten was born. Now she was still thawing out.

Her aunt busied herself arranging the tea things on the table, including red-and-green Christmas mugs. "How's the search for the star coming along?" she asked, pouring a mug for Harriet. "I am so glad you and Will teamed up."

"So far, our efforts haven't been very successful. We had what seemed like a promising lead, but in the end, it led nowhere." She intentionally left out Gerald Plum's name. Will was right. They needed to proceed with caution. In a small village like White Church Bay, openly delving into someone's life in connection with a crime, whether they proved guilty or not, could affect their reputation forever. Gerald was living proof of that.

"Well, you're trying, and that's what matters." Aunt Jinny took sip of tea and said thoughtfully, "I'm glad we agreed to tell Will the story of the origin of the star."

"Me too."

"Speaking of all this..." Aunt Jinny hesitated, and when she spoke again, her tone was tense. "There is something you should know."

"What's that?"

"It's a bit awkward. I probably shouldn't even bring it up. But I wanted to make sure you knew in case it affects your investigation. A while back, Eloise Pennington made quite a scene about wanting to borrow the star."

"Borrow it? Whatever for?" Sipping the hot tea, Harriet felt a flush of warmth begin to replace the attic's chill.

"She wanted to duplicate it in her studio and then return it." A frown creased Aunt Jinny's forehead. "As if it were a library book rather than a priceless artifact. Naturally, the church leadership wouldn't even hear of it. That star is pure silver with sapphires. The insurance premium on it is high enough. Imagine what it would be if the church started loaning it out?"

"What did Eloise do?"

"She threw a tantrum."

"What was her argument?"

"She stated that art should be accessible to all, not kept hidden away."

"But that doesn't mean you can just take it home with you," Harriet pointed out. "It's not as if galleries loan out their artwork."

"Agreed. But she insisted that it should be replicated so people could enjoy it year-round."

"When was this?"

"She started asking some years ago, with the pastor before Will. But she's been bringing it up at the church council ever since. To be honest, when the star disappeared, she was the first person I thought of."

"Why haven't you mentioned this before?"

"I didn't want to accuse someone without concrete evidence. And I felt that I might be jumping to conclusions."

"So why are you telling me now? Has something changed?"

Aunt Jinny stared into her tea for a long moment then sat up straight. "Last night she was bragging at the women's institute about her newly developed skills in silversmithing. Apparently, she took a class at the community center. She mentioned she'd be displaying her latest creation soon, as if it were some big secret." She took a peach scone. "That proves nothing, of course. Eloise has always been extremely dramatic."

"Anything else?"

Aunt Jinny picked off a bit of scone. "Eloise had a booth at the Christmas fair selling handmade crèches. She makes them from felted wool. She shapes each figure to be very realistic and then dyes them with natural colors. Anyway, she left her booth unattended, which is unusual for Eloise."

"How long was she gone?"

"At least twenty minutes. I know because she wasn't there the whole time we were cleaning up the hot chocolate."

Harriet frowned. "Twenty minutes? That's enough time to take the star and hide it then make it back to the fair. What time did she disappear?"

"About the time of the camel chase. I heard the noise and ran out to see what was happening, but I don't recall seeing Eloise."

Harriet nodded. "She might have simply been lost in the shuffle when everyone was running around. Have you mentioned any of this to Van?"

"No," Aunt Jinny said. "I don't want to accuse anyone without evidence. However, given Eloise's history regarding the star and her odd behavior at the time the star went missing—well, I thought you should be aware."

"Thank you. Coincidentally, my first appointment tomorrow is with Eloise. She's bringing in her ferret." Harriet took a sip of tea. "I'll let you know what happens."

CHAPTER TEN

Camden
March 1923

Letty let the door click shut behind her and hopped down the stoop's three steps to the sidewalk. She paused to take in the lively street. This wasn't Yorkshire, not by a long shot. She was hit by a sudden pang of homesickness—for her folks, her siblings, and those endless stretches of green back home under wide, open skies. But the longing was chased away by a spark of excitement. Camden, a borough in the bustling city of London, was brimming with the promise of something new, starting with school this morning.

Letty's parents, with a nudge from the local schoolteacher in White Church Bay, had pinched pennies so Letty could get a fancy education in London. She was staying with her aunt and uncle, walking to school in a neat uniform. Her aunt had ironed it within an inch of its life the night before, making sure Letty looked the part—serious student, mature young woman. She loved the uniform with its snug, dark wool skirt, a crisp white blouse, a tie striped with the school's colors, and a blazer proudly sporting the school emblem. Gripping her satchel, Letty stepped forward, a bundle of nerves and excitement, all set for the day ahead.

Letty made her way through Camden's streets as the city began to wake up. The tidy lines of brick houses were occasionally interrupted by cheerful shopfronts, each adding a splash of color to the city's everyday scene. She hurried past a bakery, where the aroma of fresh bread drifted out, making the street feel a bit warmer. A butcher shop showcased all sorts of meats near a greengrocer's display piled high with fresh fruits and vegetables. The strong scents of tea and coffee wafted from a diner on the corner. Each place, in its own way, helped to wake up the city, adding to the morning's hustle and bustle.

Workers hurried past her with lunch pails in hand, while groups of laughing children made their way to school. Housewives chatted as they carried their shopping baskets, sharing news with one another faster than any newspaper could spread it. Letty took it all in, the different voices and ways people moved. She felt a bit like an outsider but also, strangely, part of it all.

Trams and buses and even automobiles roared down the streets, so different from the gentle rhythms of Yorkshire. The hum of the city filled her with a mixture of awe and nervousness. Everything was new, thrilling in its novelty, and stirring a sense of adventure within her.

Letty rounded the corner and stopped short. The familiar street had vanished, replaced by a sea of market stalls that squeezed the path to a ribbon. The air buzzed with the scents of spices and the chatter of bargaining. She felt lightheaded. Her straight shot to school had just turned into a winding trek through temptations and holdups.

Letty's heart pounded in her chest, each beat screaming she was going to be late. First-day jitters transformed into panic. No time to turn back, *she thought, eyeing the packed market street. She had to get through. Gripping her satchel like a lifeline, she dove in.*

She raced forward, dodging people and stands, blurting an apology every time she bumped into someone, but unable to stop. The crowd seemed to be closing in around her, making her breath come faster. She pushed on, her mind on one thing—making it on time. She couldn't let her first impression be an empty seat.

Letty glanced up at the clock tower and saw the seconds slipping away. She sped up, dodging through the crowd like she was playing a game of tag. Her heart raced, urging her on. She burst from the market's grip into clearer streets with little time to spare.

She raced around the corner, and the school came into view. It was huge and a bit intimidating, standing tall in the heart of Camden. The school was nothing like the village school back in Yorkshire. Its size alone was overwhelming, and its old, detailed architecture was like something out of a book—beautiful but also a little frightening. Huge windows stared down like sentinels that seemed to command the street below. It was exciting to think about going to school here, learning new things and meeting new people. Her stomach lurched. She loved adventure, but this was overwhelming. Taking a deep breath, she reminded herself that this was the beginning of something great.

She bit her lip as she approached the huge front door. Would her Yorkshire accent stick out? Would what she had learned back home measure up? As Letty watched other students chatter and laugh on their way in, her sense of being an outsider grew. She took a deep breath, trying to calm the butterflies. Then, with a mixture of dread and determination, she walked through the school door.

The sable ferret whimpered as he lay on the examination table Friday morning. His unique white blaze was overshadowed by the fact that he was extremely underweight.

"Slinky is not himself," Eloise Pennington said, worry in her voice. "And he's so thin." Eloise wore her characteristic vibrant attire. Today's outfit included a cape of emerald-green velvet, its embroidery a kaleidoscope of purples, blues, and oranges, with a fuchsia scarf tied around her neck in a complicated knot. A billowy layered dress shimmered, giving glimpses of orange and turquoise. Her silver hair fell from her shoulders in untamed waves. It was like standing next to a walking art show.

"Ferrets can be tricky." Harriet picked Slinky up, peering into his face as he twitched his nose at her. She gently set him on the scale. "Yes, his weight is much lower than I'd like to see in an adult male." She placed the little ferret back on the exam table and gently palpated his abdomen. "This is your first visit with us, right?"

"That's right," Eloise confirmed, worry apparent in her voice. "Am I overreacting by bringing him in?"

"Not at all. Sudden weight loss is almost always a sign that something is wrong, and with a small animal like this, the sooner we catch it, the better. The underlying cause is likely contributing to his lethargy." She conducted a thorough examination of the ferret, assessing his eyes, inspecting his ears, and listening to his heart. "How long have you had him?"

"Five weeks. I've never had a pet before. I've never wanted one. Tethering another soul to my unpredictable path feels like clipping its wings."

Harriet had never heard that particular reason before, but she would much rather that no one had an animal unless they really wanted one. Those who got pets on a whim or simply because it seemed to be the thing to do often ended up not caring for the animal properly. "How did you choose a ferret?"

"He peered up at me from his little box, and our eyes met. It was obvious that our inner beings had fused."

"That's a lovely story." Perhaps it sounded odd, but she had certainly heard stranger reasons for selecting an animal.

"And he was cute."

"He certainly is." She admired his white mitts and bib. "Pet store find?"

"Craft fair, actually."

"That's a new one on me," Harriet admitted.

"Actually, he was outside the fair. I saw him in a cardboard box as I was walking in. No one was around, and I could tell from the state of him and the box that he'd been on his own for at least a day or two. I thought no creature as soulful as this one should be alone in this world. I took him home, and now he sleeps in his own comfy bed and roams free in the house."

"Was he this thin when you got him?" Her mind raced with possible causes.

"Plump as a butterball."

Harriet hid a grimace. If he'd lost this much weight in only five weeks, it couldn't be good. "Was he initially lethargic?"

"Playful as anything."

"He doesn't present with any immediate medical issues," Harriet mused as she handed Slinky back to Eloise. The ferret immediately burrowed into her scarf. "What are you feeding him?"

"Slinky is a vegan, like me." Her voice carried a defiant edge.

"Vegan?" Harriet tried to keep her tone neutral.

"Yes. We like to be eco-friendly. He has the freshest organic kale, sea vegetables, tempeh, and acai berries shipped from Brazil." She sighed. "But he snubs it all."

"That's because ferrets are carnivores," Harriet explained. She reminded herself that Eloise had fed the ferret incorrectly out of ignorance, not malice. And Eloise cared enough about Slinky to bring him in before things had gotten too dire for Harriet to help. "I respect your personal beliefs, but ferrets must have an abundance of animal protein in their diet, or they don't get the nutrients they need. The best thing for him would be to start with a commercial ferret food and then add in a little cooked meat every day until his weight is back up. No more plant-based diet, okay? Our systems can handle that, but ferrets can't." She jotted down a list for Eloise, starting with an excellent brand of ferret food.

"Do you mean that I've been depriving him all this time? Effectively starving him?" Eloise looked stricken as she laid a hand over Slinky, who nuzzled it affectionately.

"I don't want you to think about that. You didn't know, but you do now, and you can get him started on a meat diet. He will be a happy little ferret again in no time, and it's obvious to me that he loves you as much as you love him." She handed the list to Eloise. "Ask Polly to give you a pamphlet on ferret care. It'll help you feel more confident and make sure his needs are being met, plus enrich your bond even more. I'm glad you rescued Slinky. If everyone cared so much about animals, our world would be a better place."

"Our world could do with more care, couldn't it?" After a last cuddle, Eloise settled Slinky back into his carrier, lined with what appeared to be a vintage fur muff. "I heard you were trying to find the star. A pity it was stolen."

"Yes. A substantial loss for the church and the village." She kept her tone light but watched Eloise closely.

"Art, when hidden away, always attracts attention. Sometimes unwanted."

"What do you mean?"

"Art needs to breathe, to be seen in new light," Eloise said. "It shouldn't be guarded or gate kept."

"You mean it shouldn't be kept safe?"

"I mean, art has a life of its own. It should be allowed to roam free, like Slinky here."

"If giving it a life of its own means theft, then I can't agree," Harriet replied.

"You have a painting of the star, don't you?"

"My grandad did an oil painting of it years ago."

"And the church allowed him to take the star to his studio to paint it?"

"I think he sketched it while it was on the tree in the church. Then he used the sketch to create the painting." Harriet hesitated then dived in. After all, Eloise had brought this up. "You've always wanted to reproduce the star, haven't you?"

"Not 'reproduce,'" Eloise replied with an elegant sneer. "Increase its expression."

"You mean copy it?" Harriet spritzed the stainless-steel table with disinfectant and then wiped it down.

Eloise tucked the carrier under her arm. "I thought you of all people would understand, being the granddaughter of an esteemed artist like Harold Bailey."

"I do understand, and I don't mean copy it in a bad sense. I meant extend its influence so more people could enjoy it."

"I suppose you are referring to the rumors about me? My supposed past? My alleged scandal?" Eloise's voice was icy, each word laced with a bitterness that hung in the air.

Harriet froze. "No. I'm not aware of anything like that." Aunt Jinny had mentioned nothing about a scandal.

"Forget it." Eloise turned on her heel. "Come along, Slinky. We are going to the market posthaste. I'm thinking someone has earned himself some chicken for dinner after being such a brave boy during his appointment."

Harriet watched her go. She felt much better about Slinky's future, but she had no idea how to feel about Eloise's past.

CHAPTER ELEVEN

Later that day, Harriet stepped into the White Church Bay Library, housed in a stone cottage in the upper part of town. The building, with its big white shutters on either side of the tall windows flanking the door, had a rich history. Over the years it had been a blacksmith's shop, a pub, and even a vacuum sales shop before being converted into this quaint haven for readers and browsers. The basement housed meeting rooms, and a row of computer terminals for research and internet access added a modern touch to its historic charm.

Harriet's online search for *Eloise Pennington* revealed a mention in a 1983 article from the *London Art Review* regarding art fraud, but it wasn't accessible online. With the days dwindling until Christmas Eve, she needed to find that article fast. Time to go old-school and dig through the archives for a hard copy.

"Dr. Bailey!" A young man with curly hair and wire-rimmed glasses greeted her from the front desk, his face lighting up at her arrival.

"Hello, Oliver," she replied with a smile.

"How can I help you?" Oliver rounded the desk with the confidence of someone setting out to change the world, one overdue book at a time.

"I need the November 1983 issue of the *London Art Review*."

His eyes sparkled. "Archives are this way." He led her across the reference room then down a hallway and into a large storage room that was lined floor to ceiling with labeled boxes.

"Let's see what we can find," he murmured as he began pulling boxes off dusty shelves, each producing a puff of dust. "Ah, here we are," he finally said. He set a box on the table.

She watched as he shuffled through the worn issues. He took out the issue she'd requested and held it up to the light. "Long time since anyone asked for this one."

"Thanks." She took the neglected journal. "This is exactly what I need."

"Anytime, Doc." He grinned. "Can't wait to hear what you find."

She left the library at a run and dashed to the church. She found Will in the parish hall, arranging tables in long rows. He raised his head when she burst through the door. He appeared to be alone in his task. Perfect. They needed privacy for what she was about to reveal.

"Great to see you, Harriet." He peered at her. "Something wrong?"

"We need to talk."

"Yikes. Nothing good has ever followed those words."

She grinned. "Well, that's usually true. But you have to see this."

"Here. Sit down." He set up two folding chairs across from each other. "I need a break, anyway."

"Aunt Jinny told me something odd about Eloise Pennington. Apparently, she has repeatedly asked to borrow the star for her studio."

"I know. She complains at church council every now and then. I never give it much attention. Why?"

"She's been bragging to people about her silversmithing abilities. And she did a disappearing act during the Christmas Fair."

"Let me guess. During the camel chase?"

"You got it. Eloise brought her ferret to the clinic this morning and mentioned a scandal in her past." Harriet rummaged through her bag and removed a photocopy of the article she'd found at the library. "Look at this."

"What is it?"

She unfolded the page and handed it to him. "It's from the *London Art Review* in 1983. It's about art fraud." She began to read it over his shoulder, though she had already pored over it multiple times.

THE ART OF DECEPTION: ELOISE PENNINGTON'S RISE AND FALL SHAKES THE LONDON ART SCENE

In a seismic event that has left the London art scene reeling, celebrated artist Eloise Pennington recently found herself at the center of a scandal. The once-revered creative maverick has been implicated in the production of art forgeries. Sources reveal that the pressure to maintain her popularity in the highly competitive art world drove Pennington to replicate lesser-known pieces by prominent artists. This move has sparked intense debate in the art community about the challenges and ethical dilemmas facing contemporary artists.

Pennington used an underground art network to sell these replicas as newly discovered masterpieces. Her forgeries brought significant sums from both galleries and collectors, all driven by the possibility of owning what they believed to be a lost treasure.

The ruse was discovered when two vigilant art historians stumbled upon identical pieces in separate collections. Follow-up tests showed small inconsistencies that exposed the true provenance of the artwork.

The arrest and subsequent trial have brought out a range of public opinion about Pennington, portraying her as everything from a brilliant mastermind to an unfortunate victim of the art world's demands.

Even in the face of overwhelming evidence, Pennington has sidestepped incarceration, thanks to legal loopholes and a defense strategy that raised compelling questions about the ethics of art commerce. Instead, she faces huge fines and an indefinite professional ban, leaving her reputation tarnished but not destroyed.

"Wow." Will sat back and gaped at her. "I had no idea."

"Do you think this means that Eloise could be involved in the star's theft? That she might have stolen it to make copies in her studio?" Harriet tapped the page. "And how convenient that she already knows people in the underground art world."

Will stood and paced. "I'm not saying she wouldn't steal it for her own gain. But I wish we had a little more to go on than a decades-old article."

Harriet agreed. "We need to figure out our next move—whether we confront Eloise or take our findings to Van."

Will resumed setting up chairs. "Time is of the essence. However…"

"What?" Harriet prompted.

He paused and met her gaze. "However, be careful. Eloise may not be the harmless bohemian she appears to be."

Camden
March 1923

Letty had braced herself for the first day of school in Camden to be challenging, but she hadn't anticipated feeling this overwhelmed. She stepped into the school hallway, and the noise broke over her like a wave. Girls chattered and laughed, their voices blending into a cacophony that shook her to her core. They darted around with a purpose she couldn't begin to comprehend, leaving her feeling as if she stood still in a rushing stream.

A few steps in, she came to a halt, a group of five girls blocking her path. Their eyes swept over her, and Letty felt their judgment. It was in the way they paused, the slight arch of an eyebrow, the way their gazes lingered on her pristine uniform—a clear outsider's badge in this new world where everyone else's uniforms were comfortably rumpled. She might as well have worn a sign around her neck that read I'M THE NEW GIRL *in bold letters. The realization made her stomach twist in a silent plea for the ground to swallow her up right then and there.*

The laughter from the girls echoed down the hallway, making Letty's cheeks instantly hot. "Look at this one, all shiny in her new uniform. Greenhorn," one of the girls sneered.

Letty's face burned even more, a dead giveaway she was embarrassed. She clenched her fists. Part of her wanted to yell back, to not let them get away with their cruelty. But more than that, she just wanted to fit in, not stick out like a sore thumb on her first day. So she swallowed the lump of awkwardness in her throat and pushed past them.

Hands trembling, Letty dug through her satchel until she found a neatly folded piece of paper. It listed her classes in the precise handwriting of the headmistress. She studied it as she continued through the school's busy halls. It was unsettling to start in the middle of the term, missing any kind of welcome or orientation. And all the other girls already knew one another. No one else was new.

She checked the classroom numbers above the doors and finally located her first class, mathematics, where she hoped to find a seat in the back where she could stay under the radar. Letty paused to take in the room. This was nothing like her small village school in Yorkshire. The sheer scale of it took her breath away. Rows of polished wooden desks were neatly arranged, each paired with a chair that faced the large blackboard on the front wall. Sunlight streamed in through tall windows, casting a warm glow over the room and highlighting the dust motes dancing in the air.

Around her, clusters of girls chatted softly. Letty noticed their confident demeanor, so different from the casual camaraderie of her previous schoolmates. Here, everything seemed more formal and serious. She chose a desk and slid into the chair, trying to catch her breath. The girl across the aisle gave her a saucy smile, and suddenly Letty felt a bit better. Maybe she wouldn't be totally alone here. She lined up her composition books and placed her new fountain pen with its polished nib next to the inkwell.

Letty's thoughts drifted to her old village school, where she'd first fallen in love with mathematics. It had been a cozy, three-room building, where the students had known one another's names, and laughter often filled the air. The desks were worn from years of use, each scratch memorializing the generations who had learned there. Her teachers were more like family, guiding with patience and a personal touch that made every lesson feel like a discovery. Letty had flourished there, soaking up knowledge like a sponge. Arithmetic and a bit of geometry were as far into mathematics as they had gone, but she'd absorbed all the lessons and longed for more.

Her teacher had soon noticed her natural aptitude. He would keep her after class to challenge her with increasingly complex problems that weren't in their textbooks. Letty saw something special in the patterns and in the neat solutions. It felt like solving a puzzle. When the pieces clicked into place, they showed her a world where everything was tidy and ordered and where everything made sense.

Letty watched as the young teacher entered and took her place at the front of the room, her posture straight, commanding respect without saying a word. Her hair was pulled back tightly, not a single strand out of place. The simple elegance of her dress and the confident way she moved caught Letty's attention. Letty glanced at the paper given to her by the headmistress. Mathematics Instructor: Miss Edith Cantrell.

Letty's twenty or so classmates fell into a respectful silence as Miss Cantrell surveyed the room. Her gaze was discerning, missing nothing, and when it landed on a girl slouching in her seat, she said crisply, "Miss Thompson, please sit up straight. We're here to learn, not lounge."

Letty felt her own spine straighten at the teacher's tone.

Miss Cantrell's gaze fell on Letty. "And you must be our new student," she said in a gentler tone. "Please come write your full name in the roll book." She gestured to a book on her desk.

Letty, feeling the spotlight on her, stood slowly, smoothed the skirt of her uniform, and walked up to the desk. With deliberate care, she wrote Letitia Joy Baxter *as carefully as she could, savoring the weight of the fountain pen in her hand. Then she placed the pen precisely in its place beside the ledger and returned to her desk.*

"Today, we will focus our attention on algebra," Miss Cantrell said. "And we'll start with a review of something foundational—simple linear equations. We'll learn how to solve for X *when it is in an equation." The teacher turned to the blackboard and began to write rapidly.*

A wave of excitement washed over Letty. True, she was the new girl and everything here was worlds away from Yorkshire, but in this moment, amidst the figures and formulas of mathematics, she was in her place. Here, she felt alive and utterly herself. Letty opened her composition book, its pages crisp and clean, ready to be filled with notes.

As the teacher started detailing the principles of algebraic equations, Letty began to write, her pen moving smoothly over the paper. Whatever else came, at least she had the consistency and familiarity of numbers.

CHAPTER TWELVE

"What's this?" Will asked, pointing to a spot on the ground late that Saturday afternoon.

The clinic had closed at noon, so Harriet had met Will on the moors for a walk before supper. Now she followed his attention to the trail's edge. A hedgehog lay motionless, its flattened spines blending into the winter-brown grasses of the moor. December's feeble light picked up small dots of red. Blood? She crouched next to it for a closer look. The tiny creature should have been alert, its snout quivering with each unfamiliar scent, eyes bright and open. Instead, it didn't move, and its eyes were closed.

"Is it alive?" Will asked.

"Barely," Harriet said.

"Should we take it to the clinic?" Will eyed the hedgehog with concern.

"Absolutely," Harriet replied at once. "It'll fare better with us."

"What's it up against out here?"

"Predators, mainly," she answered. "And exposure. The moors can be unforgiving."

"Then the clinic is its best chance."

"Without a doubt." Her gaze met his. "We'll get it back on its feet."

"What's the procedure?" Will asked.

She gazed again at the hedgehog. She was struck by its delicate beauty, having never seen one so close. The pattern of its quills, in white, brown, and black, was intricate and lovely. "We don't want to hold it captive for too long. We'll nurse it then set it free as soon as it's ready. As adorable as it is, it can't become a pet."

Will gently picked up the hedgehog, wrapped it in his scarf, and then passed the bundle to Harriet. They walked back across the moor together. Harriet was determined to save the small creature they had found. As they talked about what to do when they got to the clinic and how to help their little patient, Harriet appreciated Will's kindness. It felt good focusing on something other than solving a theft.

Harriet settled the hedgehog into a small cardboard box lined with warm flannel and placed it on the stainless-steel exam table. With her stethoscope, she strained to catch the fragile flutter of his heartbeat.

Will watched with keen interest. "Well?" His hazel eyes focused on her. His unruly hair was even more tousled from their walk on the moors. And their outing hadn't spared his clerical collar, which now sported a smudge of mud.

She pressed the stethoscope to the little hedgehog once more. Still a very thready heartbeat. She carefully took his temperature and found it dangerously low. "He's barely alive. Who knows how long he's been lying out in the cold."

"He?" Will quirked an eyebrow.

"Yes." She tucked her stethoscope away and thought for a moment. "We have to raise his body temp slowly, which is gonna take some time." She picked up the box. "Let's find a more comfortable spot."

They made their way to the study. The cold air of the outdoors and the harsh fluorescent lights of the exam room made the study's soft lighting and cozy warmth even more welcoming. Will soon had a fire going in the fireplace, and she took her seat in a comfortable chair beside it. Will sank into the chair across from her. They placed the box, which held the hedgehog wrapped in flannel, on the ottoman between them.

"That should warm him up," Will remarked, peering down at the little bundle in the box.

"It should help anyway. You know, he might not make it." She shot him a concerned glance. "For an animal that tiny, the road back from hypothermia can be difficult. Maybe impossible."

"I know, but I can't bring myself to give up on him. How about I brew some tea?" he suggested. "And scrounge up a snack. I'm a bit peckish."

"I'm peckish too, but I can get it." After all, she was the hostess.

"Nonsense. I know where everything is, and I'll feel better if you're with the hedgehog."

He disappeared into the kitchen and returned a few minutes later with a heavily laden tray holding tea, a tin of biscuits, and two ham sandwiches. To her delight, he also brought the last slice of Aunt Jinny's Victoria sponge cake, which he had cut in half. "This will get us started anyway," he said as he arranged it all on the coffee table between them. "Sugar for your tea?" he offered, picking up the small tongs used to transfer sugar cubes from their bowl to the cup.

"Two, please," she said. "And cream."

"Certainly." Will doctored her cup and handed it to her then made his own tea and sat back with a sigh. "Saving animals is hard work."

"Tell me about it. It makes me want coffee. But that would keep me up all night."

"You Americans and your coffee," he teased.

"I almost gave it up when I moved here and realized I do like tea. But after two days without coffee, I couldn't brew it fast enough."

"It's only tea in White Church Bay. I can't imagine anything else."

"Do you like living here?"

"I love White Church Bay." He sipped his tea. "How about you? Are you glad you moved here?"

"Of course."

"Don't take this wrong way, but you don't sound entirely sure."

"I do like it here. But it's been a big change. I expected that, of course, but I still underestimated just how much. From Connecticut to Yorkshire as well as from working for someone else to running my own practice." Harriet set her teacup back on the saucer. "With Christmas around the corner, the distance between me and my parents feels even greater than the ocean that separates us." She suddenly felt relieved to talk about all this. She experienced a level of emotional comfort with Will that she seldom felt with other friends, especially ones she'd known for such a short time. She didn't want anyone to think she was unhappy with her choice, because she wasn't. But there were times when she missed the comforts of the life she had known before.

"You're preaching to the choir on that one," Will told her. "Navigating uncharted waters is a tremendous leap, and it can make everything familiar seem distant and small. It was the same for me when I moved from seminary to leading a church."

"Really?" She'd known he would understand, but she hadn't realized how much of that understanding would be due to personal experience.

"Absolutely. Seminary fills your head with ideals—visions of spiritual transformation, ground-breaking social justice, packed pews. But then you arrive at a parish, and suddenly you're plunged into real life—people wrestling with loss, fractured families, some barely making ends meet, and all craving a vibrant church community. And then you're not just a pastor. You're their North Star, guiding them through the chaos."

"So we're both navigating new terrains, trying to be the guides we never knew we'd have to be," Harriet mused. "I feel that way about the veterinary clinic as well. Academia doesn't prepare you for day-to-day practice. At least not entirely. You don't realize how much the animals and the owners depend on you. I constantly worry that I'm not up to it."

Will leaned back, his gaze locking with hers. "You were called to be a vet. That means God is with you. And on those days when it seems like you aren't enough, remember that He is."

"Is that what you do? Remember that God is the one filling you, the one making you 'enough'?"

"That's what I try to do." He laughed. "And when I don't, things usually get messy."

"I think I just feel a little out of place sometimes, like a puzzle piece that doesn't always fit."

At that moment, a tiny stirring came from the box. Harriet set down her teacup. With practiced ease, she lifted the bundle onto her lap and peeked at the small hedgehog. Retrieving her stethoscope, she carefully placed it on the tiny creature's chest. "His heartbeat's stronger."

"Awesome. Is that from warming him up?"

"Most likely." She swaddled the hedgehog back in the flannel and returned him to the box beside the fire. "A bit more rest should do him good."

Will smiled, his eyes fixed on the hedgehog. "Those quills are something."

"They're specialized hairs made of keratin. When danger's near, he rolls up and presents them like a suit of armor. When a hedgehog trusts the one he's with, the quills relax."

"How does he know who to trust?"

Harriet put her hand on the box. "Animals tap into instincts we can only dream of. Pheromones, hormones—you name it."

"If only my instincts were as keen as his."

Harriet laughed. "Yours and mine both."

The hedgehog's faint breaths punctuated the room's silence. After a few moments, slouched in the deep chair, Will's eyelids drooped.

"If you want to go home and get some rest, that's okay," she told him.

Will's eyes snapped open. "Absolutely not. I'm staying right here until our spiny friend is out of the woods."

"Maybe he'll come around better if he senses food," Harriet said, thinking out loud.

"He needs a name, don't you think?"

"I would like to see if he survives first."

"But giving him a name would show confidence and hope, right?"

She chuckled. "Okay, you win. What kind of name? Something to represent his rescue? Like Moses, plucked from the Nile?"

"I'd rather give him a name that reminds you of home. Any ideas?" Will asked her.

"How about Nutmeg?"

"It's cute, but why Nutmeg?"

She smiled. "Connecticut is the Nutmeg State."

"That's perfect. Nutmeg it is." He paused for a moment, his laughter gone. "Saving Nutmeg is important, but the duty I feel to find the star is overwhelming. As White Church's pastor, I have both a moral and professional obligation to get it back. And we're running out of time to have it for Christmas Eve."

"That's a lot to take on. You feel single-handedly responsible for a theft at the church?"

Will's expression was solemn. "The star has been safeguarded by every pastor at White Church since 1919. I don't want to go down in history as the one who lost it."

"You didn't lose it. Someone stole it."

"I left the library door in the church unlocked."

"It was in a safe during a church function where people needed to be able to go in and out freely," Harriet reminded him.

"With the combination taped to the bottom of a desk drawer nearby. That's like writing the PIN on the back of your debit card."

"Which, while unsafe, still puts the blame on the person who actually commits the crime of stealing. You'd never expect someone to enter the church library, climb under the desk for the combination, and steal the star after staging a camel chase for distraction and safely stowing away a cat. At least some of that was premeditated, which means that even if you'd locked the church, they would have found another way go get in." She folded her arms over her chest. "Nope. The one and only person to blame is the person who stole it. I wish we could improve our search strategy though."

"Any ideas?"

She crossed to the reading table and retrieved her notebook. Settling back into her fireside seat, she flipped it open. "First, we follow up on Eloise. I have a feeling about her and her demands to take the star home. The way she talks about it and art in general—it's not so much passionate as it is obsessive."

"Obsessive enough to steal?"

"Possibly. As soon as we can, I say we question her." She made a note with her pen.

"We don't want to spook her. If we do, she'll never reveal anything," Will pointed out.

"I know. Give me time. I'll come up with a plan."

"That's our problem. Time is running out."

"Maybe we could share what we've learned with Van. As the detective constable, he'll probably be able to do more with it than we can." Harriet closed her notebook. "The more resources we engage, the sooner we crack this case."

"Look at that," Will said as the hedgehog opened his eyes and blinked. "I think Nutmeg wants his tea."

"Back in a jiff." She dashed to the clinic, returning a minute later with a petite syringe with the needle removed, and a small vial.

"What are you giving him?" Will asked, his eyes narrowing with curiosity as she scooped up the hedgehog and cradled it in her lap.

"Electrolytes."

"I don't know what I expected, but it wasn't that," Will said with a smile. "I thought you'd give him sugar water or something."

"Never give a hedgehog sugar or anything with fats, salts, spices, or dairy. Those things can cause health problems for these little guys."

"It must be hard to keep track of what's good and bad for all the different animals you see in your practice."

"It is," Harriet admitted. "And it's a great responsibility. What if I forget something and treat an animal incorrectly?"

Will regarded her. "I doubt you would do that. In fact, I can't even imagine it."

"Unfortunately, it happens to the best of us. All I can do is try to stay on top of things." She held the tiny syringe to Nutmeg's mouth. His eyes had closed again. She massaged his chest, but the hedgehog remained unresponsive.

"Come on, buddy," Will murmured.

After a few more attempts to revive him, Nutmeg squirmed and opened his eyes. Harriet tried the syringe again, and this time, he took a bit of the solution. When he turned his face away, she capped the vial and settled him back into his flannel.

Will pushed the ottoman closer to the fire. "Once he's better, what's on his menu?"

"Live mealworms, crickets, even a bit of cooked egg."

Will chuckled. "Well, fingers crossed for breakfast with eggs."

The mantel clock struck ten. She hadn't realized how late it had gotten.

Will stood slowly, looking as exhausted as she suddenly felt. "Rescuing a hedgehog on the moors on Saturday is one more good reason for having one's sermon done early in the week."

"Go home," Harriet told him. "You don't want to fall asleep in the pulpit." She adjusted the flannel around Nutmeg. "I'll monitor him through the night. We've got a long way to go."

Will put on his coat. "With Nutmeg and the Christmas star."

CHAPTER THIRTEEN

Monday morning when she checked on Nutmeg, she found him stirring in his box. Not bad for being rescued from death's doorstep a mere thirty-six hours earlier. She thought he could soon swap his electrolyte menu for a nice mealworm or perhaps a cricket or two.

She checked her phone and found that Polly had sent her the list of appointments scheduled for the day. The afternoon was packed. First up, a dog presenting with what sounded like eczema, but she wanted to see it for herself before prescribing treatment. Then there was an Alexandrine parakeet who refused to chirp, and that might require some time.

Fortunately, the morning had a few gaps. She could definitely fit in a visit to Eloise.

As she brewed a cup of coffee, she texted Will. NUTMEG IS MOVING AROUND. STOP BY AND SAY HELLO. The doorbell's chime sounded as she hit send.

Mrs. Agatha Farrell stood on the front stoop with a pie in one hand and her pocketbook in the other, her face lined with urgency. "Good morning, Dr. Bailey. Sorry to barge in on you like this. But I need to talk with you."

"Please come in," she replied. "Is this about Jelly Bean?" She had just treated Agatha's Chihuahua for pancreatitis.

"Oh no, your treatment has made all the difference." She slid the pie onto the kitchen counter. "This is for interrupting your busy morning. But I had to come straight here."

"You didn't have to bring a pie, but thank you. Have a seat." Harriet gestured to a kitchen chair. "May I get you something? Coffee? Tea?"

"Goodness me, no." She sat down, perching on the edge of the chair, pocketbook in her lap. Her fingers drummed a nervous rhythm on the table. "This morning, when I was walking Jelly Bean—well, you know how lively a Chihuahua can be. Anyway, he slipped his collar and darted straight into Eloise Pennington's back garden. Naturally, I followed him."

Harriet felt her breath catch. "Go on."

"I wasn't snooping, mind you, but her blinds were open. I glanced up while I was trying to catch Jelly Bean and—well, that's when I saw it."

"Saw what?"

Agatha's eyes were wide. "The silver Christmas star."

Harriet's thoughts whirled. "Are you certain?"

"I'm certain. I've seen that star placed on the tree every Christmas Eve since I was a toddler. I'd recognize it anywhere. I know that you and Pastor Will are searching, right? I thought you should be the first to know."

"Thank you. We'll sort this out."

"I'll leave it up to you to contact the authorities—or whatever you think you should do." Agatha clutched her purse as she stood. "Remember, time is of the essence."

Almost before the door closed behind her, Harriet grabbed her phone to text Will again. CHANGE OF PLANS. MEET ME AT ELOISE PENNINGTON'S HOUSE. ASAP.

The midmorning sun cast a soft glow over the ivy-covered stone cottage. Harriet and Will stood at its blue front door adorned with quirky pink half-moons and yellow stars.

They had agreed to search for the star themselves first, wanting to avoid casting undue suspicion on Eloise based on neighborhood gossip. They hoped to find more solid evidence before involving the authorities or alerting the community.

Before Will even rang the doorbell, Eloise's voice floated down from an open window above. "I'll be right there!"

Exchanging a glance, they waited. Will appeared tense, and Harriet felt her own nerves flutter.

The door opened, and Eloise greeted them, all smiles and morning energy. A turquoise headband tamed her silver hair. She wore bell-bottoms, a black T-shirt topped with a paint-splattered apron, and ballet slippers.

"Good morning, Eloise," Will said. "I hope we aren't bothering you."

"Not at all," she said, beaming. "Please come in."

Eloise led them into the front room. Half-finished canvases stood on easels near jars of clouded water and brushes. Wooden crates spilled over with tubes of paint, unused canvases, and sketchbooks. A velvet sofa was adorned with three paintings of various whimsical creatures, none of which Harriet could name. A heavy coffee table held glossy magazines and an art deco tea set. Two vintage floor lamps cast a glow over a purple shag rug.

"Please sit down," Eloise said. "I heard you joined the choir."

Harriet settled into a large armchair covered with a leopard-skin throw. "Well, I'm giving it a try anyway."

"Hoping to release some inner joy through music, are you?"

"That's exactly it." She watched as Will perched on a dainty Victorian fainting couch, and resisted the urge to snap a photo for Keri Poole. They might be on the brink of something more important than a viral post.

"Now, what can I do for you fine folks this morning?" Eloise asked.

"We wondered if you would be willing to donate an art piece for the silent charity auction for the music committee. I'm sure your work would be a hit," Harriet explained. Since joining the choir, she had been talked into joining the fundraising effort.

Eloise's eyes lit up. "Of course! What would you like?" She waved her hand, signaling that the room's contents were up for grabs.

"Well, my goodness. How generous," Will said. "So much to choose from."

"How about my 'Moonbeam Meditation'?" Eloise walked to an easel. "I've almost completed it."

Harriet peered at the painting—six red and yellow cats in various positions. "What are the cats doing?"

"Yoga. On floating yoga mats."

"I love the colors," Will said. "And how the moon is so, um, green."

Eloise spun around and trotted into an adjoining room. When she swept back into the sitting room, she carried something mounted on a wood slab. "Here's another option. I call it 'Harmony Henge.' It's a miniature Stonehenge, made from bottle caps, beads, and twisted wire from old electronics. I'm proud of the rendering, and it's also eco-friendly because all its bits and pieces are recycled." She set it on the coffee table.

"That's first rate," Will said. "How about if I describe both pieces to the music committee's fundraising team and let them decide?"

"No problem," Eloise said. "I've got lots more paintings and sculptures if neither of these is quite right."

"I'd love to see more of your art," Will said.

This was Harriet's cue. She and Will had planned this move earlier. "And while you're giving him a tour of your studio, may I use your bathroom?"

Eloise pointed down the hall. "Second door on the left. Pastor Will, let's begin in the attic. I keep some of my best work up there." She started toward the back of the house with Will following. "You don't mind a bit of climbing, do you?"

"Not at all."

Harriet ducked into the bathroom, which was entirely pink. Pink sink, pink tiles, pink curtains, pink towels. She washed her hands as loudly as she could in case Eloise was listening. After drying her hands on a plush pink towel, she slipped into the narrow hall. She pushed open a small yellow door and found a room bursting with boxes and eclectic art. A painting with a haunting face reminded her that Eloise was more than just a carefree artist.

She headed down the hall and opened another door to a tiny room. A stained-glass window bathed the space in shifting colors, and a few boxes and packing crates were stacked against the walls.

No sign of the silver star. Muffled conversation from upstairs reached her. She had mere minutes, if that, before Eloise would return and catch her snooping.

Soft scuffling reached her ears, and she froze. She breathed again when Slinky's head peeked around the corner of a bookcase. She wouldn't have thought such a tiny ferret could make so much noise.

She moved to the next room, holding her breath at the door's loud creak. Sunlight streamed in through the tall windows and onto rows of potted plants on a long table. Her heart pounded as her eyes darted from ferns to hanging planters. No star. She had to find it before her cover was blown.

She heard steps thud on the pull-down ladder from the attic. She was out of time. She bolted from the sunroom and collided with a tall vase. She caught it inches from the floor and righted it.

Will's voice mingled with Eloise's close by. Spotting a partially open door at the end of the hall, she bounded across the Persian rug and ducked inside. The room was bare except for an old desk under a window. She caught her breath. On the desk, catching the morning light, was the silver star. She pulled out her phone and snapped several photos.

Solid evidence. Finally.

Will leaned back in his office chair with a groan. "This isn't our star."

At Will's pronouncement, Harriet was relieved that she hadn't given in to her impulse to grab the star and flee Eloise's house.

A closer examination of the photo on the screen showed that Eloise wasn't their thief after all—at least, not based on this.

"How do you know it's not the one that belongs to the parish?" Van asked. Harriet had called him on the way to the church from Eloise's place, and he'd met them there.

Will indicated the screen. "The original star had a delicate, almost undetectable engraving on the back, called a maker's mark. This star has nothing."

"The angel with outstretched wings, right?" Van asked.

"That's it."

She leaned forward and peered at the spot on the star where the angel should have been. "Maybe the lighting in the room obscured it." She'd intentionally captured the front and the back of the star, but the job had been a hurried one.

"Maybe." Will's voice sounded hesitant. "But here's another problem. Look at the sapphire in the middle. On the original, the gemstone is centered perfectly. But here, it's slightly askew."

Harriet slumped into the club chair next to his desk, echoing his earlier groan.

"It would seem that Eloise isn't our thief." The lines of stress in his face eased, reminding her how much the idea of a guilty church member troubled him.

"That's good, isn't it?" She tried to assure herself, wanting to believe that she truly felt relieved about it and not disappointed. "I like Eloise. And Slinky."

"Excuse me?" Van stared at her, his eyebrows lifted. "Who's Slinky?"

"Her ferret."

"Of course." Van grinned.

"You know what else this means?" she asked.

"What?" Will raised an eyebrow.

Harriet grimaced. "It means that we're back to square one."

CHAPTER FOURTEEN

They trekked across the moors, heading into the biting wind, the late afternoon sun offering little warmth.

After realizing they were no closer to finding the star, Harriet thought focusing on a positive note would help, and Nutmeg the hedgehog was definitely that, as it was time to release him back into the wild. With treatment that included warmth, food, and liquids, the little guy was energetically snuffling and scratching to get out of his box. Harriet didn't want to set him loose too soon, but it wouldn't help Nutmeg to keep him confined. He was meant to live in the wild, and she wanted to get him back as soon as he was ready.

Once the clinic was closed for the day, she had met Will, carrying the box where Nutmeg actively scurried about.

"So where do you think his new home should be?" Will asked, stepping over a clump of heather.

"Someplace where he can get food, water, and easy access to shelter. Ideally, an area with all the resources he'll need for survival."

They reached the spot on the trail where they'd first found him but kept walking in search of a better location, as he clearly hadn't fared well there.

Will pointed to a secluded copse with lots of fallen leaves, where bracken and heather grew thick. "How's that for ideal real estate for a hedgehog?"

"Plenty to burrow into."

"Nice neighborhood, good schools, easy commute."

She laughed. "And an all-you-can-eat buffet of nutritious insects."

"Did you hear that, little guy?" Will said to the box. "No more takeout for you."

They set Nutmeg on the frosty ground beside an abandoned rabbit burrow. It would provide a cozy winter haven. His small snout twitched as he examined his surroundings. Then, after a parting glance, he scuttled under the blanket of leaves and was gone.

"Godspeed, Nutmeg," Will said softly.

"You know, he was near death when we found him," she observed during their walk back to the village. "But with a bit of care, he's ready to carry on with his life."

"I imagine he'll meet a lady hedgehog named Cinnamon or Cardamom. Settle down, have a litter of little hedgehogs. What are baby hedgehogs called?"

"Hoglets."

Will squinted at her, as if trying to figure out whether she was serious. "Are they really?"

"They are."

He burst into his contagious laugh. "You make life fun. Do you know that?"

She smiled. "I'm glad you think so. I usually hear that I'm too serious."

They walked in a pleasant silence for a bit. The cold air carried the faint scent of woodsmoke from the village, and the moor stretched behind them.

"Nutmeg seemed unsure at first when we let him go," Will said, breaking the silence. "Made me wonder if he wanted to jump back into the box."

"He probably did. But then he went for it. No looking back."

"That's right." He met her gaze. "No looking back."

Late that night, after she had said goodbye to Will, Harriet stared at the calendar that lay open on her cluttered kitchen table.

It was December ninth. Ten days since the star was stolen, and she hadn't made any progress in finding it. The table was buried under a chaotic mix of notes, turning it into an impromptu headquarters. To anyone else, it might seem like clutter, but Harriet saw order in the chaos—every single piece was crucial. Next to the avalanche of paper was her favorite mug, the contents still warm. Charlie, the clinic cat, dozed next to her on the table, unfazed by the photographs of Calvin in his pen before and after his legendary romp through the village.

Central to all the information was a glossy photo of the missing star. Even in the soft kitchen light, it shone with a silver glow. Every time she saw it, Harriet thought of Letty and Albie. That photograph was her mission and her muse, a silent demand for resolution.

Somewhere in this chaos of details and disorder had to be the breadcrumb that would lead them to the truth. Shaking off a rising feeling of frustration, she gathered the scattered crime-scene photos she'd taken after Van had left the day the star had been stolen. She rearranged them, each image showing the disarray in the church library and the church secretary's office.

She placed the photo of the boot print at the far-left corner of the table. Beside it, the plant toppled on its side. Next the turned-over lamp. A little farther down, she centered the image of a fallen Bible, its pages splayed open to Psalm 97.

She greeted Maxwell, who rolled in and looked up at her expectantly. The long-haired dachshund had been hit by a car before she'd come to White Church Bay, leaving his back half paralyzed. He now got around with a wheeled prosthesis her grandfather had outfitted him with. She removed it and helped him lie down on a braided rug near the kitchen heater, tucking his favorite blanket around him.

Returning to the table, she scrutinized the evidence. There had to be a pattern. These clues were not arbitrary. They told a story as detailed as any patient file at the clinic. If only she could diagnose the theft as readily as she could an illness or condition.

Her phone pinged. Polly had uploaded a new photo to the clinic website. Harriet's face broke into a smile at the sight of Dottie, Lloyd Throckmorton's pet armadillo, clad in a tiny knit sweater that Harriet had recommended for the cold season. Armadillos weren't common in Yorkshire, except for a few kept by private breeders, and she rarely saw them as a vet. But she always enjoyed the chance to work with an animal she didn't know well.

She laid the phone on the table and took a sip of her now cold coffee. Her gaze was fixed on the scatter of notes, waiting for a brilliant idea. But nothing came. Her cell phone pinged again, this time with a text from Keri Stone. She had attached a photo of Harriet and Calvin at the live Nativity, requesting permission to post it.

Gazing at the photo, Harriet thought she didn't look too bad. Her hair wasn't at its best that day, but it didn't matter much. After all, she was a country vet, and messy hair was an occupational hazard. She texted back, GO RIGHT AHEAD.

Harriet finished her coffee and rose to make a fresh cup. As she stood by her coffee maker, its hum a familiar backdrop, her mind wandered to a conversation she'd had with Marvin Jenkins. Earlier that day, while she'd administered parvo shots to his new puppies, he'd mentioned his search for videos of Calvin's escape on the church website. He had mused about the oddity that the internet-savvy Keri hadn't posted such a potentially viral moment, then wondered whether Keri could channel her social media skills into helping find the missing silver star.

Returning to the table with additional brain fuel, she mulled over his words. If Keri was always on the lookout for the next big post, why hadn't she recorded Calvin's escape? Harriet was certain she'd seen the social-media maven at the live Nativity, shooting photos and talking to people. All of this begged the question—where was Keri during the theft of the star?

But as she thought about it, she had to wonder whether Keri would even want the star. Why would someone like Keri care about a Christmas tree ornament? Would she even have a way to sell it? Unless…

Harriet grabbed her pen and opened her notebook to an empty page. Unless the theft of the star provided the perfect opportunity to grab more online attention. Was that motivation enough to steal?

She made a few notes and then browsed the church's online photo gallery. Taking a long sip of her coffee, she attempted to refocus. Today at the clinic had been nonstop. She and Polly hadn't even taken a break for lunch, working through every minute. And now, as the clock chimed eleven, the weight of exhaustion pulled at her. But she couldn't quit. She felt like she was close to figuring something out, even if she wasn't sure what it was.

The church's website displayed photos Keri had snapped at the Christmas fair. Among them were two shots of Calvin. One as he was being unloaded from the transport truck, and another of him in his enclosure, contentedly munching hay. If only Keri had managed to photograph Calvin just before or during his escape, Harriet might be able to spot who had tampered with the gate of his pen.

Unless it had been Keri herself.

Harriet typed *Keri Stone* into the search bar, and instantly her screen was inundated with videos, blog posts, and endless selfies. There was also a link to a podcast, *Keri Unfiltered*. She recalled that Will had hired Keri as the church webmaster because of her prowess with social media. He had envisioned expanding the church's online presence, and Keri seemed perfect for the job. The church's website was uplifting and meaningful, tailored to be family-friendly and appropriate for all audiences.

Now Harriet found that Keri's personal online participation was in sharp contrast to her presentation of the church. Her blog, website, social media, and podcast were whirlwinds of color, humor, and daring pranks. With thousands of followers hanging on her every post, she combined the outrageous with the comedic and garnered a lively response.

Harriet scrolled until she found Keri's entry from the day of the Christmas fair, a video of Keri trying to make Yorkshire pudding at the Happy Cup Tearoom and Bakery. The young woman sported a holiday-themed apron and a slightly askew Santa hat. Her deliberately mismatched earrings seemed to jingle with the promise of festive cheer and whimsy.

As the creator of a popular podcast, Keri would be always hunting for that next viral hit in a relentless pursuit of internet fame. The theft of the star—or playing the hero in its recovery—could skyrocket her online presence. A story like that was pure gold for someone whose goal in life was more likes and shares.

Browsing Keri's online presence, Harriet noticed that the young woman had an uncanny ability to find herself at the heart of exciting situations, each conveniently translating into content that captivated her audience. But although the star's disappearance offered all the elements Keri loved to exploit—a mystery to unravel, a chance to be seen as a community-minded savior, and, most importantly, a story that could capture the imaginations of thousands online—it was nowhere to be found.

But was this concrete evidence of her guilt? Suspicions and a lost opportunity to gather clicks weren't enough to accuse someone of theft. Harriet wrote down all the reasons Keri could be the culprit.

Like so many others, she'd had the opportunity—she was at the church when key events unfolded, proven by her photos. As the church's webmaster, she might have an office key. She might even have learned the hiding place of the combination. In other words, Keri possibly had the means to pull off the theft.

But she also had motive—her constant quest for viral content. The theft of the silver star wouldn't be just any story. It would be a sensation, a high-stakes drama perfectly tailored for an internet craze. Something she could post everywhere—not only on the church's webpage. With one well-executed theft, Keri could not only dominate local gossip but also capture the attention of a much broader audience, feeding into her status.

Harriet pulled a fresh notecard from the stack and wrote *Keri Stone* at the top. She pivoted to her laptop and printed a photo of Keri. Placing the photo and the card in the center of the table, she felt a surge of both anticipation and dread.

Could the bubbly young woman with pink hair have really masterminded something so criminal as the theft of a priceless piece of art?

After Wednesday night choir practice, Harriet rummaged for her keys in the parking lot of White Church. Gerald had announced extra practices for the Christmas Eve service now only two weeks out. This year, they planned to sing classics like "Silent Night" and "Joy to the World," plus a folk hymn called "The Wexford Carol" that was sure to stand out.

Harriet had her doubts about hitting every note perfectly, but she was enjoying the chance to meet more people from the church. Her breath formed little clouds, and she wrapped her cashmere muffler tighter around her neck.

Choir members spilled out of the brightly lit church, their chatter and laughter filling the chilly air.

Keri, her hair streaked red and green for the holidays and wearing a black wool coat that nearly reached the tops of her shoes, strode toward a silver Mini Cooper parked a few spots away.

Harriet seized the chance. "Hey, Keri!"

The young woman faced her, tugging on a purple knit beret. "Hey, Dr. Bailey. Great practice tonight, huh?"

"You were amazing, hitting those high notes in 'The First Noel.'"

Keri grinned. "Aw, thanks. I'm posting a video on the website."

Harriet could see Keri's face clearly in the glow of a nearby streetlight. "By the way, I noticed you didn't post any pictures or video of the camel escaping from his pen. It seems like that would've been a golden social media moment."

Was it her imagination, or did something flicker in Keri's eyes? "Oh, I heard about it. Would you believe my rotten luck in missing the whole thing? I was in the parish hall the entire time. Hot chocolate spill. You can't imagine the cleanup effort."

"That's too bad. You missed quite an event."

"A day in the life, right? I'll see you later."

Keri waved goodbye, and Harriet watched her walk across the parking lot. Then Harriet ducked into the vehicle she'd inherited from her grandfather—a Land Rover she had dubbed "the Beast"—and called her aunt.

The phone rang only once before her aunt answered with a voice bubbling with cheer. "Well, hello, my dear. What's going on?"

"Just got out of choir practice," Harriet told her.

"I still can't believe you're in the choir. Your parents were in disbelief when I told them."

"Hey, I did it for a good cause."

"I know. Do you actually sing?"

"A little."

"Are you on key?" Aunt Jinny pressed.

"Well, I thought I was, but then tonight Gerald offered to give me a private lesson. Said I could use a little 'tuning up.'"

Aunt Jinny burst into laughter. "Only you, Harriet."

"Thanks for the support," Harriet replied dryly. "Quick question. You were in the parish hall for the duration of the Christmas fair, weren't you?"

"Until I heard you were chasing after a camel, at which point I left and ran to find you."

"And you witnessed the big hot chocolate spill, right?"

"Indeed," Aunt Jinny confirmed. "No one was hurt, but it was very sticky."

"Did you happen to see Keri Stone helping with cleanup?"

There was silence on the other end of the line, and Harriet could practically hear the wheels turning in her aunt's mind as she searched her memory. At last, Aunt Jinny replied definitively, "No. She wasn't there for the spill or the cleanup."

"Did you see her at the fair at all?" Harriet pressed.

"At the very start, when we were setting up tables. Not at all after that."

Before her first appointment the next morning, Harriet hurried to the church to update Will on her suspicions about Keri. She found him at work in his office. "Are you busy?"

"I'm struggling with Sunday's sermon. I'm not sure who's winning yet."

"Do you always start on Thursday?"

"I try to start earlier, but Thursdays are my big writing days."

"Well, I won't keep you then," Harriet said briskly. "Here's the deal. Keri claims she was in the parish hall when Calvin took off. But Aunt Jinny says she wasn't. That means her alibi doesn't hold up."

Will's brows knitted together. "I had hoped we wouldn't have to consider another church member."

"I know. I'm sorry." And she genuinely was, but they couldn't ignore the facts.

"What makes you suspect her? I mean, besides lying about her alibi?"

"Think about it. Keri is always so eager to showcase her life online, chasing likes and shares. Yet a camel runs amok at a major church event, and she posts nothing? An influencer like her would be sharing it everywhere she could."

"Fair enough. She would have had the opportunity to get pictures of Calvin. Even if she was somewhere else taking pictures when he got out, there was enough commotion that she would have been able to get some shots of the chaos and us bringing him back. The church paid her to stay all day and take photos for the website."

"Well, that's another thing. She wasn't at the church the whole day."

Will sat up straighter in his chair. "What do you mean? Where was she?"

"She was at the Happy Cup Tearoom, demonstrating how to make Yorkshire pudding. She has video on her website."

"Was she there when Calvin escaped? Doesn't that mean she didn't take the star?"

"I don't know," admitted Harriet. "I don't know what time of day she was at the tearoom. But that shouldn't be hard to find out."

Will ran his fingers through his hair. "What about the boot print? I can't see Keri in that style of boot."

"True. But she might not have been alone, which would mean that the print could have been from her accomplice."

"How would she know the combination to the safe?"

"The same way anyone would. She searched Claire's office for it."

Will frowned. "She just doesn't seem like a common thief to me," he said.

"What if it's not about the star itself?" Harriet said. "I was wondering if she's thinking beyond simple theft. Maybe she sees it being stolen as a way to boost her online presence."

"How would that work?" Will asked.

"She could base her podcast on the theft, coming up with different suspects, motives, etc. You know, like those true crime podcasts that are so popular right now. People would follow along to find out what's happening, what the latest news is about the star. Then at some point, she anonymously returns the star and ties up her podcast in a neat little bow. "

Will rubbed the back of his neck. "So she's using the star and will eventually return it?"

"Right. Creating an aura of mystery around the star could be her aim, rather than outright theft."

"But isn't she taking a huge risk that she could get caught?"

"Of course. But she's young and ambitious and thinks she can pull it off. It's risky, but it fits her profile better than theft."

"You think she's that clever?"

"I wouldn't put it past her. And don't forget, an influencer will go to all sorts of lengths to get content that might go viral. It's how they make their living, after all. There was an influencer who climbed a skyscraper in New York City with no safety gear and recorded the whole thing. He gained over a million followers from that stunt."

Will shook his head. "Americans."

"It's not limited to us. I've seen influencers from all cultures and backgrounds doing such things."

"I suppose it's plausible. She's got the resources and a reason. Plus, her alibi's no good." Will massaged his temples. "It all makes my head spin."

"Sorry, but we're running out of options. And time."

Will nodded. "If Keri's our thief, we need solid evidence."

"As we would for anyone. You write your sermon. I'm on the case." Harriet stood. "Actually, before I do any star investigation, I've got some Christmas shopping to do. I'm running out of time for that too." She didn't mention that his gift was one of the ones she was stuck on. He wasn't easy to shop for, but she had some ideas.

"Don't you also have patients to treat today?" Will asked.

"Actually, I do have a miniature dachshund with a back problem. Since they have such long torsos compared to the rest of their bodies, they are prone to issues with their backs."

He raised an eyebrow. "Sounds like I'll brave the endless parish meetings and sermon headaches while you take on pint-size pups with bad backs."

Her smile matched his. "And other Christmas crises."

CHAPTER FIFTEEN

Later that day, Harriet sat behind the reception desk of the quiet clinic, finishing an inventory of waiting room amenities. Assorted pet leashes and colorful pamphlets on pet care lay in neat piles on the desk, and samples of dog treats filled a box on the counter. Beside her, a cup of tea sent up a gentle wisp of steam. Polly was in the back making more tea.

Ethan Grimshaw, the farrier, came through the door. "Hello, Harriet."

"Hi, Ethan," she replied. "How are things?"

"I just finished shoeing two geldings out at the Pickwells' farm."

Harriet nodded. "They spoke highly of how you dealt with their new mare the other day. I'm sure they'll offer good word of mouth for you."

"I'm glad to hear that. It was easy. A little hoof trimming, and she was ready to ride."

Polly emerged from the back with two cups of tea. "I thought I heard someone out here with Harriet. Can I talk you into a cuppa, Ethan?"

"Easily. Thank you." He accepted the cup and busied himself drinking it for a few moments. "Do you have any other referrals for me, Harriet? I have tons of work, but I don't want to leave you in a lurch when you've been so kind to me since I arrived."

"We're all set at the moment. But I'll certainly let you know if that changes."

"Good." Ethan crouched to give Charlie a scratch behind the ears, the cat purring in approval. "Hello, lovely. I'm a horse guy, but you aren't so bad."

"Not bad?" Polly laughed. "She's adorable. Aren't you, Charlie?" She tossed a dental treat to the cat, who happily gobbled it up then flopped onto her side, inviting more pets.

"I'm only joking. I love cats." Ethan set his empty teacup on the counter. "I'd better be going. Merry Christmas!"

As the door shut behind him, Polly refreshed their tea and then began to put away the inventory that had already been accounted for. "Quiet for a Thursday," she remarked.

"It is. We might close early, since we both have more Christmas shopping to do. But first I want you to see this." Harriet clicked to a different screen on her laptop.

Polly set her tea down and leaned in to get a better view. "Oh, Keri's Yorkshire pudding video? I haven't seen that yet."

Harriet pressed play. Keri appeared on the screen, frantically trying to master Yorkshire pudding in the homey setting of the Happy Cup Tearoom and Bakery. They watched as she made a mess of it, flour and other ingredients flying.

Polly chuckled in appreciation.

Pausing the video, Harriet pointed to the date in the corner. "Keri shot this the same day the star disappeared. At least an hour after it was stolen."

Polly leaned closer, her eyes narrowing. "Knowing her, Keri's bakery antics started way before we saw her video."

"What do you mean?"

"Keri is all about the perfect shot. Despite her off-the-cuff vibe, she's meticulous. She once told me that setting up a video shoot could devour her whole afternoon."

"And that means what?"

"That at the time of the theft, she was likely knee-deep in dough, not deceit."

"But how can we be sure? It's a stretch from 'likely' to 'definitely.'"

Polly's fingers flew over the laptop keys. She pulled up a series of behind-the-scenes shots Keri had posted on her website. "We can tell from these. They show her at the bakery. Check the time stamps. Do they give her an alibi?"

Harriet peered at the photos. Sure enough, the times on at least four or five of the photos showed that they were taken right when Calvin escaped from his pen.

And just like that, Keri Stone was no longer a suspect.

Early the following morning, Harriet walked into the parish hall as Keri unrolled her exercise mat. The room had undergone its Friday morning makeover—foam mats arranged in rows and a small group of women chatting and laughing while they stretched. Less than two weeks until Christmas, and she still didn't have anything for Aunt Jinny. Maybe a membership to the exercise group? A month of free classes?

"Hey, do you have a minute?" she asked, approaching Keri. The young woman might have a foolproof alibi, but why had she lied about cleaning up the hot chocolate? Harriet intended to find out.

"Sure," Keri said, her smile camera-ready, as usual. "As long as you don't mind if I stretch while we talk."

"Not at all," Harriet replied. She decided to jump right in. "You told me you were cleaning up hot chocolate when the star went missing."

Keri's face flushed. All around them, the hall was gradually filling with exercise enthusiasts.

Harriet waited, allowing the silence to make the younger woman uncomfortable enough to speak first.

"Yeah, so?" Keri finally said, dropping her arms and glaring at Harriet before facing away from her.

"I heard that you weren't in the parish hall except at the very beginning of the fair, and then I saw your video." Harriet moved to stand in front of Keri once more. "Which you recorded at the Happy Cup that afternoon. Is that where you were when the star was stolen?"

Keri's expression softened. "I was torn, you know? The church hired me for the day, and I didn't want to let anyone down. Shooting a baking video during the fair—it felt like I was trying to be in two places at once." She chewed on her lip, regret flickering in her eyes. "I owed Pastor Will my time. I promise you—and if you watch the video, you'll know—I tried to blend both worlds, creating content that also spotlighted the fair. I talked about it while I made the pudding. It was my way of making up for it, hoping to drive more attention and ideally visitors to the event, since I have a larger following than the church does. I didn't want to disappoint anyone, especially not Pastor Will."

"So why lie? You could have told me that."

"I was afraid of being judged for trying to do both. I thought if I told you, you'd see it as me not taking my job seriously. But honestly,

I was trying to promote the fair in my own way. I messed up by not being clear from the start. I'm really sorry for any trouble this caused."

"We thought you might have swiped the star."

"What? No way. Why would you suspect me?" Keri looked stricken.

"Because you lied about where you were." Harriet looked her in the eye.

"I get that. I'll make it right. If Pastor Will gives me another chance, I'll be fully committed."

"I'm glad to hear it," she said, offering the distraught young woman a warm smile. The music kicked in, and the instructor began the class. Harriet ducked out the door, feeling better.

Until she realized that, once again, she was back to square one.

CHAPTER SIXTEEN

London
January 1933

The early morning London air was crisp, biting Letty's cheeks as she stepped out of the flat she called home. She wrapped her coat tighter around herself, a shield against the January chill, and took a moment to breathe in the city—a blend of soot, fresh bread from the nearby bakery, and the faintest hint of the Thames.

Twenty-three-year-old Letty had found her footing in London. She loved her neighborhood of Bloomsbury, with its busy streets softened by the green of garden squares and the hum of students and artists discussing ideas over tea. The redbrick buildings and a few bookshops made Bloomsbury feel cozy, like a little village in the middle of the big city.

This place reminded her of a bit of home in White Church Bay. She had spent the week after Christmas with her family in Yorkshire, and even though she loved being with them, she was happy to get back to her flatmates and her own life in London. Letty's flat, shared with a group of girls who had quickly become like sisters, was a cacophony of laughter, late-night confessions, and the occasional teasing over who had left the teapot empty. They were all young women carving out a place in the world, each with dreams as vivid and interesting as the city itself.

She loved her job as a bookkeeper at Selfridges, one of London's grand department stores, a short walk from her flat. The luxury store buzzed with energy and elegance, but for her, it was a place where she could lose herself in ledgers and numbers, a language she'd always understood better than any other.

Letty's morning dash through the bustling streets of London had become as routine as tea and toast. This morning, she was on her usual path to work when a sudden gust of wind whipped through the street, scattering the bundle of papers she held in her arms. These weren't just any papers. They were ledger pages she'd brought home from the store to work on. She raced to grab the flying sheets, trying not to lose any of them.

To her surprise, a chap in a long pea coat suddenly stopped to help her pick them up. His suit was sharp and crisp, fitting him in a way that suggested confidence and an eye for detail, traits Letty found appealing even in the middle of her mini disaster.

As their hands met—hers slightly trembling from the morning's rush and his assured and steady—over a flying ledger sheet, Letty looked up into his eyes, which twinkled with a spark of amusement, a silent chuckle shared between two strangers over the absurdity of the moment. It was an expression that seemed to say, "Well, this is a fine mess, isn't it?" Letty couldn't help but let a genuine smile break through her embarrassment.

"I'm Cecil Bailey," he said, his voice like a warm blanket on a chilly morning.

"Letty," she replied, feeling the corners of her mouth lift in a smile she hadn't planned on giving so freely today. "Thank you." She took the final paper from him, their fingers brushing briefly in a touch that lingered like a promise. "You've rescued both me and my job from certain doom."

"Anytime, Letty," he replied, with a grin that suggested he'd enjoyed their little adventure on the pavement as much as she had.

For the next five mornings, Letty scanned the crowd for a glimpse of Cecil. Despite telling herself it was silly, hope leaped within her with each step she took toward work, though every day passed without sight of him. By Friday, she had resigned herself to the fact that their meeting was nothing more than a fleeting London encounter.

And then, there he was, his gaze finding hers across the tangle of morning commuters, and with a smile as warm as the first rays of sun.

Stopped at a red light, Letty watched him check left and right before he dashed across the street, ignoring the signal on his way over to her. Up close, he was as handsome as she remembered from their quick encounter over the windblown pages. He was tall without being intimidating, his presence solid and comforting.

"Hello again," he greeted, his voice carrying a mixture of warmth and amusement that she had begun to suspect was his usual tone. Letty could detect the subtle scent of sandalwood, a comforting and unexpectedly intimate note that made her heart flutter anew.

"Hi," she managed to reply. Standing with him so close, she took in the finer details—the way his suit seemed to embrace him and how his impeccably-styled hair held a rebellious wave that caught the morning light.

"I hoped I'd see you again," Cecil said. "I've been carrying an extra umbrella in case London decided to be London and rain on your papers."

Feeling heat in her cheeks, she stammered, "H-how thoughtful."

"Listen, I'm sorry if this is too forward, but could I convince you to have a cup of tea with me? I know a cozy place down the street."

"If we hurry. I do have to get to work." Letty was suddenly grateful that she'd made an early start that morning so that she had this extra time.

"Of course. So do I."

He escorted her to a quaint little tea shop where they were welcomed by a warm atmosphere teeming with the bustling chatter of patrons and the delicate clink of teacups against saucers. The aroma of freshly baked pastries enveloped her, a sharp contrast to the brisk chill of the city street outside.

As they settled at their table, a flutter of nerves danced in Letty's stomach. For the past week, she had been on the lookout for Cecil, half-convinced she would never see the mysterious man again. Yet here he was, sitting across from her. She was charmed by the way his deep brown eyes crinkled when he smiled, and he always seemed to be on the verge of laughter.

He scanned the small menu then asked her, "What would you like?"

"Something daring," she replied, a playful smile on her lips. "Maybe Dragon Well green tea."

He laughed. "So you're adventurous? I thought you might be. I, on the other hand, will stick with Earl Grey."

"You're a traditionalist," she observed.

"Not with everything, but definitely when it comes to tea," he said.

Letty soon found herself at ease with Cecil as the conversation flowed. She shared details about her job at Selfridges. For some reason, she felt compelled to express how important this job was to her. He listened carefully, asking insightful questions that showed he genuinely cared.

Then he described his career as a veterinarian and that he was in London for a conference.

"Where's home?" she asked before she could stop herself.

"I'm from Yorkshire, born and bred," he explained.

"You are?" she asked, delighted. "I'm from *Yorkshire. I grew up right outside a little town called White Church Bay."*

"You never," he said. "My family has lived in White Church Bay for generations, and I plan to set up my veterinary practice there. How did we never meet as children?"

"I grew up on a farm and went to a little country school. Our paths probably never crossed."

Cecil met her gaze. "Well, I'm glad they've crossed now."

She hadn't talked so easily with a young man before, nor been so interested in the conversation. Yet, as much as she wished to linger in the moment, she was mindful of the time. One was not late to Selfridges. "I have to go," she said reluctantly.

"Me too," Cecil replied, rising. "I'm on a panel this morning. I've really enjoyed this though."

"As have I. Thank you." She pulled on her coat and grabbed her handbag. Time had flown, and she would need to run to get to the store on time.

"Do you like churches?" he blurted.

"Excuse me?" She blinked in surprise.

"I'm sorry," Cecil said. "I'm a bit of an architecture buff, especially when it comes to old churches."

"I love them," she said. "They're fascinating."

"I would like to take you to see some of London's most amazing old churches this Saturday, if you're interested."

"Is this a date?" Letty asked.

"It is if you want it to be." The tips of Cecil's ears seemed a little pink.

She beamed at him. "I'd like that."

"Wonderful. How about if we meet here Saturday morning for tea first?" Cecil suggested, his smile wide.

"Saturday morning it is. I'll see you then."

Though she felt as if she floated on air to work, Letty arrived right on time.

CHAPTER SEVENTEEN

Have another," Doreen Danby urged, sliding a plate of Eccles cake across the small kitchen table toward Harriet.

The late morning sun streamed through the windows into the bright, cheerful kitchen. As she selected a second cake, Harriet wondered if she should have stayed at the parish hall to participate in the exercise class with Keri. People in the village always offered her the most delectable sweets, especially her neighbor Doreen.

The aroma of the Eccles cake, thick with currants, nutmeg, and cinnamon, mingled with the scents of a wood fire in the potbellied stove. It conjured an almost tangible sense of home. Harriet took a deep breath, letting the richness of her surroundings relax her. She felt worlds away from her usual bustling life, and the change couldn't have been more welcome.

Doreen leaned forward, her usually composed face taking on a challenging edge. "You'll never find that star, you know."

That statement jolted Harriet back to reality. "Why not?" She took a bite of cake, reflecting that she had merely stopped in for a friendly visit. She was beginning to grow tired of every conversation coming back to the star.

"Because if the person I suspect is responsible, then I'm afraid the star might already be beyond our reach."

Harriet sat up straight, her interest in the cake momentarily forgotten. "Who?"

"Do you know Lloyd Throckmorton?"

"He runs Thistle and Thatch Antiques, right? He brings his armadillo to me. But why would he have anything to do with the theft?"

Doreen shifted uneasily. "I really shouldn't speculate. It's not my place. And I'd hate to cast aspersions without any proof."

"But you think there's a reason?" Harriet pressed gently.

With a reluctant sigh, Doreen leaned in, as if the walls might be eavesdropping. "It's just that Lloyd has made a couple of attempts to purchase the star from the church."

"But the church wouldn't sell it?"

"Wouldn't even consider it. I was on the church council at the time."

"Why would he want it?"

"To sell to one of his London buyers, no doubt. He went on and on about how much it was worth."

Harriet wondered why Will had never mentioned this to her. "What was his reaction when the church wouldn't sell it?"

"The first time, he was obviously disappointed and annoyed. But he walked away peacefully. The last time, though, was a different story. He came back to the council with an even more generous offer, and when they refused him again, he was furious. He said the star could bring in a lot of money at an art auction and that it was irresponsible of the church to pass on that."

"What did Pastor Will have to say about it?"

"It was before he was here."

That explained why he hadn't mentioned it to Harriet. Doreen picked up the teapot and replenished their cups.

"Wow. So he really wanted it. But enough to steal it?"

Doreen paused, and the sound of the oven timer pinging cut through the tension. "That would be my gingerbread. I'll pack some for you and Polly to enjoy with your tea. It's best to eat it while it's warm."

It wasn't lost on Harriet that Doreen hadn't answered her question.

Harriet left Doreen's and hurried straight to Lloyd's shop. She opened the door to Thistle and Thatch Antiques and felt like she had stepped into the 1940s. Vintage lamps cast golden pools of light on tables cluttered with porcelain figures and classic toys. Sepia photos were carefully preserved in ornate frames. Victorian brooches, cameos, and lockets on velvet populated a glass display case. On a scarred buffet table, a line of manual typewriters stood as a testament to days gone by. She almost expected to see Beatrix Potter in a corner, sketching in the margins of an old book.

She feigned interest in a display of vintage lace while she tried to figure out how to broach the subject of the stolen star with Lloyd. Perhaps she should have considered that before she came.

Thoughts of Letty and Albie, Aunt Jinny, and Grandad crowded her mind. She had to get the star back for them.

"Is there something I can help you with, Dr. Bailey?" a gruff voice asked. Harriet looked up to see the tall older gentleman coming toward her. He sported a short gray beard and rimless glasses and wore a dark blue cardigan.

"Hello, Lloyd. How are you? How's Dottie?"

"I'm fine. Dottie is better. She loves her new heat lamp."

"Good. Armadillos hate to be cold."

He peered at her over his spectacles, exuding impatience even though she appeared to be the sole customer in the store. Was the store a front for something more lucrative than antique toys and Victorian lace?

"I'm hoping to find a Christmas present for my aunt Jinny."

"Dr. Garrett?" he asked.

"That's right. You know her?"

"Everyone does. And I knew Old Doc Bailey, your grandfather, quite well. We often enjoyed a cup of tea and talked about our favorite books."

Harriet nodded. "I got my love of reading from my dad, and he got his from Grandad."

"Indeed. Our chats wandered from Byron and Yeats to John Grisham."

Harriet laughed. "I never knew he liked Grisham."

"Harold might have been an astute intellectual and a brilliant artist, but he still loved a good thriller. If you're after something for Dr. Garrett, you might try the rare books section. I believe I have a leather-bound copy of *The Apothecary's Almanac.* It's a collector's item with medieval woodcuts."

"That sounds great. I was also hoping to find an ornament for her tree this year."

"I see. Follow me." He led her to the back of the store, where a long shelf displayed intricate Christmas decorations.

"These are perfect." If she wanted to start a conversation about the star, it was now or never. "I've been thinking about the silver Christmas star at the church and how much Aunt Jinny loves it. She's really upset that it won't be on the tree this year."

A shadow flashed over Lloyd's features. "Yes, bad business. Most distressing."

"I was wondering if I might find something here that could serve as a sentimental reminder of the church's star. Especially if the real one isn't recovered in time for Christmas."

"I highly doubt that the star will be recovered," Lloyd replied. "It's a valuable piece, and whoever took it has likely already sold it."

"You sound very certain about that."

"A person doesn't take the risk of stealing something like that and then put it on top of their own Christmas tree." He picked up an ornament, a whimsical silver star. "Here's a lovely Christmas decoration for your aunt. Not exactly the silver star from the church, but similar enough to serve as a pleasant reminder."

"Thank you. It's lovely." She took the star from him and admired it, trying to sound casual. "Tell me, how hard would it be to sell the church's Christmas star?"

Lloyd paused for a moment. "It's difficult to say. I don't deal with the underground market. All my transactions are legitimate, and I sell mostly to locals. However, if you were connected with the right people, I would imagine you could sell it rather quickly."

"Do you have any thoughts about who might have taken it?"

He gave her a sharp glance. "How would I know who stole it?"

"I simply wondered if you might have heard something, since you deal with antiques and know others in that community," she said.

"I wouldn't classify it as merely an antique." His eyes narrowed. "It's over a century old, handcrafted in Yorkshire. It's a work of art. As I have told the people of White Church on numerous occasions." He adjusted his spectacles. "As for who might have stolen it? If I knew, I would have called the detective constable by now."

"Good point." She selected a music box from a nearby shelf and wound it. The haunting notes of "Für Elise" broke the silence. "Quite a shock, its disappearance during the Christmas fair."

"Very. And a rather daring thief."

"Did I see that you had a booth in the parish hall that day?" She kept her tone light.

"We have one every year."

"Must've been loud with the commotion of the camel escaping."

"I wasn't there. Herbert Aynesworth, my assistant, was in charge. He's a university student who handles the tech stuff, including my accounting. For years, I managed quite well with a ledger and pen. I never touch a computer. You see, I don't merely sell antiques—I'm turning into one." He gave a wry smile.

"I get it. Without Polly, I'd be a mess." She examined the music box as though it were the most interesting thing she had seen in years and added casually, "Did you keep the shop open on the day of the Christmas Fair?"

Lloyd hesitated for a moment. "I closed briefly for year-end inventory." His gaze darted to the front. "Quite the tedious chore."

"I struggle to get through inventory projects too. Does Herbert help you with that?"

"Most times, yes."

"But not this time?"

"No."

Which meant that unless Harriet found someone who could corroborate Lloyd's story, he didn't have an alibi for the theft of the star.

"Lloyd Throckmorton? Seriously?" Will said, leaning against the stall door, his arms folded. He had met Harriet in a church member's barn, where she was examining the owner's pony. The warm, musky scent of hay and horse filled the barn, and a single lantern hung from a wooden beam. "He really doesn't seem like the type."

She had just finished telling him about her conversations with Doreen and Lloyd. It was almost evening and late for a vet appointment. But she wanted to make sure Buttercup was okay—her owner had sounded anxious on the phone. Harriet noticed Will had traded his black shirt with the tab collar for a cozy cable-knit sweater and well-worn jeans.

"There's a type?" she asked.

"Well, I guess not. But he's an elderly man whose greatest love is his pet armadillo."

"How can you be sure?" Squatting down, she rested her hand on the pony's front right hoof. "Easy now, Buttercup. Almost done." She could feel warmth emanating from the hoof, confirming her suspicion. Buttercup had developed an infection or abscess, a common issue. As a farrier, Ethan would have been able to treat it, but he had told Harriet he would steer clear of medical issues to avoid taking business from her. Harriet would be able to treat it easily.

"What's the word, Doc?" Will asked.

"Ethan Grimshaw was right. He fitted Buttercup for shoes yesterday and mentioned that she seemed off. Then her owner called me. I figured I'd better check her out."

"That's good of you." Will got back to the theft. "Lloyd's an old-school sort, not one to steal from a church—or anywhere else for that matter."

"The perfect cover. And if you're going to steal something, you wouldn't exactly wave a flag, right?" Harriet pointed out. "And maybe he wasn't the one to do the actual stealing. His assistant, Herbert, was in charge of Lloyd's booth at the fair, and he could have taken the star for his boss."

"True, but Lloyd's always struck me as the type who respects antiques, not the type who wants to make quick money from them."

"No red flags at all? He's never made any threats?"

"None. Although..."

Harriet raised an eyebrow as she drained the abscess then applied an antiseptic bandage so that it would continue to drain. Buttercup would be back to normal in no time.

Will took a deep breath. "It's probably nothing. But a month ago, Lloyd delivered an antique credenza to the church for the library. He noticed the safe and asked if that was where we kept the star."

Harriet ran her hand along the pony's velvety neck, murmuring praise in her ear. Then she stepped out of the stall and packed up the contents of her medical bag, each instrument snug in its familiar place. "What did you say?"

"I told him we locked it up in there and only brought it out on Christmas Eve." He stood across from her, frowning. "He asked to see the star. I didn't think there was any harm in it. He's a professional, so I let him have an up-close look."

"Where exactly was he when you entered the combination and opened the safe?"

Will closed his eyes and pinched the bridge of his nose with his thumb and forefinger. "Looking over my shoulder. I thought he was merely excited, but—"

Harriet finished the sentence for him. "But he might have been casing the joint."

CHAPTER EIGHTEEN

Harriet descended the narrow stairs and made her way along the hall, toward the hum of conversation. The church knitting group met in the youth room every Saturday at one o'clock. It sounded as if they were a lively bunch, which was good for Harriet's mission. The members of this group, chatting and laughing as their needles clicked, knew everything there was to know about White Church Bay. According to Aunt Jinny, they were the town's unofficial information network. Harriet figured if anyone had the scoop on Lloyd and what he was up to, it would be them. She planned to listen in and maybe ask a few casual questions, without making it obvious that she was digging for information.

She pushed the door open and stepped in, glancing around at the colorful posters and artwork that brightened the otherwise plain walls. A flat-screen TV hung on one wall, sharing space with a framed print of Jesus carrying a lamb on His shoulders. Dust motes floated in a beam of light coming through the single window.

Knitters were gathered in a circle on the upholstered couches, overstuffed chairs, purple beanbag, and lone rocking chair. The click of needles set the beat of the room as if pacing the conversation.

She noticed that each knitter had their own distinct style of dress. She knew several of them. Mildred sported a brown cardigan over a faded housedress. Sarah, a single mom of three, wore sleek black leggings paired with an oversize jumper. Tina, in her T-shirt and ripped jeans, wore one earbud but was in an animated conversation with Sarah. Sixty-something Frank was the solitary male, balding with a thick silver mustache.

In the middle of the room, a table held a tea tray with mismatched cups around a teapot. On another tray were slices of checkered pink-and-yellow Battenberg cake on paper plates.

"Good to see you, Harriet," Mildred greeted her, her smile warm. "We could use some youthful energy around here." Mildred went around the room and introduced everyone to Harriet.

Harriet smiled. "Lovely to be here. I hope you don't mind me dropping in."

A woman named Judith, her eyes magnified by large-rimmed glasses, nodded toward the empty chair beside her and managed to not miss a stitch. "Have you been knitting for a long time?"

"I've never knitted, actually," Harriet confessed. "I always thought it required patience I didn't possess."

Frank, juggling three knitting needles for some reason—Harriet didn't know people used more than two at a time—said, "Patience is hardly a prerequisite, but it's often a result. Knitting is almost meditative and has been shown to improve mental health. And then you have a beautiful product at the end."

"Well, I do like beautiful products." She took the offered seat. "And a challenge."

Judith rummaged around in her large knitting bag and retrieved a pair of needles and a skein of soft blue yarn. She handed them to Harriet with a smile.

Harriet accepted them, wondering how she'd gotten herself into this. First, the church choir. Now knitting. She didn't have time for either. Not to mention she lacked any actual skill. But the White Church Knitters were a font of information. If village gossip about Herbert or Lloyd existed, the knitters would know it.

Mildred pushed an ottoman next to her and sat down, her own skein and empty needles in hand. "Here, let me show you how to cast on and then the basic knit stitch. Trust me—you'll have it in no time."

Harriet watched carefully and tried to replicate Mildred's movements, which looked so easy, but somehow her fingers wouldn't cooperate. But when she finally produced her first stitch, the group erupted into applause as if she'd climbed Mount Everest.

As she fumbled with the knitting needles, she reminded herself that she wasn't there to knit but to fish for information.

Fortunately, Mildred saved her the trouble of having to start the conversation. "Have you seen my pictures of the Christmas fair, Dr. Bailey? There are some brilliant ones of you."

Harriet pounced at the chance. "No, but I would love to."

Mildred pulled out her phone. "Here, check these out."

Harriet admired several photos—the sheep, the goat, the rabbits, Mary and Joseph, and some great shots of Calvin. A blurry photo of Calvin breaking free from his pen caught her eye.

"You got a photo of the camel escaping?" She felt a spark of excitement.

"Didn't mean to. I was taking a picture of him, and then he started stamping his feet and pushed through the gate."

"Did you see anybody standing near the pen?"

Mildred swiped through a few photos. "No. I had switched to video, and it was all I could do to get it right on this confounded thing. My granddaughter says she'll upload the pictures for me—wait, is it upload or download?"

"I think it's upload. How much time elapsed between the photo and the video?" Harriet asked.

"Maybe twenty or thirty seconds," Mildred said. "They're awesome action shots, don't you think? I'm entering a couple of them in the parish photo contest."

"You should," Harriet said. "Would you mind sharing them with me?"

"Of course not." Harriet rattled off her phone number, and Mildred swiped and tapped several more times. "There you go."

Tina removed her earbud. "I can't believe the Christmas star was stolen while that camel was running around."

"I can't imagine Christmas Eve without it," Frank said.

"It's a disgrace," an elderly woman named Doris said. "Who would steal from a church?"

"Had to be an outsider. None of us would do such a thing," Frank said. "The star is a beautiful piece of art, a symbol of the season."

"When someone messes with that, they mess with all of us," said Doris.

Harriet decided to take the plunge. "Speaking of the Christmas fair, I heard Herbert Aynesworth ran the Thistle and Thatch Antiques booth. I've heard he's very good with accounting. Did anyone see him that day?"

"I think he was there, but he wasn't doing much work. Glued to his mobile," Tina said.

"Didn't seem the least interested in any sales, to be honest. Didn't even respond when I offered him a fresh scone." Judith squinted through her spectacles at the paper pattern smoothed out in front of her.

"I know how important the Christmas fair is to Lloyd. He never misses it. So, when I saw that young lad not even trying to sell anything, I called him," Mildred said, her voice indignant. "I was keeping an eye on my friend's booth while she was at lunch, so I couldn't leave," she explained when Harriet looked questioningly at her.

"Good for you," Judith said. "What did he say?"

"He never picked up. So I swung by his shop after my friend got back from lunch to let him know that Herbert might not be the best person to watch his booth, and also to get a gift for my niece. She collects old apothecary jars with the original labels still on them, and Lloyd always has just the thing. But the place was closed up tight. I even went around back and knocked on the door. Sometimes he works late and doesn't hear if someone's up front. But there was no answer, and I didn't see any lights on."

Perhaps Lloyd hadn't been at the shop doing inventory during the Christmas fair after all. Harriet supposed it was possible that he'd merely been ignoring his phone and the door to focus on the task. But if not, where had he been and why had he lied about it? The knitting group had proved to be every bit as informative as she had hoped.

"Have you got a knitting project in mind?" Tina asked her. "We all have something we're working on, and we share updates online. Keeps us motivated."

She would actually have to knit. Perhaps while rehearsing the alto part of "O Come All Ye Faithful." She swallowed a groan and asked, "Well, what's a good starter project?"

"Usually, I recommend starting with a square or rectangle shape, like a dishcloth or scarf. If you want something slightly more challenging, you could make a sleeve for your phone." Tina held up her own black phone sleeve, adorned with a lime-green stripe. "You make a rectangle, fold it in half, and sew up the sides. Then you have the perfect thing to protect your mobile, and you have the satisfaction of making it yourself. I'd be happy to give you a private lesson."

Well, at least her mother would be impressed with her new skill. She'd been encouraging Harriet for months to get involved with something besides the clinic and snooping around town. "I'd like that," Harriet told Tina.

Will had the easy job. As a pastor, he just had to flash a smile and chat—no need to moonlight as a warbling alto or an enthusiastic knitter to bag a good lead.

The bell overhead chimed as Harriet entered Thistle and Thatch Antiques again. She had left the knitters and gone straight to see Lloyd. It was a good thing the clinic closed at noon on Saturdays.

An old register, a relic in its own right, sat on the counter. A sleek laptop was open beside it, its screen glowing. An interesting juxtaposition—a shop and owner that both reveled in the past, yet with someone plugged into the present.

Lloyd emerged from the back room, looking disheveled. Gone were the crisp shirt and tailored trousers, replaced by a worn coat, a bulky red scarf, rumpled khakis, and hiking boots. "I'm about to close the shop for a few hours, Dr. Bailey. Could you return later, perhaps?"

"I can be quick. I only need to pick up a few Christmas gifts." She couldn't leave without getting some information. "I'm stumped on what to give my parents. They're always tricky to shop for. Oh, and for Pastor Will. The gifts you recommended for my aunt Jinny were perfect."

He glanced at the clock, eyebrows pinched together. "I've some very nice brass candlesticks, new from London. They would add a touch of elegance to any room."

She followed him to a crowded shelf and examined the ornate candlesticks, envisioning them on her parents' dining table. "Those will work perfectly. Thanks."

"I can't think of anything right now for Pastor Will, but I'll keep my eye out."

"Thank you. I would really appreciate that." She could use all the help she could get in that department.

As Lloyd printed the receipt for the candlesticks, her gaze wandered across the counter and settled on a stack of books beside a tall vase. She leaned over for a better view. *The Journal of Gemology* sat next to *Warman's Antiques & Collectibles Price Guide* with *An Illustrated Guide to Collecting Silver* beside them. She committed the titles to memory as best she could.

"I'm thinking of asking Herbert to look over the clinic's financial software. Seems like he's got a knack for it."

Something flickered over Lloyd's expression. "Herbert is quite indispensable." He wrapped brown paper around the candlesticks.

"Probably makes it easy to do things like taxes, budgets, and inventory, doesn't he?"

"Indeed," he said dryly, sliding the candlesticks into a bag.

"It's too bad you had to stay here at your shop and missed the Christmas fair."

"I detest the fair." He handed the package with the candlesticks across the counter to her. "A gaggle of old women selling knitted dish towels and jars of jam. I have better things to do."

"Oh?" She felt her cheeks grow warm as she fumbled through her prying questions. But if the star was to be found, maybe a little awkwardness was the price to pay.

It didn't matter, because Lloyd ignored it. "If that completes your purchases, Dr. Bailey, I really must close. I have a pressing commitment."

"Nothing wrong, I hope." She had truly become shameless. Next time, Will could do the interrogating. She wondered if he was bound by the Seal of Confession not to disclose anything someone confessed to him as a pastor. Or was that only for Catholic priests?

Lloyd answered with a silent stare as he buttoned his coat.

"Right then. Merry Christmas." She pushed through the door onto the chilly sidewalk, noticing he didn't return the holiday wishes.

Harriet started the picturesque walk to the isolated house on the moor, wrapped up against the late morning chill but enjoying the bright sun and sharp air. It was a beautiful day for a brisk walk, even if it meant doing a bit of work on her day off. Sunday after church was usually a feet-up, tea-in-hand kind of day, but today she was making an exception.

An elderly client had called while she was still in church. Her dog meant everything to her, so even though his symptoms didn't seem like a true emergency, Harriet had decided to go out and see what was happening.

While walking, she reflected on Will's sermon that morning. It had hit all the right notes about sticking together and helping out. It didn't hurt that he was pretty sharp in his Sunday best. There was something about him—maybe the way he genuinely cared, or maybe how he managed to come off as both serious and a little charming at the same time.

The farm lay beyond the moors, promising a splendid midday stroll. The cliffside path was a narrow ribbon snaking its way along the craggy edges of the coast. Gulls screeched overhead, the sound carried away by a brisk, salty wind that nipped at Harriet's cheeks and nose. The walk was lovely, but by the time she finished examining the dog, she wished she had driven to the farm. She would have loved to jump into the Beast, blast the heater, and be home in slippers in under twenty minutes. Instead, she was trudging back along a beautiful but cold trail across the moor.

An old stone cottage, desolate and weather-beaten, appeared a short distance off the trail. Wisps of smoke curled from its chimney. Will's mention of his childhood growing up on the moors flickered in her mind as she eyed the cottage covered with ivy and moss. She realized that she had never asked for any details about his childhood. It seemed that all they talked about lately was the Christmas star. In fact, they planned to meet for breakfast the following morning to discuss the progress they'd made on the case.

Lost in her thoughts, she almost missed a sudden movement up ahead. An older man, tall and thin, wearing a bright red scarf and clutching a small bundle, strode across the field toward the cottage. *Lloyd.* She was fairly certain he hadn't seen her.

She watched as he reached the stone building. With a quick glance over his shoulder, he opened the door and slipped inside.

She waited and watched. She was about to give up and start walking again when the door creaked open and he stepped out. He now walked with a noticeable spring in his step, but his hands were empty. Whatever he had carried into the cottage, he had left it there.

The only reason anyone would venture down this lonely path with a bundle in their arms would be to conceal something. The secluded location made it a perfect place to hide something valuable. Something like the silver star.

CHAPTER NINETEEN

That old place is on National Trust land," Van said, frowning in the empty reception area at the clinic. "And in bad enough shape that it's dangerous. I don't want anybody mucking about out there, especially an older gentleman like Lloyd Throckmorton."

"We have to go," Harriet insisted. "What if the silver star is there?"

"I agree," Will added. "But I'd feel a lot better if it was the three of us together." He gave Harriet a concerned look. "Especially since it will be dark soon."

Van nodded. "I'll need to talk to the owner and get permission. Otherwise, I'll need a search warrant." He turned to Will. "Great sermon this morning, by the way. Why do I feel like you're talking directly to me each time?"

Will laughed. "I'm not, but I'm glad you feel that way. Most of the time I'm preaching to my own needs and praying it helps someone else."

It had been a good sermon, but all Harriet could think about right now was the possibility that the silver star was stashed away in that old building. "Do you know the owner?" she asked Van.

"We play in the same rugby league. Let me give him a call." Van used his cell phone, putting the call on speaker.

After a few rings, a cheerful voice boomed in answer. "Gareth speaking."

"Gareth, it's Van Worthington. I hope I'm not catching you at a bad time. I need a favor." Van's tone was professional yet slightly apologetic for the intrusion.

"Not at all. What can I do for you?" Gareth's voice was warm.

"We've come across something at your cottage on the National Trust land. I need to have a peek inside. Would you grant permission for law enforcement to access the building?"

"Of course, mate. I haven't been out there in ages, though, so I can't speak to what sort of state it might be in. What's going on? Do you need me to come down there?"

"No need, Gareth. I'm checking out a possible trespass. If I have your verbal consent, I can check it out. I'll document this call for our records."

"Keep me updated," Gareth said before they exchanged goodbyes and ended the call.

Van turned back to Will and Harriet. "Let's go."

Twenty minutes later, they were at the cottage. Van opened the door and stepped in first, switching on a light then signaling the all-clear. As Harriet and Will entered, they halted abruptly. Will let out a low whistle.

The interior was nothing like the crumbling exterior. Vintage charm abounded with old oak furniture, two brass oil lamps, and Persian rugs. Cheerful curtains framed the sea view. Van turned on a battery lantern, and it cast a warm glow over untouched cookies and a thermos on a makeshift table. Apparently, Lloyd had transferred a collection of furniture and decor from his antique shop.

Van clicked on two more lanterns and scanned the room. "This doesn't strike me as a thieves' hideout. It looks like someone lives here, but it's not like anything Gareth would do."

"This furniture is from Thistle and Thatch. He hasn't even removed the price tags from some of this stuff," Will said, examining a love seat.

"So Lloyd has a secret hideaway," Van said. "Who would've thought?"

"A secret hideaway that's tasteful and elegant, without a hint of criminality," Harriet mused. "But that doesn't make him innocent."

"Doesn't make him guilty either," Van reminded her. "I say we go through the place. We've got permission to be here and came all this way, so we might as well make it worth our while." He walked into the small kitchen, and in a moment Harriet could hear cupboard doors being opened and closed.

She crossed to the rickety door at the back of the cottage and pushed it open. Surveying the sparse room, her eyes lingered on a makeshift table—a weathered door balanced on two sawhorses. A tattered armchair stood in one corner.

Against the far wall was an old wardrobe. She tugged open the wardrobe's door. It appeared empty, but then she spotted a lockbox on a top shelf. The box was large and heavy, clearly meant for keeping valuable items safe. It wasn't the usual antique she'd expect from Lloyd. The box was new and shiny, with a simple lock and no decorative details. She hauled it off the shelf and carried it into the kitchen.

"Will you look at that?" Van said, rising from his crouched position by a low cabinet as Harriet set the box on the table.

"Why would someone hide a lockbox in a decrepit cottage like this?" Will asked.

"To keep a secret safe," she said. "Can you open it, Van?"

"Not without a key, and I wouldn't get your hopes up that the silver star is inside." Van spoke evenly, but Harriet didn't miss the hint of excitement in his voice.

"Think about it," she pressed. "Lloyd hides a lockbox in a cottage that seems to be abandoned. Obviously, this is a secret hideaway."

"And you saw him arrive this afternoon carrying something," Will said.

"Did it look like this box?" Van asked.

"No. More like a cloth bag from the grocery. But the star could have been in the bag, and he brought it here to put in the lockbox. It's a perfect place to keep stolen goods."

"Do you think that's what it is, Van?" Will asked. "If not the star, then other loot?"

"And can you bring him into the station on a suspicion of theft?" Harriet added.

Van held up his hands to stop the onslaught of questions. "We'd have to catch him in the act of transporting the goods. If we find something stolen and show it to him, he'll claim that it isn't his and he has nothing to do with this place. After all, someone else could have brought things here from his shop." They followed Van as he put the lockbox back on the wardrobe shelf. "I'm not confiscating it for now. I want to start by giving Lloyd a chance to explain."

While Will led the men's Sunday evening Bible study at church, Harriet and Van paid Lloyd a visit at Thistle and Thatch Antiques.

The cozy charm Harriet had once felt was gone, replaced by a hint of unease. Having Van by her side was a relief, as her view of Lloyd was changing. He no longer seemed like the amiable gentleman she had thought him to be. His smile didn't feel as warm, his actions less straightforward.

They found him standing behind the counter, his back hunched as he shuffled through a box of tarnished spoons. He adjusted his spectacles and gave a slight cough at the sight of them. "Ah, Detective Constable Worthington. Dr. Bailey. To what do I owe the pleasure?"

Van cleared his throat, his voice courteous but firm. "Lloyd, we'd like a word."

"Christmas shopping?" he asked, his voice hopeful in its feigned cheerfulness. He gave the impression of someone who knew what was coming but couldn't accept it.

"In private, maybe?" Harriet suggested.

A few customers at the back of the shop were watching a train circle a pine tree village. For a moment, it reminded her of the toy train that used to chug around her family's Christmas tree. She shook off the memory and the bittersweet nostalgia that followed it.

Without a word, Lloyd spun on his heel, and they followed him behind the long counter, down a short hall, and through a narrow door marked OFFICE.

A gangly twentysomething man slouched in front of the laptop she had spotted earlier.

"Herbert," Lloyd said to him. "Pop out and run the cash register."

The three of them waited while he closed the laptop and tucked it under his arm then left without a word, pulling the door shut behind him.

"Sit," Lloyd said, his voice clipped. So much for the old-world charm. Harriet wished Will was with them. He was good at drawing people out without putting their guard up—no doubt a trait every effective pastor needed.

Van lowered himself into a creaky folding chair, and Lloyd sat in his chair behind the desk. She perched on an ornate ottoman. It made her a foot shorter than the two men, but it was either that or stand the entire time.

Lloyd steepled his fingers. "It isn't often I get a visit from the village detective constable and the village veterinarian. Quite the dynamic duo."

"It's merely a friendly conversation," Van said, his voice casual. He gave Lloyd a warm smile. "Not a big deal. I brought Dr. Bailey here because she has observed you and I wanted her in on the conversation."

"She has observed me? What am I, one of her patients in need of a wellness check?" He kept his eyes on Van as if Harriet weren't in the room. "And where, pray tell, has Dr. Bailey 'observed' me?" The sarcasm in his voice was no longer a thin veneer, but full force.

"Entering the old cottage next to the cliff walk," she said. "You carried something in, and then you came out empty-handed."

He raised an eyebrow. "I'm surprised that you don't have better ways to occupy your time than spying on an old man. Do your alleged 'observations' violate the law?"

"No. But the cottage isn't yours to use. It's privately owned and on National Trust land," Van said.

"And I wasn't spying. I was walking by," she added.

He ignored her. "That building has sat abandoned for a decade. I hardly think I've done any harm."

"Why do you go there?" Van asked, his voice still light.

"It's a quiet place, away from prying eyes."

"If someone were prying, what would they see?"

"In this village, any activity can serve as fodder for gossip."

"Are you providing fodder?" Van's tone was light, but Harriet could tell from his face that he meant business.

"Not at all," Lloyd replied, his voice icy. Rising abruptly, he straightened to his full height, his posture rigid. "My personal life is none of your affair. I am far too busy with my shop to entertain such nonsense. If you insist I vacate the cottage, so be it. I shall cease and desist."

"Sit down, please," Van said. "You're right. Technically, this isn't my business, and you don't have to answer my questions. But if you don't answer, it might look like you're hiding something."

Lloyd looked from one to the other and slowly sat back in his chair. "Fine. To end this absurd questioning of my integrity, I will tell you the truth. I visit the cottage to meet a friend away from the village gossip. Her husband passed away a year ago. You know how people talk, and I don't wish to expose her to nasty rumors. We both love history and literature. Old manuscripts. Cartography. It is seldom that one makes such an unexpected connection, and we wanted to protect it."

"You've certainly fixed up the place," Van said. "Made it quite cozy."

"Is it against the law to be a little comfortable when you meet the love of your life?" Lloyd's voice trembled. "We have afternoon tea and conversation."

"Nothing wrong with that. Can you explain why there's a lockbox in the wardrobe?"

Lloyd's fingers twitched, and his sophisticated facade cracked. "How do you know about that?" he demanded. "What were you doing in there?"

"I had permission from the legal owner of the building to check it out for possible trespassing," Van replied.

"It's just a place to keep something valuable. Nothing illegal, I assure you."

"Mr. Throckmorton, where were you during the Christmas fair?" Van asked abruptly.

"You mean when the star was stolen?"

"Yes."

"At the cottage," Lloyd answered quietly.

"Alone?"

"No. I was with my friend."

"I'm sorry, but I will need her name," Van told him. "I can assure you I will do my best to maintain your privacy as well as hers in this matter."

Lloyd hesitated until Harriet thought he would refuse to answer. At last, he whispered, "Clara Jones."

"The retired librarian? Oliver took over for her recently, didn't he?" Harriet asked.

"Yes. She's a lovely woman."

"I'm glad you've found each other," she told him, and she meant it. "Grandad would have been happy for you too."

Lloyd's expression softened briefly before snapping back into a stony glare. "And what would Doc Bailey have thought of his granddaughter accusing an elderly man of theft?"

"He would realize that I am not accusing anyone of anything, but doing what I can to return a priceless heirloom to the church." She fought to keep her tone even and reasonable.

"Can Mrs. Jones corroborate your alibi?" Van asked.

"Of course. But I would prefer that you leave her out of this."

"I'll do my best, but I can't promise anything."

"Can you open the lockbox and show us the contents, Lloyd?" Harriet asked. "It could clear your name."

"I have no interest in clearing my name." Lloyd stood again. "I think it's time for the two of you to leave. I've answered all your questions. I will move my things out of the cottage, including the lockbox, which, by the way, is my personal property."

"Lloyd, I didn't want it to come to this, but now I'm afraid it has. I will need you to show us the contents of that box, or I'll be forced to confiscate it." Van rose to his feet, his towering height and considerable build overwhelming the small office.

Lloyd eyed him with defiance then slumped in defeat. "Come with me."

Lloyd switched on the table lamp, and Harriet blinked against the sudden brightness after the dark ride up from the village.

"How did you get all of this up here?" Van asked, glancing around.

"Herbert and his university mates will do anything for a bit of cash." Lloyd wore an expression of both resignation and pride.

Van moved to the bedroom and reemerged with the lockbox. "Open it, please," he said.

Lloyd retrieved a key from his coat pocket, inserted it into the lock, and lifted the metal lid. He took out a swath of blue velvet and unfolded it, revealing a small ring box inside. He opened it, and even in the dim light, the diamond sparkled back at them. "Satisfied that I'm not hiding the silver star in here now?"

"Is it for Clara?" Harriet asked.

Lloyd nodded.

"It's beautiful," she said.

His face softened. "I'm going to ask her to marry me. I don't see any reason for either of us to be lonely ever again."

"You can't use the cottage for it," Van said, his voice firm.

Lloyd's disappointment was palpable.

"Van, could they meet here one more time so Lloyd can propose in their special dating spot?" Harriet asked. "It would be more romantic that way."

Hope lit Lloyd's eyes. "Would that be permissible, Detective Constable?"

Van sighed. "With the owner's permission. And knowing Gareth, he'll probably think it's a lark. But after that, you need to move your things out and don't come back."

"I give you my word, DC Worthington." Lloyd clasped the ring box to his heart. "I've waited a long time for this moment, an old bachelor like me."

"I'm happy for you," Harriet said. "A lot of people will be."

He gave her a brilliant smile.

"Let's be on our way," Van said, moving toward the door. "I'll call Gareth for you, and I'm going to suggest that he install a padlock."

"Understood. And Detective Constable?"

Van looked back, one hand on the door handle.

"Thank you."

CHAPTER TWENTY

Harriet carefully navigated the slippery flagstones, her mind on the previous day's visit with Lloyd. The sun had sunk below the horizon, and the temperature had plummeted, turning the afternoon's cold drizzle into a thin layer of ice. The yard light sent out a weak beam, throwing long, twisted shadows across the frozen garden. Above, the clouds were a heavy blanket, smothering any hope of moonlight.

Maxwell's barking inside the dark house cut through the stillness, a welcome sound even as she regretted not leaving the kitchen light on. Each step toward the house reaffirmed her goal—slippers, robe, and a cup of tea.

A client had called her with an emergency as the altos were about to practice their part. With relief, she had dashed out of choir practice, the tune of "Lo, How a Rose E'er Blooming" still in her head.

Dairy farmers usually managed things solo, so the client's emergency call meant he was worried. He'd been right to be. His cow would have been in real trouble if he'd waited until morning to call Harriet. Three frantic hours later, drained of all energy, she trudged back to her car, blasted the heat, and pointed the Beast toward home.

As she slid her key into the kitchen door lock, something caught her eye. A white envelope, its corner sticking out from under the welcome mat. She stooped to tug it free and found that it was blank on the front and the back. It looked like an invitation or, more likely, a thank-you from a satisfied pet owner. This was one of the many things that made her job so meaningful. In a small village like White Church Bay, people often showed gratitude with personal touches like an apple pie, a bundle of fresh rhubarb, or in this case, a handwritten note.

She slid it into her pocket and started to push the door open—then froze. A sharp, prickly feeling on the back of her neck told her someone was watching her. Her heartbeat kicked up a notch. She spun around but saw only the deserted yard with Aunt Jinny's dower cottage casting a silent, looming shadow. It must be her imagination.

She hurried into the house, flicking on a light and kicking off her Wellingtons in the mudroom. Slinging her parka over a chair, she greeted Maxwell and Charlie. She tossed the note onto the kitchen table.

She put the kettle on and listened as the grandfather clock chimed ten. She was running on fumes, up since early that morning. The kettle's whistle sliced through the quiet, and she busied herself making tea. The ritual was familiar and comforting, and she chose a blend of herbal lavender and chamomile to help her relax. She carried the steaming pot and her favorite mug to the table, where the envelope waited.

Pouring the tea, she tried to shake off her unease. It was simply another night, another long shift making her too tired to think straight. But as she settled in, the warm mug in her hands, the feeling of being watched crept back in. With a sip to steady her nerves, she reached for the envelope. That would cheer her up.

She broke the seal and slid out a plain white card. A chill ran down her spine as she read:

Cease your quest, or you will rue
Knowing secrets not meant for you.
Dare not to speak the truth aloud,
Or risk that you might wear the shroud.

She swallowed hard, a cold sweat prickling. Someone must have placed it under her welcome mat after she left for choir practice. The realization sent a wave of nausea through her.

She grabbed the card and headed to the study. The fireplace ignited with a click, and soon flames danced in it. But tonight, their usual comforting effect was lost on her. She barely registered that the fire burned. Maxwell had already found a cozy spot near the fire. She guided him out of his prosthesis and settled him on the soft rug. He curled up, gazing at her.

Her heart racing, she sank into the club chair across from the fire. Charlie came in and leaped onto the arm of the chair, purring softly as if to offer some comfort. The flicker of the flames sent shadows jerking across the walls. Even Charlie's soothing purr echoed weirdly in the room. Max seemed uneasy too, lifting his head to sniff the air as if he sensed something was wrong.

She read the card again. A tight knot formed in her stomach. The writing was all curves and flourishes, with each letter on point, as if the author wrote with an expensive pen. The ink was a deep, velvety black. She shivered. No matter how beautiful the handwriting was, the words were nothing short of creepy.

Worst of all, the threat was clear in the rhyme. Someone out there didn't want the truth to come to light.

Harriet showed the note to Polly first thing Tuesday morning.

Polly immediately wanted to cancel the morning's appointments so Harriet could talk to Van, but that was unthinkable for Harriet. She couldn't bring herself to make her patients wait. But as soon as the final patient, the little tortoise, left with a positive prognosis, she raced to the police station.

She burst into Van's office and slapped the note down on his desk. "I found this last night under the mat at my door."

He picked up the envelope and pulled out the card. After a moment he said, "This is disturbing. Do you have thoughts on who might have left it? Any angry pet owners or anyone else you might've rubbed the wrong way?"

She folded her arms over her chest. "No one who'd leave a morbid threat written like a nursery rhyme. The only person I can think of who's been upset with me lately is Lloyd, and that's been resolved, so I doubt it would have been him."

The door banged open to admit Aunt Jinny with Will on her heels. "Oh, thank goodness!" she exclaimed, gripping Harriet's shoulders and peering into her face. "How are you holding up, love?"

"Polly rang you?" Harriet guessed.

"She did. I found Will, and we came right over." Aunt Jinny turned to Van, her eyes piercing. "So, what's your plan?"

"Now, Dr. Garrett, stay calm. I don't think we want to jump to conclusions."

"A threatening note shows up on my niece's doorstep, and you're telling me to stay calm?" Aunt Jinny's normally twinkling blue eyes seemed to snap. "I am far from calm."

"May I see that?" Will's uncharacteristically sharp tone startled Harriet. He examined the card closely then read the note aloud.

Aunt Jinny grabbed Harriet's hand. "I know I'm the one who asked you to, but now I want you to stop searching for that star," she said. "Please."

Glancing between Will and Aunt Jinny, Harriet sensed a shift. The quest to unravel the star's mystery, once a challenge and homage to her great-grandmother, had suddenly morphed into something dangerous.

She hesitated. "I'm sorry, Aunt Jinny, but I can't."

"Why not?" her aunt demanded.

"Because backing down out of fear gives someone else too much control over me."

"Sometimes backing down isn't about giving in. It's about being smart and safe," Will said.

She shot him an annoyed glance. "As if you would do it."

"Hey, I might," he said. "I know you don't want to hear it, but I'm with your aunt on this."

"I'm not quitting. Not with Christmas Eve so close."

"Who knew about your plans last night?" Van asked.

She thought for a moment. "The emergency call wasn't planned. Choir practice is common knowledge, though, and Will announced at Sunday service that Gerald has us doing extra practices."

"You didn't stop by the clinic to pick up equipment or anything for the emergency call?" Aunt Jinny asked.

She shook her head. "Everything I needed was in the Land Rover."

"Did you see anyone when you got home after?" Van asked.

"No. But..."

"But what?" Will prompted.

"It probably sounds silly, but I felt funny. As if someone was watching me."

"But you didn't see anyone?" Van pressed. "Hear anything?"

"Nothing. It was just a creepy feeling. Like someone was there, in the shadows."

"You live alone, it was late, and you were tired. Do you think you could have been imagining things?" Van asked.

At that, Aunt Jinny's frustration boiled over. "Van, you know Harriet better than that. She's not one to fabricate tales or indulge in flights of fancy. This is no mere figment of her imagination."

"I'm not saying she's imagining things, but I am trying to remain objective." Van turned to Harriet. "Does Ethan Grimshaw ever work late, maybe on one of the horses boarding in the barn? Could he have seen something?"

Harriet shook her head. "He does work late sometimes, but he's been away at a conference since Sunday."

"And you're certain he attended?" Will asked.

Harriet scowled at him. "Absolutely. He keeps me apprised of things like that in his schedule as a professional courtesy."

Aunt Jinny leaned forward, her curiosity evident. "How well do you know Ethan?"

Harriet shrugged. "Well enough, I suppose. He's a graduate of the farrier school where Grandad served as a trustee. Grandad always held their graduates in high regard, and people like Ethan's work."

Aunt Jinny's eyebrow arched. "Didn't he show up at your doorstep asking for a job?"

"Yes, that's true. I couldn't hire him full-time or anything, but I welcomed having a qualified farrier to recommend to clients. After I did my due diligence by checking his references, of course."

Van leaned back in his chair, considering. "He's new to the village."

Harriet fought to suppress a sigh, intimately familiar with the implications of being a newcomer in a tight-knit community like White Church Bay.

Will redirected the conversation. "Where's the conference being held?"

"Kingston upon Hull," Harriet replied.

"That's over an hour's drive from here," Van said. "When will he be home?"

"Late tonight," Harriet replied.

Will grabbed his cell phone and tapped the screen. "Found the conference website," he said after a few moments. "According to this, Ethan is one of the workshop leaders."

"Then I really doubt he'd skip it," Harriet said.

"Could you drive by the clinic regularly? At least when she's there alone?" Aunt Jinny asked Van.

He shook his head. "I'd like to, but the department is stretched thin." He turned back to Harriet. "Do you have a security system?"

"No. I've never needed one."

"Perhaps you should consider it." Van stood.

"That's your solution, Van?" Aunt Jinny snapped. "Harriet pays for a security system she's never needed before, and you do nothing?"

"Right now, the only thing I can do is check this note for fingerprints," Van said.

"I know," Aunt Jinny grumbled. "I don't mean to take everything out on you."

Van touched her arm. "We literally have nothing else to go on."

"For now," Harriet said. "Until another note shows up."

"I'm worried," Aunt Jinny announced.

Harriet found comfort in her aunt's snug front room, with its cozy fire and bright decorations of twinkling lights and holly. Yet she found it hard to hide her concern when her aunt was so upset.

"That note is more than a little troubling," Aunt Jinny said as she paced.

"It is," Harriet said. "I hope Van can discover something helpful from the paper or envelope."

Aunt Jinny's frown deepened. "I encouraged you to search for the star. If something happens to you because of that, I will never forgive myself."

"I chose to search for the star, remember? You suggested it, but I made my own decision."

"I feel responsible for your safety. I didn't tell your parents about the note because I didn't want them to worry." Aunt Jinny's anxiety spilled out in her voice.

"Would you please sit down?"

Aunt Jinny settled into a chair across from her, her expression weary. "It's more than the note. I'm worried about the impact of this search on the village."

"What do you mean?" Harriet asked, surprised.

"People are becoming discouraged, thinking that we might have a Christmas without the star. And worse, they're starting to gossip and conjecture even more than usual. I don't like it."

Harriet's stomach churned. She hated that this friendly, peaceful little village was on edge.

"There's no denying it. This search is affecting you and the village. They're counting on the star being back by Christmas Eve. If it's not, they'll be really let down." Aunt Jinny's voice was heavy with concern.

Harriet stayed silent, feeling the pressure on her intensify. Suddenly the room felt small and tight.

She straightened in her seat, squaring her shoulders. Maybe she was in over her head. But she couldn't give up on this search. It had become too important to her.

"I understand your worries, and I appreciate them," she said. "But I need to see this through. For me, for the village, for Letty."

Aunt Jinny appraised her for a long moment then nodded. "Just be careful. Please. Nothing is worth more than your safety."

CHAPTER TWENTY-ONE

The great hall of Lord Miltshire's estate made Harriet feel as if she had been transported into a coffee table book. Oriental rugs, sunlight through lead-paned windows, and polished wood panels all radiated history and elegance. She scanned the crowd and spotted Will on an ornate settee upholstered in red plush. She suddenly realized that Tuesday was Christmas Eve. Here it was the Wednesday before and she didn't have a present for him. She wanted it to be something special but was still at a loss for what.

He had convinced her to attend Lord Miltshire's annual yuletide event to celebrate fine art and cuisine. It was a well-attended affair each year, showcasing a talk by an art critic and then a selection of gourmet meals prepared by local chefs. At this year's gathering, Percival Thorne from the Royal College of Art in London would speak about the oil paintings in Lord Miltshire's collection.

"You made it," Will said with relief. "I was getting worried."

"I just diagnosed a dog with diabetes," she explained as she settled next to him on the settee. "I had to show the owner how to administer insulin shots."

The room was packed with villagers. She realized she had begun to identify the people of White Church Bay by their pets. That small older woman had brought a Great Dane into the clinic and controlled him very well during his examination and annual vaccinations. The man over there had a potbellied pig with arthritis, and he absolutely doted on her, dutifully applying the liniment Harriet had prescribed.

Will leaned toward her. "The art is incredible, isn't it?"

"Stunning." Even though she had a limited knowledge of art, especially compared to Will or her grandad, she knew what appealed to her, and these paintings definitely caught her attention. Each brushstroke was intentional and deliberate, the color choices perfect for the subject matter as well as the overall mood of the piece. Seldom had she seen such grandeur up close likc this.

"They're mostly from the Dutch Golden Age of art," he added. "Notice the attention to detail. It almost feels as if you could touch an image and it would come to life."

"It really does."

The room quieted as Percival Thorne approached the podium. Slender, with a neatly trimmed beard and finely tailored suit, he was every inch the London art critic. His sharp gray eyes scanned the audience with a hint of condescension. Will had told her that Percival's reputation as an art critic and dealer was unparalleled.

She enjoyed the lecture immensely. Percival was a bit stiff when he began, but as he talked about each painting, his demeanor changed, and he drew her in with his animated and engaging descriptions. She was astounded by how much one could learn from dissecting an image and examining its individual parts. It reminded her of making a diagnosis—a careful accumulation of detail-oriented observations.

As the seminar concluded, Percival invited questions from the audience. Hands shot up, with inquiries ranging from the type of paint used to the enduring popularity of Dutch art.

After a few volleys of questions, one of the villagers in the back raised his hand. "You know, Mr. Thorne, this village has a piece of art that we feel is every bit as valuable as these paintings. Some have even deemed it priceless."

The room went silent.

Percival's eyebrows rose in curiosity. "Indeed? Tell me more."

The man recounted the tale of the Christmas star, from its donation to the church in 1919 to a recap of the theft. He left out the camel chase.

Percival frowned in apparent thought. "Can anyone offer a more detailed description of the piece itself?"

"I can. I also have photos." Will stood and gave a meticulous description of the star then took his phone from his pocket, swiped the screen a few times, and handed it to Percival. The room was completely silent as everyone waited.

After what felt like an eternity, Percival spoke. "I regret to inform you that I've seen this star, or at least a remarkably similar one, on the international market. I believe it's been sold."

A collective gasp swept the hall.

"Is there any way to find out for sure whether it was sold, and if so, who bought it?" Will asked. Harriet could hear the hint of desperation in his voice.

Percival shook his head. "No. If the star that I saw was yours, I believe it was sold to an anonymous buyer. Once an item like this is stolen and subsequently sold, it essentially vanishes. The seller probably fabricated a provenance for it and everything."

"Can't the authorities trace something like that?" Will inquired.

"It's harder than you think," Percival replied. "Otherwise, items like the Rembrandt from the Isabelle Gardiner heist would have been recovered long ago."

"Where did you see the star?" Harriet asked.

"At a private showing in Istanbul that was otherwise legitimate," he responded. "I cannot give you any other information about it."

Another villager shot to his feet. "It was stolen less than three weeks ago. How could it have ended up all the way in Istanbul already?"

Percival shrugged. "Stranger things have happened. The people who steal art and sell it like this are extremely good at what they do. Getting it out of the country and overseas is to be expected. They have a better chance of getting it away from the rightful owner or anyone else who might recognize it and report it stolen."

"Are you sure it was this star?" Will asked quietly, hopelessly.

"Not entirely, but it certainly looks familiar." He gave Will a sympathetic glance. "I'm sorry, Pastor."

"Are you saying that there's no hope of recovering our Christmas star?" Lord Miltshire asked.

Percival appeared regretful. "If that silver ornament is indeed the one I spotted, I fear it has likely disappeared forever."

After the evening's event, Will and Harriet hiked together across the moor, the landscape a monochrome of dried brown grass under a sky heavy with brooding clouds. The silence between them was dense, echoing their unspoken worries and doubts.

"So, what do you think?" Will asked, his voice dogged with weariness.

"I don't know," she replied. "Percival wasn't sure it was the same star."

"He seemed pretty convinced. He's an expert with a highly trained eye, and our star must be rather unique. Otherwise, he would have said so. And if it's already been sold internationally to an anonymous buyer..." He trailed off, leaving his unspoken fear hanging between them.

"But that's just it, isn't it? He admitted that he wasn't sure it was our star. It still leaves room for doubt." Her attempt at optimism sounded hollow, even to her own ears. "I texted Van and told him what Percival said. He's checking it out."

"Good." Will paused. "I'm so tired of chasing shadows. I don't want to give false hope to the church and village."

"What about my threatening note?" Harriet pointed out. "Doesn't that mean the thief and the star are in the village?"

"Not necessarily. The note could mean that the person who stole it might have simply been a local person hired to steal it and then hand it over. Since you and I are still investigating, they're likely panicking that we will find them out. They want us to back off."

She felt as if Will had stolen her last shred of hope. She stopped walking and stared out over the vast moor. They both stood without speaking for a long moment, the weight of their disappointment settling around them like the cold front that had rolled in.

Will's expression shifted from despondence to contemplation. "I hate the thought that we are walking into a dead end, that after all this there's nothing we can do and no justice to be had." His words were hesitant, but at least they lacked his earlier resignation. "At the same time, I can't bring myself to quit."

Harriet felt her determination hardening, the knot in her chest giving way in the face of clear resolve. They resumed their walk.

"I must tell you," Will said. "I am still disturbed by the note under your mat. Someone is obviously unhappy with the fact that you're involved with this. They think you're vulnerable. And they're right about that."

"I'm not thrilled about the note either. But I'm hardly vulnerable." She couldn't even admit to herself how much the situation terrified her. Someone had come onto her property and deliberately tried to scare her into giving up on the star. Sometimes she wondered if she should, especially if she lost Will's support.

She pointed to a spot next to the trail. "That's where we found Nutmeg."

His tone lightened. "You're right. I wonder how he's doing. No doubt fat and happy in his deluxe new home." He grew serious once more. "Nutmeg was certainly no quitter."

"And we didn't quit on him."

"No, we didn't. We stayed with him until he was out of danger. Until he found his way."

Harriet took a deep breath. "I say we go back to the beginning. Reexamine our steps. Follow any lead, no matter how small. We're not giving up. Not yet."

He grinned. "So, it's once more unto the breach?"

"Once more unto the breach." She returned his smile.

With that, they retraced their steps to the village. The town came into view with the familiar sight of smoke curling up from chimneys. It was an image of home and comfort, and she thought it must feel that way to Will as well.

Yet there was no doubt that somewhere in their peaceful community, a thief lay in hiding, desperate to keep his secret safe.

CHAPTER TWENTY-TWO

London
October 1940

Letty paused in her letter to Cecil.

He had been stationed at Aldershot in Hampshire, giving her some comfort in the knowledge he was still in England. But last week, he had been deployed to France. The thought of it left her terribly unsettled. Uncertain if her letters would even reach him, she persisted in writing, clinging to the hope that they would somehow find their way to him. It was her way of keeping him close, of refusing to let the war make him feel farther away than he already was. With each letter, she poured out her feelings, imagining him reading them somewhere and smiling at her words.

Their romance had blossomed rapidly in the months after their first date when they wandered through London's ancient churches. Beginning their excursion at the tea shop near Selfridges, they'd meandered past a variety of historic landmarks. She marveled at Cecil's depth of knowledge as he talked about each site. By the time they visited the final church, she knew she had fallen deeply in love. After six months of frequent visits between London and White Church Bay, they had exchanged vows in her beloved White Church.

To Letty's parents' delight, they settled in Cecil's ancestral home of Cobble Hill Farm. She didn't mind giving up her job at Selfridges in exchange for doing the books at Cecil's budding new vet clinic and teaching math to local schoolchildren. However, Hitler changed everything, and all too soon, Cecil was called to serve in the Royal Air Force.

Without Cecil, she couldn't run the clinic, and she soon grew restless alone in the large country home. Fortunately, some of her old friends from school and Selfridges invited her to visit them in London and perhaps resume her old job with them until Cecil came home.

Because he must come home. She could not even imagine another outcome.

She soon realized how the hustle and bustle of the big city kept her too busy for worry. She quickly fell into the rhythms of accounting at Selfridges during the day and talking with her friends late into the night.

But the war outside grew harder and harder to ignore.

One night the sudden wail of sirens sliced through the quiet of the flat. Her flatmates were out, but she'd chosen to stay in and write to Cecil. "Not again," she whispered to the empty room, her heart racing as the reality of the war invaded her sanctuary.

She moved quickly, shoving papers into her desk drawer and grabbing her coat and satchel—always packed, always ready. She prayed her flatmates had heard the sirens and were hurrying to the nearest shelter as she was. The once-bustling sights and sounds of London at night were replaced by the cacophony of sirens and the hurried steps of the people in her neighborhood. The air was thick with tension, each breath a mix of fear and determination.

The bomb shelter, a mere block away, felt miles distant as Letty navigated the panicked crowd. The entrance was a bottleneck of chaos, drawing her and dozens of others toward the promise of safety underground. Inside, the dim light cast long shadows across the faces of those huddled together. Letty found a space against the cold concrete wall and crouched with her knees drawn up to her chest. Around her, whispered conversations and soft sobs filled the air.

"I heard the East End was hit last night," a woman murmured nearby, her voice barely above a whisper.

"Hush. Don't scare the children," her companion chided gently, nodding to a sleeping toddler cradled in her arms.

Letty closed her eyes, the distant thud of bombs a grim lullaby. She thought of Cecil, facing dangers far greater than this in some unknown location. She thought wistfully of the life they had planned, now on hold as so much of the world was. Stay safe, my love, *she thought, a silent prayer among many.*

She huddled closer to the wall of the bomb shelter, the cold seeping through her coat. Around her, others whispered prayers and platitudes or sat in silent vigil, their faces barely discernible in the dim light. The shelter, a cramped refuge from the destruction above, vibrated with each bomb that fell from a seemingly infinite supply. In these moments, London felt worlds away from the life she had known on the Yorkshire moors.

Letty closed her eyes against the fear, seeking solace in her memories of those moors. So vast, so free. *She could almost feel the wind in her hair, the smell of the grass, the endless sky above stretching out like a promise. There, freedom wasn't just a word. It was the air, the land, the very essence of being.*

A sudden, louder explosion jolted her back to the present, but her mind clung to Yorkshire. She remembered one afternoon in particular, the setting sun turning the sky into a canvas of golds and pinks. It was the day she and Albie had found the silver star in an abandoned badger's den. To Letty, the star had been a sign of hope, a beacon in simpler times.

Now, as the shelter trembled with another nearby hit, Letty wondered about the star. Did it still sit atop the Christmas tree in a church full of people she'd known almost from birth? Did it still catch the light, reminding others to hope even in such dark times? A sense of warmth briefly displaced the chill.

"Are you all right, miss?" a man asked beside her. "I was talking to you, but you seemed lost."

She adjusted her coat around her legs, noticing that her hands were grimy from sitting on the concrete floor. The kindness in his eyes nearly brought tears to her own. "I'm fine," she replied, managing a smile. "Or as fine as anyone can be here. I guess I was so lost in my thoughts that I didn't notice anything around me."

"That's just as well. It's good to escape this mess, if only for a moment in our dreams."

As she sat there, jolted back to reality by the terrible destruction overhead, Letty clung to the image of the Yorkshire moors and the church where a piece of her heart still lingered, embodied by the silver star. It was a reminder that some parts of the world, some parts of her, remained untouched by the war's reach.

Finally, the all-clear siren cut through the early morning silence, a signal that the night's terror was over—for now.

Letty stepped out of the bomb shelter and into the first light of dawn. The familiar streets were unrecognizable, littered with debris and the remnants of what once was. Buildings that had stood for centuries were reduced to mere skeletons. The air was thick with dust, painting the world with a hue of despair.

She walked on, each step taking her closer to what she feared most. People passed her, some in tears, others in a daze, but all united in their loss. Letty wrapped her coat tighter around herself, a futile attempt to ward off the chill of the morning and the reality of her situation.

Her favorite bakery had been reduced to rubble. It had been a landmark on her daily walks, a place where the smell of fresh bread brought a semblance of normalcy to her wartime life. Now it was gone, like so much else.

Her pace slowed as she approached the building that held the flat she shared with her friends. She stopped in her tracks. The entire structure was now a hollowed-out shell. Walls that had held her life, her laughter, her conversations with her dearest friends, had caved in.

A sob caught in her throat as she took in the devastation. This can't be happening. *If only she could deny the reality before her eyes. Her dear London, where she'd sought refuge from her loneliness, had proved to be no haven at all.*

Nearby, a child wailed, a sound that mirrored the ache in her heart. Letty spotted a young girl sitting on the curb, clutching a ragged doll, her parents nowhere in sight. Letty knelt beside her, putting an arm around her. "It's going to be okay," she said, as much to herself as to the child.

As she comforted the girl, Letty knew that London was irrevocably changed. The war had taken so much from so many, and now it had taken her home.

In that moment, with the sun rising over a city of ashes, Letty made a decision. It was time to return to Yorkshire and her family. It was time to face her real life, haunted as it was by Cecil's absence.

CHAPTER TWENTY-THREE

Bright morning sunlight filtered through the stained-glass windows of the old church, casting patterns of red, blue, and gold squares on the stone tiles of the floor. Dust motes swam in the air. The space was silent in an expectant way.

An empty church sanctuary held undeniable power for Harriet. She slid into a back pew and sat there in the stillness, breathing deep. Will had stopped by the office and asked her to come by the church, saying that he wanted to discuss something. She pondered yesterday's conversation when they had agreed that they would not give up. She was glad of that. Without Will's energy and optimism, she would have a hard time continuing.

Pulling a hymnal from the rack in front of her, she flipped through the pages, stopping to hum through a few of her favorites. Listening to herself, she wondered if the frequent choir practices weren't helping after all. She found she could almost capture the tune of "All Creatures of Our God and King."

After sliding the hymnal back into the rack, she tapped her cell phone screen. Where was Will? In twenty minutes, Lloyd Throckmorton would arrive at the clinic with Dottie, who had stopped eating her regular diet of snails, larvae, and fresh fruit. Harriet mentally went over the list of possible ailments, as well as a list of supplements that might tempt the armadillo. She had been afraid that her professional relationship with Lloyd would suffer after she suspected him of stealing the star. But he seemed to have risen above any negative feelings he might have harbored. Lloyd was, as her grandad would have said, a stand-up fellow.

She studied the front of the church, imagining where the Christmas tree would stand. At the top, she pictured the silver star with its sapphire stones scattering light around the room. Worries about her safety and the star being lost forever clouded her thoughts, but she shoved them away. No way was she going down that rabbit hole right now. She wasn't about to give up.

Finally, the heavy door opened, and Will stepped into the sanctuary. A wave of unexpected gladness washed over her at the sight of him.

He hurried toward her. "Sorry for being late. I was held up by a call."

"That's okay," she replied. "But I don't have much time before my next appointment." She noticed the weariness in his features and how his posture sagged slightly. He avoided direct eye contact, which was strange for someone as open and straightforward as Will.

"You did a wonderful job with that budgie, by the way. What exactly was the issue?" he asked.

Had he really pulled her away from her busy day to talk about a budgie? "A feather mite infestation. Common among birds and easily treatable. I applied a topical spray and told her owner to clean out the cage." She folded her arms over her chest. "Honestly, Will, do you really want to discuss mites in budgies?"

"No, of course not." But he stared straight past her toward the door, as if waiting to be told what to say.

"What then?"

He finally met her gaze. "You won't like this, but I've been thinking, and I think we need to stop looking for the star."

"What?" This hadn't even been on her top ten list of things he might want to tell her.

"I couldn't sleep last night because I kept thinking of that note you got. I know I said the exact opposite yesterday, but I've had more time to think about it."

Harriet stood up and walked a few steps away from him to the spot where the tree would soon stand. Suddenly, all she could hear were nasty voices in her head amplifying the self-doubt that had begun to underscore her every move in the case. And now it felt as if Will doubted her too. "I thought you said yesterday that you weren't giving up."

"It's not giving up altogether. Van is still on the job, and he'll keep us in the loop."

"We've put all this work, effort, and time into finding the star, and now with a few days to go, you want to stop looking? That sounds like giving up to me." She hated that her voice sounded bitter, but she couldn't help it. She'd reached her limit.

"It's just too dangerous, Harriet." He stood and approached her.

"What happened to 'once more unto the breach'? No quitting, no looking back? Have you been talking to my aunt?"

Will ran his hands through his hair. "She stopped by the church," he admitted. "She's worried about that note, and I am too. I feel like this is spinning out of control. And I'm a little cross with Van for not doing more."

She leaned against the end of a pew. "Van is doing everything he can. I've been impressed with him."

"But I don't feel like he's taking the danger seriously."

"If there was genuine danger, I think he would."

He faced the altar. She wondered if he was picturing the tree and absent star. "I need to start thinking of another way to close the Christmas Eve service. As the pastor of the church, it's my responsibility to plan for such things."

"I'd like to think that our plan is to find it. At least give the search one more serious try." She was surprised to realize that under her frustration was hurt. She loved thinking of them as a team. She had thought he enjoyed it too.

They turned at the sound of echoing footsteps. An older woman with streaks of gray in her neatly pinned bun came toward them with purposeful steps.

"Mrs. Mortimer," Will said. Harriet heard a strain in his voice. She knew that some parishioners were a little demanding, and she wondered if Mrs. Mortimer fell in that category. "You must be here for the altar flower vases."

"Pastor Will," she said, stopping in front of them, seemingly indifferent to any disruption she might have caused. Her glasses magnified the sharpness of her blue eyes, while her crisply tailored dress gave a sense of no-nonsense authority. "The flower vases are the least of my concerns. Did I hear you suggest we won't recover the star in time for Christmas Eve?"

"That's not what I said," he replied.

"I distinctly heard you say the words 'another way to close the Christmas Eve service.'" She fixed steely eyes on Harriet then Will.

"Everyone believes the two of you will find the star. Is that belief misplaced?"

"We've done our best," Will replied, his usual patience obviously worn thin. "But Christmas Eve is mere days away."

She laid a hand on her chest. "Well, I never. I always thought you two would find the star. I am most disappointed." Her expression softened. "You must, you know. This village needs that star." She spun abruptly and walked back down the aisle, her heels clicking on the stone tiles. They watched as the door closed behind her.

That evening, Harriet trudged up to her bedroom, the dim light casting soft shadows over plush pillows on her neatly made bed.

She had put in a good, long day at the clinic, followed by dinner with Aunt Jinny. She and Polly had decorated the office for Christmas. Polly loved decorating and was a genius at it. She knew where to put the garlands and exactly the right number of lights. She'd found a great spot for a small Christmas tree that was safe for pets. She made the waiting area cozy with holiday-themed cushions, and stockings hung on a cardboard fireplace. All in all, the day's work had been hard but also fulfilling. Harriet appreciated more and more how satisfying it was to be a vet in a small community.

She splashed water on her face, brushed her teeth, and changed into comfy flannel pajamas. Her mother had given them to her before she'd left Connecticut, with a reminder of the cold winters in Yorkshire. The glow from the single lamp on her bedside table cast a warm ambiance over the room. Wooden beams crisscrossed the ceiling. Underfoot, a plush rug muffled her steps from the bathroom to her bed. The old furnace kicked in with its usual pipe banging. She smiled, feeling her weariness slip away before a surge of optimism. The old house made her feel safe, content. There hadn't been another note, and nothing bad had happened. Maybe there was still hope that she would find the star. She felt bad over the argument she'd had with Will, but she couldn't let him dissuade her from doing what she could to find something that meant so much to her family.

She climbed into the walnut four-poster bed that had been in her family for three generations. The covers enveloped her like a soft cocoon, and she reached to switch off the lamp. Her gaze fell on the framed photo on the mantelpiece of the small fireplace. The picture captured a proud moment—Harriet in her graduation robe, flanked by her beaming parents. She smiled and whispered good night to the two of them.

And that was when she saw it. A shock of white against the dark wood of the mantel.

Her pulse quickened. No, it couldn't be. Not inside the house. Not in her bedroom.

She slid out from under the covers and raced across the room. A white, square envelope, identical to the one under the doormat. She snatched it and darted back to bed, where she yanked the covers up around her. She took a deep breath then tore it open.

Time to return whence you came, my dear,
For in shadow, evil unseen lurks near.
Go back, or face what waits for thee
In tenebrous dark—your destiny.

A spike of anxiety pulsed through her, making her heart race. She reached for her cell phone on the nightstand, but it wasn't there. Where was it? She always kept it close.

After stuffing her feet into slippers and throwing on her robe, she began a frantic search. Her phone was her lifeline, her link to the outside world, and tonight, her only hope for safety. She made herself stop and think. Maybe she'd left it in the kitchen. But the idea of walking through the big, empty house terrified her. There was a landline in the office downstairs, but that posed the same obstacle.

Then it hit her. She'd shoved her phone into the Beast's center console during a puppy delivery, a mental note lost at the day's end. She'd bet it was still there, silent and waiting. She bounded across the room and slammed her bedroom door shut then locked it.

Back in bed, she read the note again before dropping it into the top drawer of the bedside table. She'd show it to Van first thing in the morning. He'd told her earlier in the day that no clear fingerprints were found on the first note, but maybe this one would be different.

Harriet pulled the handmade quilt up to her ears. As illogical as she knew it was, she felt safer under the covers.

She strained her ears for any sound of an intruder. Every creak, every rustle, made her shudder. Fear coursed down her spine. Had she locked the doors? What about the windows? Did it even matter? If the person who left the note had gotten in once, they could get in again.

And who was to say they'd vacated the house after depositing the note? After all, the poem spoke of unseen evil in the shadows. Then she thought better of that. If someone was in the house, Maxwell, down in the living room, would be barking his head off.

But then a creak on the stairs shook her to the core, followed by another. Her heart pounded wildly. Another creak, then a meow that drained the anxiety from her. Charlie. She climbed out of bed again and opened the door. Charlie strutted in. "Kitty, you might need to cut down on the treats," she said with a shaky laugh. "You're a little heavy on the stairs." She closed and locked the door once more, grateful for a soft, purring ball of warmth to join her in bed.

Perhaps the intruder had gotten in when Polly went to lunch. Someone could have easily slipped out of the waiting room, down the hall, and up the steps. Harriet pulled the covers tight. She had never felt so alone in her entire life, even with Charlie curled up beside her.

Someone had been in the house, had invaded her personal haven. How on earth would she ever get to sleep?

She jolted awake, sitting straight up in bed with a start. Her heart was pounding, a stark contrast to the stillness of her bedroom.

The vividness of the nightmare lingered, its unsettling images blurring the line between the dream and reality. In it, her parents stood on the bank of a river while she shouted to them from the opposite side. The dark water rushed past. Finally, she jumped in and tried to swim toward them. But the current caught her. The last bit of the dream was her shouting out as she was swept away. She woke drenched in a cold sweat.

She glanced at the clock. Almost six, and the sky was lightening from black to gray. She listened but heard nothing. She forced herself to take deep breaths. Was the current of her life sweeping her away? She felt like she was at risk of drowning in everything that was happening in White Church Bay. The village had felt tranquil and festive with its Christmas decorations and good cheer. However, she had now received two threatening notes. The first one had rattled her for a day or two, but she'd moved past it when nothing terrible had happened. Christmas songs were sung, and people talked about presents and parties. She had worked with wonderful clients and their pets, laughed with Polly in the office, and talked with Will.

A shadow crossed her mind when she thought of their last conversation. They had parted badly. She was angry about his decision, and he was annoyed that she wouldn't see it his way.

But she valued his friendship and realized she needed to apologize for reacting so badly. He had the congregation to worry about, and he did owe them a backup plan. Instinctively, she reached for her phone to text him, only to realize there was no phone. The darkness seemed to engulf her, and the shadows took on an eerie presence. Reaching over, she switched on her desk lamp, but the light didn't seem to pierce as far as it usually did.

She would never leave her phone in her car again. Maybe Aunt Jinny was right, and everything had truly gotten away from her. But if she gave up now, she felt as if she would be failing Letty's memory, to say nothing of the memory of her grandfather. He had cherished the star and the tradition that came with it. More than that, generations of villagers had looked to the silver Christmas star as a symbol of God's love, strength, and light. She couldn't stop now. She wouldn't. Some bully leaving scary notes wouldn't make her give up and hide.

She threw off the covers and got out of bed, pushing her feet into her slippers and sliding on her robe. It was time to stop cowering at every noise and flinching at her own shadow. She had work to do. Time was running out.

First on her list this morning, though, was to call Van and report the note.

CHAPTER TWENTY-FOUR

Exhausted from a nearly sleepless night, Harriet shuffled into the reception area of the clinic.

Polly looked up from her desk, worry etched into her face. "Your aunt Jinny called me about the note. I think she's about to bring in Scotland Yard."

"I know. It's not good," Harriet replied, rubbing her temples.

"Jinny said that they left it in your bedroom." Polly's normally rosy cheeks were pale. "This can't go on."

"Agreed, but I don't know how to stop it."

"I do," Polly said firmly. "Stop the star search. Make it public that you couldn't care less about the silver star or who stole it."

"I'll keep that in mind, but I'm not ready for that yet."

"Okay, but it's starting to freak me out."

Harriet sighed. "You and me both. Let's talk about something else."

"I wish I knew how." Polly took a deep breath, clearly trying to calm herself. "Sorry, it's just everywhere right now. Last night, Van and I went to that Victorian Christmas market in Fylingthorpe, the one where you can make your own ornaments. It was supposed to be a fun little date. But even then, this whole situation was all I could think about. And judging by how quiet Van was all evening, he felt the same way."

"Did he say anything about it?"

"He thinks we should be extra careful, especially now. He even mentioned that he's trying to figure out how to station a patrol car at the clinic. He's really worried about you, Harriet. We both are."

Polly's words warmed Harriet's heart. Despite the fear and uncertainty, the support of friends like Polly and Van reminded her of the strong bonds she had formed in this tight-knit community. "Thanks, Polly. And thank Van for me too. It means a lot to know you're both watching out for me."

Polly smiled, a bit of the worry easing from her features. "Of course. We're in this together, right? So let's figure out our next move. And maybe, just maybe, we can find a way to enjoy Christmas despite this mess."

Harriet pulled her scarf up over her nose, bracing herself against the brisk wind sweeping across the moors. The afternoon sun was already sinking.

She peered down the path toward the village, wondering what was keeping Will. Church duties or a parishioner's emergency, maybe? With the Christmas Eve service three days away, he could have gotten caught up in planning or working with the worship team. Today was Saturday. He might have gotten engrossed in the final touches to tomorrow's sermon. It would be the last Sunday in Advent, and he would want his sermon to be especially good.

She glanced at her cell phone and saw a text from Polly. After the clinic closed at noon, Polly and Van had headed to a care home on the outskirts of White Church Bay, where Van's football league was hosting a Christmas tea for the residents.

Polly had texted, FATHER CHRISTMAS HAS ARRIVED. An image of Van in a beard and red suit handing out candy canes accompanied the message.

She texted back, HAVE FUN!

STAY SAFE.

ALWAYS.

As she slid the phone back into her pocket, Harriet felt a twinge of envy, not so much for Polly and Van's budding romance—she was truly happy for them—but about missing the simple, happy events that seemed so hard to find in her own chaos right now.

Where was Will? Their rambles on the moors had become something she had started to really look forward to. The fresh air, the open space, and the friendly chats had become a highlight.

Her phone buzzed with a text. CAN'T MAKE IT. PARISH EMERGENCY. SORRY. She stared at the message, a mixture of confusion and hurt bubbling up. No explanation, no promise of a rain check. Just a few words, as cold as the December air.

Her stomach knotted. Was it the search he was weary of? Or her company? The possibility lodged itself in her mind, a shadow over her thoughts. She turned back toward the village, retracing her steps. The vast moors lay behind her, as alone as she was under the fading evening light.

"Easy there, girl," Harriet murmured to the nervous chestnut mare.

Alberta Clark's horse farm was a frequent destination. Formidable Alberta demanded excellence, but Harriet appreciated that as well as how meticulously Alberta cared for her horses. The mare's deep brown eyes watched her, nostrils widening. Gently, Harriet ran her hands over the mare's neck and withers, feeling the solid muscle beneath the sleek chestnut coat. She was glad when Diamond Ridge's ears flicked forward. It meant she was relaxing. She loved the opportunity to treat such a stunning horse, grateful that her veterinary work provided a wide variety of patients and challenges.

Being here and focusing on Diamond Ridge took her mind off Will. She knew him to be an honest person, so she believed him about the emergency. But she couldn't help feeling as if he was drifting away from her, creating distance between them.

She stepped back to better observe her patient, paying careful attention to the mare's stance. Diamond Ridge clearly was uncomfortable, keeping her weight off her left foreleg. Harriet gently ran a hand over the knee, feeling warmth and swelling as her fingers touched the joint. The mare flinched.

"Sorry, baby," Harriet said.

Slipping out into the brighter light of the aisle between the rows of stalls, she sorted through her medical bag until she found what she wanted.

She was about to reenter the stall when Alberta came into the barn. Even in her late seventies, Alberta Clark's stride was deliberate and steady, reminiscent of a seasoned dancer. Harriet had heard that, in her youth, Alberta had been a contender for the National Ballet. Her transition from ballet slippers to riding boots was evident in her graceful manner.

"Any news, Doctor?" she asked.

"A simple sprain in her left front knee," Harriet assured her. "I'm treating it with an injection to get the pain and swelling down, and she'll need to stay off it as much as possible."

Alberta followed her into the stall and held the mare's halter while Harriet administered the injection. "I have had other horses suffer sprains, so I'm familiar with the treatment. Thank you for helping her. I trusted no one but Doc Bailey with my horses, and it's a relief to know that I can now trust you."

"I'm sure he appreciated your trust, and I know I do." Harriet capped the syringe and slid it back into her bag. "You should see improvement in Diamond Ridge quickly. But reach out to me if you don't, or if you have any other issues."

"I will." Alberta slid the stall door shut behind them and fell into step beside Harriet as she walked up the stable aisle. Horses nickered a greeting at Alberta, which told Harriet volumes about their regard for her.

"Are you enjoying village life?" Alberta asked as they left the barn and moved into the weak December sunlight.

"I am," Harriet said. "White Church Bay is a lovely place."

"And you like being a vet out here by the sea?"

"I love it. Taking over Grandad's practice has been an exciting challenge. And it's kept me busy." Harriet opened the back of the Beast and placed her bag in its usual spot beside the sneakers she'd brought with her. Then she sat beside the bag and changed out of her wellies.

"I've heard you've been busy with things other than veterinary practice," Alberta said.

"Do you mean the church choir and the knitting club?" Harriet laughed. "I'm not sure those things are keeping me busy, but I'm enjoying them so far."

"I mean other things." Alberta waited, her eyes narrowed.

Harriet stood and stretched her stiff back. She knew what Alberta was referring to, but she wasn't about to encourage the topic. "Other things?"

"I heard you've been searching for the stolen Christmas star. Have you made any progress?"

"No. But there's still time."

Alberta huffed. "Not much. You think it was someone here in White Church Bay?"

"At the start, I thought that. But now I'm not so sure."

"I heard what the expert at Miltshire's art soiree said about its possible sale in Istanbul." She emphasized the word *expert*, her tone dripping with skepticism. "I'm assuming you've decided it wasn't a local thief based on that."

"It seems less likely to have been masterminded by a local, at least."

"Interesting."

"Why is that interesting?" She wished Alberta had stuck to a conversation about horses.

"You underestimate the village, Dr. Bailey. We may seem like a sleepy town of rural folk, but we're not, I can assure you."

"I didn't say that, but it doesn't seem likely to me that anyone from White Church Bay would possess the connections to sell it on an underground art market. Are you saying you think the thief was local?"

"That is precisely what I am saying."

"If you have any information, I would advise you to give DC Worthington a call." Harriet slid into her car and closed the door then lowered the window. "Call me if the mare doesn't improve in a day or two."

"No need to rush off so perturbed, my dear," Alberta remarked.

"I have other patients," Harriet replied.

"You're friendly with the pastor, are you not?"

"Yes." *Sometimes. I thought.* Harriet checked her rearview mirror. "Why?"

"I heard that the two of you have adopted a bit of a sleuthing partnership."

"No. Not really." She tried to sound casual, but her instincts were alert. "Will is simply as concerned as I am about the star."

"You heard about his trip to London then?"

"Will is swamped with his parish duties, especially with Christmas so close." She felt a surge of hurt. It was unlike him to head to London without a word to her.

"Curious, isn't it?"

"What is?" she asked, even as she hated herself for prolonging this conversation.

"That in the middle of the last week of Advent, he abandons the parish and spends two days in London with no apparent explanation."

"What are you saying?"

"I'm saying that Pastor Will Knight may not be who he appears to be." A faint, knowing smile played at the corners of her mouth.

Harriet clicked her seat belt. "Will is my good friend and my pastor, and I know him better than that. You couldn't find a more upright and honest man." She might be mad at Will at the moment, and even hurt about his pulling away from her, but she wouldn't stay silent while someone else hinted he might be a criminal.

"You don't need to get offended. I'm merely suggesting that he might not be the innocent choirboy you think he is." Alberta took a slight step back, her expression transforming into a frigid mask. The air around her seemed to chill, as if an icy breeze had swept through. "I'm not the only one who's wondering about him. He had every opportunity to steal the star, and you know it. And no doubt he possesses the sophistication—and the contacts—to sell it."

"Have a good day, Mrs. Clark." Her eyes straight ahead, Harriet raised the window and drove away.

The shadows had grown long while she was at Alberta's, and Harriet's mood had darkened right along with them. She didn't think for a moment that Will had stolen the star. Even the thought of someone accusing him made her furious. She gripped the steering wheel, her knuckles white.

She clicked on the radio, hoping the sound could distract her from her swirling thoughts. After a moment, she turned it off. Memories raced through her mind, times she and Will had laughed, brainstormed, and leaned on each other. She remembered the day they found the hedgehog and the days that followed as they nursed it back to health.

But now what was she to think? Did he have the same feelings about her? And what were her feelings exactly?

A horn blared. She yanked the wheel, realizing she'd drifted over the center line. Home was the place to think about her next move, not in the car, and especially not when driving on the left side of the road.

Not that she'd get any clarity at home either.

CHAPTER TWENTY-FIVE

White Church Bay
December 1941

Letty scanned the newspaper headlines with a heavy heart. The world was engulfed in a tempest, its reverberations reaching the serene moors of Yorkshire. She was used to battles waged against the elements and the demands of farming. As happy as she was to be back in White Church Bay, away from the bombs pummeling London, she desperately missed Cecil. His absence was a painful void in her life, transforming her daily routine into a perpetual waiting game, each day stretching somehow longer than the last.

She soon found that she could not face the Baileys' big empty house without him, and she spent so much time at her parents' home that they asked her to move in with them until Cecil's return.

She hated to admit it, but even with London being bombed every night, she missed her job at Selfridges. She missed her friends in London and worried for their safety. She tracked the news obsessively, trying to get any idea whether they might be okay.

Letty had always pictured herself as a mother, but she and Cecil hadn't started a family yet. She couldn't help but wish they'd had the chance to welcome a little one before he'd had to leave. But Letty remained optimistic, clinging to the hope that when Cecil returned and life found its rhythm again, they'd start a family together at long last.

Cecil's rare letters were always filled with love, but he barely mentioned what was happening on the battlefield. Letty knew he was trying to keep her from worrying too much. They both hoped the war would end soon and England would still be England. The nights grew longer, filled with restless thoughts and fear that crept into the corners of her mind.

But her restlessness was about something else too. She felt the urge to do something, to help with the war effort. More than knitting socks and rolling bandages. Not that those efforts weren't heroic in their own quiet way. But what else could she do? She helped her parents on their farm—not that they needed her help, still being young and strong—and went back to teaching mathematics to schoolchildren. That could hardly translate into something that would help win the war. But she felt the urge to try.

Her days in Yorkshire were filled with the simple pleasures and challenges of rural life, a stark departure from the complexity and chaos of London. And she deeply enjoyed her parents' company. Yet the tranquility of the countryside could not fully shield her from the storm raging across the globe. Each letter from Cecil, every headline in the newspaper, served as a stark reminder of the uncertainty that defined these times.

Her husband was out there in the vast, uncertain expanse of war-torn Europe, risking his life every day while she enjoyed the relative safety of the countryside, teaching mathematics to children who complained about homework, blissfully unaware of the full horrors of war. The disparity of their contributions weighed heavily on her.

Letty dropped the newspaper and switched on the wireless, tuning to the ever-playing broadcasts about the war. She listened as she put the kettle on and then sat in the dim glow of the farmhouse kitchen, sipping her tea. The crackling voice from the radio filled the silence of the night. Her parents had long since gone to bed. The clock struck eleven, and she listened to the chimes, a desperate longing for Cecil sweeping over her.

Letty gave herself a shake to clear the fog of her own sorrow and focus on the present—just in time to hear an announcer's voice coming over the airwaves.

"A civilian organization known as the Air Transport Auxiliary, or ATA, is now training women to fly, to serve their country by ferrying aircraft from factories to airfields. They will serve in as crucial a role as the men fighting on the front lines."

Letty sat back in her chair, gaping at the wireless as the words clicked into place in her heart.

As the announcement continued, detailing the ATA's call for female pilots, her thoughts churned. The idea of flying, of directly contributing to the war effort, ignited a flame of excitement she hadn't felt since before Cecil's departure. It was a chance to break free from the sidelines, to take control in a world where so much was determined by forces beyond her reach.

Letty switched off the wireless then slipped into her coat and stepped out into the cool embrace of the night. The Yorkshire moors stretched out before her, an expanse of undulating heather and whispering grasses bathed in the soft hues of twilight. The beauty of the landscape, untouched by the chaos of war, offered a stark contrast to the turmoil brewing within her.

As she walked, the vast, open skies above the moors seemed to echo the possibilities the ATA represented. Letty imagined herself soaring above these very hills, no longer a mere spectator of the clouds but a commander of the skies, contributing to the war effort in a way she'd never thought possible. The thought was both exhilarating and terrifying.

Letty knew that her decision would not be without its sacrifices. Joining the ATA meant leaving behind the safety of the farmhouse, her family, and the students she'd grown to care for. And what if she didn't come back? But that was everyone's fear in the world they all faced.

The moor, with its rugged beauty and timeless presence, whispered with each gust of wind that brushed against her cheeks. Here, in the solitude of nature, Letty found clarity. She wasn't Letty the teacher or Letty the farmer's daughter or even Letty the accountant. She was a woman determined to serve her country, to make a difference in the world's tumult.

As the clouds parted to reveal a full moon, Letty's decision solidified. She would enlist in the ATA. With a resolve as steadfast as the ancient landscape around her, she turned back toward the farmhouse, the path ahead clear. This was her moment to step beyond the shadows of doubt and into the light of action. For Cecil, for herself, and for the countless others fighting their own battles.

The next morning, in the fading light of the farmhouse kitchen, Letty stood before her parents. The kitchen, usually a haven of familial unity, now felt like an arena.

"Ma, Da," Letty began, her voice carrying a blend of conviction and trepidation. "I've made a decision. I'm going to join the Air Transport Auxiliary, the ATA. It's a civilian organization vital to the war effort. I'll be flying aircraft from factories to airbases to ensure the Royal Air Force remains battle-ready."

Her father's reaction was swift. "The ATA? A woman flying warplanes? It's unheard of. The skies during wartime are no place for a lady. It's dangerous enough for seasoned pilots."

"But that's just it, Da. The ATA is revolutionary. They've seen the potential in female pilots that the traditional military hasn't."

Her father leaned forward, his face red from working in the fields. "I can't accept it. It's not right. No daughter of mine will—"

She didn't let him finish. "I'll be flying Spitfires, Hurricanes, even Lancasters straight to the war zone. You're the one who always taught me that I could do anything I put my mind to."

Her mother looked almost sick with worry. "But Letty, the risk. Those planes aren't meant for joyrides. They're war machines."

"I know, Ma. But the ATA trains its pilots rigorously. They undergo the same training as men, learning navigation, aircraft mechanics, even how to handle different types of aircraft. It's not about taking joyrides but making sure the airplanes reach where they're needed most. And yes, it's dangerous. But in times like these, we all must do our part."

Her father paced, grumbling under his breath.

Her mother laid a trembling hand on Letty's. "The thought of you up there alone terrifies me."

Letty squeezed her mother's hand gently. "I won't be alone, Ma. You know that."

"What do you even know of flying?" her father asked, his voice softer this time.

"I don't need to know anything. The ATA's training is top-notch. They teach men and women who've never flown before to fly like pros. It's not the same as fighting on the front lines, but when so many are risking their lives for our freedom and safety, how can I do any less?" Letty felt a knot form in her stomach. She peered into her mother's eyes, saw the unwavering support there, and took a deep breath. "I'll be careful. I really will."

Her father paced the length of the kitchen and back several times. The creak of the floorboards under his weight punctuated the tense silence. At last, he faced Letty, his gaze intense. She hoped he no longer saw the little girl who once chased fantastical adventures on the moors, but a determined woman on the brink of defying societal expectation.

"Letty," he began, his voice a blend of resignation and paternal concern, "it's not you I don't believe in. It's the world I question, its readiness to accept the change you're so willing to be a part of." He paused, the lines on his face deepening. "In my day, women supported the war effort from home, working family farms or in factories so the soldiers had a country to return to. War is no place for a woman."

Her mother spoke up. "And what if you don't—"

"Don't even think that. I'll come back. I will," Letty interrupted firmly.

"You've always pushed for what you believe in, Letty," her father said. "I doubt there is anything I can say to stop you."

"We're proud of you, love. Know that." Her mother's voice broke, and then, taking a breath, she continued. "Just make sure you come home to us."

Letty reached over and clasped hands with both her parents. "I will." Her eyes filled with tears. "I will make you both proud."

CHAPTER TWENTY-SIX

"You look like you've seen a ghost," Aunt Jinny said.

Harriet had come from Alberta's and gone straight to Aunt Jinny's cottage, her port in every storm. She settled back on the kitchen chair, her hands wrapped around a hot mug of tea. She traced the rim of the mug, gathering her thoughts. "It's Will. He's different."

Aunt Jinny pushed a plate of oatmeal cookies toward her on the coffee table. "How so?"

"He's become kind of distant. Not cold exactly, but not warm either."

"I thought you two were close. I was just telling your mother how happy I am that you've found a friend as good and kind as Will."

Harriet bit her lip. "I might have messed that up the other day. Will told me that he wanted to give up looking for the star, and I kind of flew off the handle about it. I think I felt as if he was telling me he didn't believe in me, which wasn't the case, and I reacted poorly. And now I can't get him to talk to me at all. I feel as if I've lost him, and I can't even blame him for it."

Aunt Jinny sat back. "May I ask you a nosy question? You don't have to answer it if you don't want to."

"Of course." She slipped off her shoes and tucked her stocking feet beneath her.

Her aunt peered into her face. "Do you have romantic feelings for Will?"

"No. Of course not," Harriet replied immediately.

Aunt Jinny watched her. "Are you sure? You don't have to tell me. I want to know whether you're aware of what's going on in your heart and whether you're being honest with yourself about it."

Harriet stared into her teacup. "You might be right. Maybe I was starting to think of him that way." She was stretched much too thin and was too worn out to have this conversation. She suddenly wished she had kept her feelings to herself. At the same time, it was sort of nice to say it all out loud. She did have romantic feelings for Will. "But even if he once felt the same way, I don't think he does anymore."

Aunt Jinny gave her a small smile. "I wouldn't be so sure. I've seen how he looks at you."

Harriet pressed her lips together, not trusting her voice. "Maybe a week ago I would have believed you," she finally said, "but not now. Things have changed."

"How so?"

"He took this out-of-the-blue trip to London and didn't say anything to me. If he thought I was more than a friend, he would have told me he was going out of town, right?"

"How do you know he went to London?"

"Alberta Clark just told me."

"Alberta is a notorious gossip. I wouldn't put stock in anything she says."

She immediately decided not to tell Aunt Jinny about the accusation Alberta had made against Will. She refused to spread something so vicious, even to someone as trustworthy as her aunt. "But still, why wouldn't he tell me he was going?"

"Why are you asking me that instead of him?" Aunt Jinny replied, her tone not unkind.

Harriet blinked away tears. "Every time I try to connect with him now, we seem to miss each other. As cliché as it sounds, we're like two ships passing in the night, unaware of the other's course."

Aunt Jinny sat back and stared into the fire for a moment before she answered. "Life has a way of throwing us curveballs. It's important to remember that not everything is as it appears on the surface."

"But as women trained in science, don't you and I often find that things are exactly as they seem?"

"We're not talking about science," Aunt Jinny countered gently. "We're discussing matters of the heart, where people don't always follow logic or scientific principles."

"I'm trying to stay rational about it." Even as she said it, Harriet knew she was failing miserably.

"Then consider this rationally. It's nearly Christmas, and a man who clearly cares a great deal about you, in spite of a minor tiff, suddenly makes a trip to London."

"What exactly do you mean?"

"That this is the season of miracles." Aunt Jinny's eyes twinkled with mischief. "Perhaps it would be best to wait and see what Christmas morning brings before jumping to conclusions."

Harriet groaned. "That reminds me—I have nothing to give him."

Just then, her phone rang. Her curiosity piqued by the sight of Lloyd Throckmorton's name on her screen, she answered. "Hi, Lloyd. Is Dottie okay?"

"She's doing grand, Doc. You fixed her right up as usual. But that's not why I'm calling."

Harriet's stomach churned. Surely he wasn't going to rehash their issue over the missing Christmas star. "What can I do for you?"

"Actually, it's what I can do for you. Are you still hunting for a gift for Pastor Will?"

Harriet sat bolt upright. "Yes. Why do you ask?"

"I think I just got in the perfect thing. Why don't you swing by the shop?"

A mystified Harriet arrived at Thistle and Thatch Antiques within a half hour. She walked through the front door and called, "Lloyd?"

He emerged from the back of the shop, holding a small box. "Harriet, wait until you see this."

She met him at the counter and watched as he opened the box. Inside was a beautifully carved camel, its wood gleaming golden in the soft light of the shop. "Wow," she murmured. What a perfect memento of her and Will's adventure with Calvin's escape during the live Nativity, if not the aftermath of it.

"I thought of Pastor Will right away," Lloyd explained. "This is hand-carved olive wood from Israel. Whoever the sculptor was, they obviously took great pains with their work. It certainly has the air of something from the Holy Land."

Harriet ran gentle fingers over the camel's smooth surface. "I can't think of anything more appropriate. Thank you, Lloyd. I'll take it."

He smiled at her. "I'm so glad you're pleased. I'd like to put our past behind us and move forward as friends."

"I'd like that too."

As Lloyd carefully wrapped the wooden camel, Harriet prayed that her rift with Will might be mended so easily.

As soon as she returned home, she kicked off her shoes, made a cup of tea, and sank into the plush club chair in the cozy reading corner. This spot was her haven, the perfect place to lose herself in the pages of a good book. But not tonight.

Tonight, she was drowning in a weariness that ran so deep, it felt like an invisible anchor tied around her neck. Even Maxwell's presence beside her and Charlie's purring bulk on the chair's headrest couldn't ease the ache.

With her feet tucked beneath her, she turned from the window and stared into the fire. The past month had been one failure after another with the Christmas star. She couldn't begin to imagine how she'd find it in time now. Then there was Will, their once-bright friendship seemingly a thing of the past.

Her gaze fell on Letty's journal, resting on the oak desk as it had since the night she'd vowed to recover the star. She padded across the cold floor and brought the journal back to her chair. Opening its leather cover released the scent of aged paper and ink. She flipped to the end, hoping that Letty's last entries might offer her some comfort.

A yellowed newspaper clipping slipped out onto the braided rug. She picked it up and carefully smoothed it flat under the lamp's amber light, seeing that it was an article from the *Daily Herald*, dated September 1945. As she read, everything else faded away.

FROM BOOKKEEPING TO BRAVERY, FIRST OFFICER LETTICIA BAILEY SOARS ABOVE ALL!

Hold on to your hats, folks! If you thought the war skies were just for the gents, think again! Yorkshire's very own Letticia "Letty" Bailey, First Officer in the British Air Transport Auxiliary, gives the boys a run for their money.

After swapping her ledgers for flight gloves, this dazzling dame from the north proved that flying for King and Country was just as important to the war effort as folding bandages and knitting socks. Danger? Pish-posh! It was all in a day's work for the fearless First Officer Bailey. This courageous woman showed us all that the British spirit knows no bounds.

Early one morning, as the fog hung low over the English Channel, First Officer Bailey was delivering a Spitfire from a factory in southern England to an air base near the Scottish border. As she maneuvered through the heavy cloud cover, her aircraft was intercepted by a stray German fighter plane.

Without a bullet to her name and in the midst of fog as thick as London's pea soup, our heroine had precious few options. Drawing from her well of flying finesse, Bailey pulled off stunts that would leave the best male pilot agog. A nail-biting quarter of an hour later, she emerged, leaving that German plane lost in her misty wake.

After touching down safely at her Scottish haven, she coolly reported her airborne escapade, her poise unshaken. The chaps at the base, having caught wind of an ATA plane being chased by a German fighter, greeted her with both sighs of relief and hearty cheers for her pluck.

As England bathes in the glow of victory, let's tip our hats to the fearless femmes of the ATA. Their tales, etched in the blue yonder, are bound to inspire many a young lass for generations to come. In Britain's stormiest hours, they've shown they're second to none.

In the stillness of the room, a single thought emerged through Harriet's own fog. Her great-grandmother had stared down a German fighter and still made good on her promises. How could Harriet even consider giving in to her own discouragement? How could she let herself be dragged into such depths of despair when she carried Letty Bailey's DNA?

She rose to her feet and crossed the room to the fireplace. She lifted the framed photograph of her grandfather, captured in front of the clinic wearing his barn coat and wellies, grinning into the camera.

No retreat, no surrender. Come what may, she'd find that silver star in time for Christmas Eve.

She mentally ran through their efforts so far. She had scoured the village for potential suspects, focusing on those with means, motives, and opportunities to steal the cherished Christmas star. None of that had gone anywhere.

Then again, she had basically called it quits when the threatening notes started appearing. They had shaken her resolve, revealing a level of malevolence that went beyond the typical motives of village residents. The thief wasn't some mere opportunist from town. This person was someone serious, perhaps even sinister. She had backed off. And not for a good reason, but because she had been afraid.

Maybe she should explore where she had the most intimate connection—her grandfather. As an artist, he had a unique perspective on the world. If her great-grandmother's courage could reinspire her, perhaps her grandfather's brilliance could spark new ideas.

She scratched behind Charlie's ears. "What do you think, girl?" she murmured. "Do you think Grandad can help us? He might have some papers or documents stashed away that might give some insight."

Charlie purred, and Maxwell leaned against Harriet's leg, their love giving her strength.

First thing tomorrow morning, she would get back to business.

CHAPTER TWENTY-SEVEN

Undisclosed Location
January 1942

As dawn broke, painting the sky pink and orange, Letty stood on the cold, wet grass at the airfield, feeling the chill through her uniform. Her heart raced with a mixture of nerves and excitement. It was 1942, in the middle of the war, and there she was, lined up with a group of women ready to join the Air Transport Auxiliary.

Letty wrapped her arms around herself, which provided little in the way of protection against the morning air but offered a semblance of comfort, a way to hold herself together in the face of so many unknowns. She was consumed with thoughts of Cecil stationed somewhere in France, his own heart committed to the fight for freedom. The thought of his steadfast courage was now a source of strength rather than merely deep, aching worry that kept her awake at night.

Now that she was here, Letty really started to feel what joining the ATA meant. She was about to do something completely outside of anything she had ever attempted. The airfield stretched out in front of her. She forced herself to take a deep, calming breath, which succeeded only in making her lightheaded rather than calm.

The planes they'd soon learn to fly were more than simple war machines. They represented new roles for women to fill, roles traditionally filled by men. She felt the weight of such a massive challenge—not just learning to fly but also showing everyone she could do it.

But even with all these thoughts swirling around, she still felt a surge of excitement. How could she be terrified and elated at the same time? It reminded her of her first day of classes in Camden. The chance to fly and be part of a movement that went beyond herself was something she had hardly taken time to think about in her rush to put her affairs in order and get to training. Now, it was about to happen.

She studied the other women on the airfield. Their expressions reflected her own feelings of anxiety and determination, and it was somehow comforting to see she wasn't alone physically or emotionally. They were all about to step into something new together, with an understood promise that they would look out for each other.

"All right, ladies, line up! Shoulders back, heads high!" The command sliced through Letty's gathering nerves, snapping her into sharp focus. The instructor, a woman whose presence commanded instant respect, had eyes like searchlights, piercing and all-seeing. "Forward, march!"

The women started across the training field, their line wobbly but enthusiastic.

The instructor called a halt, and Letty managed to keep her place in line.

The air was charged, each woman an electric current of potential as they gathered under the watchful eye of their instructor. As the formidable figure moved down the line, inspecting each recruit with a scrutiny that felt as if it could peel back the layers of Letty's resolve, a heavy weight settled on Letty's shoulders. The sheer gravity of the moment felt like a test.

"You're here to serve your country, to show you're as capable as any man in the skies. I expect nothing less than your best. In fact, I demand even better." The instructor's voice, stern yet threaded with an undercurrent of momentum, moved Letty.

She would meet this challenge, this call to rise higher than she had ever imagined.

After that day, she spent all her time in the classroom, far from the skies she dreamed of.

She greedily absorbed every lesson. She learned to identify planes on sight, getting to know the different controls and designs of the many machines she'd one day fly.

Flying solo, without help from radio navigation, she'd depend on the maps and compasses she was taught to use.

She practiced plotting her path using landmarks to guide her way. Figuring out directions and distances came naturally to her, a way for her to connect with the plane and the ground below.

Understanding the weather was another crucial lesson. She got into the habit of reading weather reports and forecasts, learning how to make safe choices and then continuously check those choices against the sky itself. Knowing what the clouds were telling her could make the difference between a good flight and a bad one.

She learned the basic mechanics of aircraft, as well as foundational repairs that would allow her to keep flying even when there were small problems.

Her instructors drilled her in the strict rules of wartime flying. She was soon familiar with where she could and couldn't fly, what to do in emergencies, and how to communicate when flying. Each flight she'd take in the future would show how well she understood these rules, silently agreeing with the sky that she was meant to be up there, away from the ground.

She reminded herself that each day was a step closer to the skies, each lesson a building block in the foundation of her goal. In the quiet moments, when doubt whispered in her ear, she would silence it with her determination, reminding herself of the journey she had embarked upon and the destination that awaited her.

She had moved into the lodgings provided by the ATA, which soon felt like a second home. There, she and the other female pilots found a strong sense of community and friendship.

Letty appreciated how the ATA treated female pilots the same as the men, giving them equal pay for the first time ever. She allowed herself to hope that one day, perhaps even in her own lifetime, that approach would be the standard rather than a noteworthy exception.

The training honed not only Letty's flying skills but her character. She learned to lead with a steady hand during flight operations, her innate empathy and patience drawing respect from her peers. When faced with complex issues—whether navigating under challenging conditions or troubleshooting airplane malfunctions—she discovered an inner resilience and problem-solving ability.

By the end of their training, the transformation was evident. Letty and her fellow recruits moved with a newfound confidence, their competence in the air a testament to their hard work and dedication. The training had prepared them for the technical aspects of their duties and had also woven them into a tight-knit group, united by their unique journey.

Letty adjusted the strap of her leather helmet, feeling its now-familiar weight settle against her brow, and checked the fit of her goggles one last time. She was about to fly solo for the first time, the final test before beginning the mission that had brought her here in the first place.

The air carried the scent of oil and aviation fuel, an invigorating combination. She glanced up at the clear blue sky, watching as wisps of clouds drifted overhead, and felt a surge of anticipation.

Her instructor's voice crackled over the radio, guiding her through the preflight checks with practiced efficiency. Letty's hands moved deftly as she inspected the aircraft. It was a de Havilland Tiger Moth, a simple biplane used for training pilots. It had a wooden frame covered in fabric, a reliable engine, and relatively simple controls. It was perfect for teaching beginners how to fly because it was stable and easy to maneuver. The open cockpit let pilots feel the wind and excitement of flying up close.

Her fingers traced the familiar contours of the propeller and wings. Each bolt, each cable, was a lifeline, a connection between herself and the machine that would carry her into the skies.

With a deep breath, she climbed into the cockpit, her pulse quickening as she settled into the pilot's seat. Her instructor spun the propellor, and the engine roared to life beneath her. She ordered herself to stay calm and focus on her work. She was used to an instructor in the plane with her, a port in any airway storm. But now she was alone for the first time—and with any luck, not the last.

She taxied onto the runway and then opened the throttle. The aircraft surged forward, its wheels leaving the ground with a gentle bounce. Letty's heart soared as she felt the familiar lift and the wind rushing past her cheeks. She'd completed her first takeoff.

In the solitude of the cockpit, muscle memory took over. Letty found herself lost in the rhythm of flight—the steady drone of the engine, the gentle sway of the wings against the wind. With each graceful turn and climb, she felt herself growing more confident, more attuned to the subtle nuances of the aircraft's movements.

Beneath her, a patchwork quilt of fields stretched out in all directions, a tapestry of green and gold bathed in the warmth of the sun. All too soon, it was time to return to the airfield. She guided the aircraft back to the runway, feeling a gentle bump as the wheels made contact with the ground once more. Perhaps it was silly, but she imagined the Tiger Moth was as disappointed to have left the great blue sky as she was.

She taxied to a stop. She had done it—she had flown solo. And in that moment, she knew with unwavering certainty that she was exactly where she was meant to be.

CHAPTER TWENTY-EIGHT

Harriet had found nothing, and it was already Christmas Eve. She had spent the past few days frantically searching, hoping for something that would give her a reason to believe that the Christmas star could still be found in time. The attic held a treasure trove of her grandad's past. Under normal circumstances, she might have been enthralled with the window into his world.

But she was on a mission with a clock ticking.

She checked her phone, horrified to see the afternoon ticking away. Since it was Christmas Eve, she had closed the clinic at noon. Polly had given her a tight hug, saying, "It'll be all right. Everyone knows you tried your best." An uncomfortable stillness had settled in as the door shut behind her. Harriet had stood in the empty clinic, alone with the echo of Polly's words and the drum of freezing rain against the window.

Staring at yet another box, she realized how tired she was. Her head pounded, and her body ached from sitting too long in the freezing attic. Sleet hit the window, and the wind's moan added to her unrest. Her mind wandered to the upcoming midnight service at the church, which made her think of Will and wonder what he was doing. The thought of him triggered a fresh bout of homesickness. She'd tried calling her folks earlier in the day, but they hadn't answered. It wasn't odd for them, busy as they were. But on Christmas Eve, it felt different to be unable to get ahold of her parents.

She stood and stretched her legs, reaching her arms above her head, then went back to the box. Most of its contents lay in a heap on the floor. The last thing inside was a crisp manila envelope, its freshness stark against the other yellowed items. It was labeled, *Hereford School of Farriery*. Ethan's alma mater and the school where Grandad had been a trustee.

She picked it up and carried it down to the kitchen table. She doubted it would lead anywhere, but she might as well check it out before making tea. In the envelope she found a mix of papers. A worn photo of a smiling older man holding a farrier's hammer in one hand and a set of clinchers in the other, three horseshoe receipts, and a graduation program. It was from the year Ethan had graduated, if she recalled his résumé correctly. According to the program, Grandad had been the graduation speaker.

She had just started to look it over further when Maxwell let out a low, guttural growl. It took a lot to upset the dachshund. He was lying in bed, but his head and ears were up.

The sound was matched by frantic whining from Rocky, a scrappy terrier boarding in the clinic for the night. Usually, she kept boarders other than cats in the barn's kennels, but Rocky was recovering from a minor stomach issue and she'd wanted him close so she could hear if he needed anything. And now he was in a frenzy.

Shoving everything back into the envelope and tucking it under her arm, she tried to clear her unease. The house was locked up tight. There was no need to get spooked. "It's okay, boy," she told Maxwell, hoping to convince herself as well as him.

He gave her a dubious expression.

She slipped down the hall toward the clinic, flipping on lights as she went.

Harriet checked on her boarders in the clinic. Two cats curled up in their respective cages, and little Rocky quieted at her approach.

"How's everyone doing tonight?" she asked in her most soothing tone.

At the sound of her voice, Rocky's tail beat a welcoming rhythm against his bed.

"Big day for you tomorrow," she told him. "Your family will be here bright and early, and that's going to be the best Christmas present ever, isn't it?" She made her rounds, ensuring each animal was cared for and had everything they would need for the night.

She put the kettle on in the kitchen then went back into the clinic and sat at the reception desk. The wind had picked up outside, and the freezing rain pinged against the windowpane. She realized that she even missed Connecticut weather. She made her tea and carried it back to the desk, where she sat down and opened the envelope. She began with the graduation bulletin, scanning the photos on the inside cover. There was her grandfather, smiling for the camera in cap and gown.

The class photo showed twenty-one graduates in neat rows. She skimmed the names, pausing at Ethan's third from the bottom on the second page. But something was wrong.

The photo captioned *Ethan James Grimshaw* wasn't Ethan.

This student had short, ginger hair and a round face, not at all like the dark-haired, slender Ethan. Had the printer accidentally put Ethan's name under the wrong photo? She looked for the photo of Ethan, guessing his picture would have the name of the ginger-haired student, but she didn't see anyone who resembled him.

She hurried to the filing cabinet and tugged open a drawer. There it was—Grandad's old card file, a relic from the '90s. Polly had a way of keeping things, insisting that she never knew when they might come in handy. Harriet owed Polly, since right now she desperately needed a phone number.

She resumed her spot at the reception desk and flipped through the tabs in the card file. She quickly found what she needed—a card for Hereford Farrier School. She plucked it out and read the single name written in Grandad's tight script. *Professor Anne Thornton, Academic Dean.* It was a long shot, given that it was midafternoon on Christmas Eve, and who knew whether Dean Thornton still worked there? But it was worth a try.

She picked up the receiver to the landline. Dead. The storm must have knocked out the lines. She picked up her cell phone and punched in the number. Holding the phone to her ear, she listened as it rang. Just when she was about to give up, a crisp voice answered, "Hereford School. Dean Thornton speaking."

Harriet was so taken aback that she had actually reached the dean on the first try—or at all—that she was momentarily speechless. "Um, hello. Thank you for picking up on Christmas Eve."

The woman at the other end laughed. "You caught me at my desk. I am no doubt the last member of the faculty still on campus. It's the best time for me to work though—when everyone else has gone home. How can I help you?"

"If you have a moment, Dean Thornton, I have a rather unusual question. My name is Dr. Harriet Bailey. I believe you were acquainted with Dr. Harold Bailey, my grandfather."

The woman chuckled with evident pleasure. "My goodness. Harold Bailey was a brilliant vet and a delightful chap. And you've taken over his practice?"

"He left it to me."

"I heard he had passed. I'm sorry. I'm glad his practice stayed in the family. I'm sure you're filling his large shoes wonderfully."

"I'm certainly trying to," Harriet replied. "I was wondering if I could trouble you for information about one of your former students, Ethan Grimshaw."

The dean was silent for so long that Harriet thought the call had dropped. When she finally replied, her voice was tight. "Of course I remember Ethan. He was one of our top students. How do you know him?"

"He runs a farriery business near me."

"I'm quite certain that he does not."

A chill ran down her spine. "Why do you say that?"

"Ethan Grimshaw died in a car accident a week after he graduated."

Harriet caught her breath. Had she entrusted the care of her patients to a fraud? Heat swept through her body, followed by a wave of panic. She remembered how Ethan had impressed her when he'd knocked on the clinic door, searching for work as a skilled farrier. She had called his references before recommending him.

"Are you saying that the person I know as Ethan Grimshaw is… someone else?"

"Can you describe him?" the dean asked.

She stammered out a physical description of Ethan.

"It sounds like you may have encountered Daniel Hartley. He was a student in the same class as Ethan. We had to expel him from the program for theft, just a few weeks before he would have graduated as a fully licensed farrier."

"But I called his references. They sang his praises."

"Daniel was a brilliant con artist. I am sure he was able to pay someone to say those things."

"I've recommended him to horse owners all over the county," she said in growing horror. "People who know and trust me."

"Fortunately, he really is a farrier. Not licensed, but he knows his stuff." The dean stopped for a moment. "Dr. Bailey, you need to be careful. Daniel Hartley is neither a good person nor an emotionally stable one. I think he'd do anything to get what he wants."

In light of what she'd learned, Harriet had to wonder if he already had.

After she disconnected the call, she set her phone in the charging station by the door. If the landline was dead, she needed to make sure her phone was fully juiced. She wasn't about to get caught without a phone again—not with a con man who might be threatening her on the loose.

She dropped into the chair at Polly's desk, her pulse quickening. The clinic door swung open, letting in a gust of cold air and sleet. "Merry Christmas," Ethan boomed, shutting the door behind him. "Or should I say Merry Christmas Eve?"

Icy fear washed over her, and she hastily slid the graduation bulletin under the envelope. "Merry Christmas Eve to you too."

A small smile played on his lips. "Working late? I thought you'd be at your aunt Jinny's by now."

"Soon. I just have a few things to finish up here."

"I almost forgot." He handed her a gift wrapped in red paper with a bow on top. "For you."

"You shouldn't have," she said. Her words came out steadily, but her fingers betrayed her, trembling as they worked at the ribbon.

He laid a hand over hers. "Don't open it now. Later. When you're alone."

She froze. "Sure."

"I'll be in the barn. I think we're in for a winter storm, and I want to make sure your equine boarders are settled for the night. This way you don't have to brave this weather." He turned toward the door.

"It's Christmas Eve. Don't you want to go home?"

He nodded at the file that covered the graduation bulletin. "Like you, I have things to do."

Harriet forced herself to smile. "Right. Thanks for the gift. Oh, and nice boots, Ethan."

"Thanks. They've served me well."

From the clinic window, she watched him stroll to the barn. As soon as the door shut behind him, she ripped open the package. On red tissue paper inside lay a small white envelope. Her hands shook as she opened it.

Speak not the truth, or in agony reside.
In umbral deep, secrets hide,
A word too much, a whisper's cost,
Unveil it all: a friend is lost.

Dropping the card on the desk, she got up and reached for her phone, but it was gone. The charging station was empty. Ethan—or, rather, Daniel—must have taken it on his way out. She raced into the kitchen and stared at the hook by the door where she normally hung her keys. It was empty too.

Aunt Jinny was at the church, setting up for the Christmas Eve service. With no landline or cell phone and no car keys, Harriet was on her own with a man who wasn't who he claimed to be. She had to get away.

She threw on her outerwear and pushed open the kitchen door. The wind yanked it from her hand and banged it against the farmhouse wall.

Startled by the loud noise, she glanced toward the barn.

Daniel stood in the doorway, a faceless silhouette backlit by the barn light. He raised his hand and waved.

She ran.

CHAPTER TWENTY-NINE

She had to find Will. It was Christmas Eve. Surely he would be at the church getting ready for the service.

A cold knot of anxiety settled in her stomach. She tugged her cap down over her ears and quickened her pace. She had sprinted the distance from the clinic to the church. Now her breath came in gasps, and she had a stitch in her side, but she ignored it.

She barged through the church door and found Aunt Jinny outside the office. "Gracious, Harriet. What are you doing?"

She disregarded the question. "Is Will here?"

"I don't know, I haven't seen him yet. Why? Is everything all right?"

She didn't want to alarm her aunt. "I just need to find him. Can I borrow your phone?"

Aunt Jinny handed it over with a perplexed expression.

Harriet dialed Will's number, but there was no answer. She gave her aunt's phone back, her sense of dread increasing.

"He might be ignoring it in favor of prayer and meditation to prepare himself for tonight's service," Aunt Jinny suggested. "Check the parsonage. Do you want me to come with you?"

"No, you have enough going on with getting the church ready for tonight," Harriet said, hoping she sounded more reassuring than she felt. "I'll see you later." She trotted next door to the parsonage and knocked on the door.

No answer. The windows were dark. Where was he?

The words from the note suddenly took on meaning. *A friend is lost.* Who else could it be but Will, the friend who was investigating the missing star with her?

Daniel must have thought that she and Will were getting close to uncovering the truth. That meant that Will was in danger. Van needed to know immediately. She wished she'd thought to call him on her aunt's phone, or at least thought to borrow the phone. But she didn't want to take the time to go back to the church. Besides, she didn't think she could put off Aunt Jinny a second time, and seeing Will, making sure he was okay with her own eyes—that was top priority.

If her conclusions were correct, that it had been Daniel who had stolen the Christmas star, she would get the information to Van soon. But not until she found Will. The revelation was jarring. Ethan Grimshaw was an impostor. He had skillfully deceived every single person he'd come in contact with. A wave of anger washed over her. Anger at both the con man and at herself for allowing him to fool her so completely. She'd played right into his scheme.

Now that she thought about it, he really was the only suspect who made sense. She'd bet anything that his boots matched the print left in the mud under the window. He'd said he loved cats, so of course he would have made sure Cocoa was out of his way but safe and comfortable. Harriet had even spoken to him near Calvin's pen. She wouldn't have been surprised if that had been when he'd tampered with it so the camel could escape. And he surely would have known about a camel's love for sweets.

How would someone unconnected to White Church Bay even know about the star to steal it? More importantly, what was his next move? Did he already have Will someplace? He'd seen her fleeing Cobble Hill Farm on foot. He would know that she'd opened the package and seen his latest poem. Would he follow her? Or would he go back to wherever he was keeping Will and—she cut off the thought.

Something made her stop. She pulled off her hat and listened. At first, all she heard was the wind and waves. But then it came again—a dog's bark, faint but fraught with panic. Who on earth would leave a poor creature out in this weather?

She hurried toward the seaward side of the church building, where the air was charged with the briny scent of salt water. The pelting sleet seemed to merge with the fine mist rising from the sea below. She heard the bark again, spun around, and came face-to-face with the entrance to the church crypt.

Three stone steps led down to a heavy oak door set in the crumbling stone. The wood was splintered with age. Rusty iron bands spanned its width, and a heavy iron ring functioned as a handle. She remembered Will telling her that the underground vault of the church hadn't been used in over a hundred years.

Her pulse thrummed in her ears. She wanted nothing more than to turn back, get Aunt Jinny, or call Van.

But from the depths of the crypt came the sharp bark again, a little louder this time. A dog was trapped inside, and she couldn't leave it there a second longer than she absolutely had to.

She found the small flashlight she'd gotten into the habit of carrying for emergency calls in the pocket of her coat then scrambled down the steps to the door. Her flashlight beam caught words inscribed in the stone over the threshold. *Memento Mori.* She knew enough Latin to figure out what it meant. *Remember you must die.*

She grabbed the heavy iron handle and pulled. It yielded easily—too easily for a door that had been shut for decades.

She propped it open with a large stone then stepped into the dark space, her eyes straining to see beyond the flashlight's beam. The air was eerily still, a stark contrast to the rain and wind outside.

She swept the flashlight in an arc. Massive stone blocks formed the walls, interrupted at regular intervals by small, weathered alcoves. She refused to examine the contents of those alcoves. As she ventured into the vault, the change in atmosphere was immediate. Not colder, but heavier, as if saturated with a bleak history she couldn't see but could feel in every breath.

The dog's bark pierced the silence. Willing herself to stay calm, she pressed on toward the sound. The low ceiling felt as if it closed in on her, while the stone pillars stretched ahead into pitch darkness. She rounded a corner. Her heart skipped a beat. Someone had placed candles in the sconces that lined this section. Their flicker threw strange shadows on the walls.

The realization hit her like the freezing rain outside. She wasn't alone. Someone had lit these candles. Every cell in her body screamed at her to retreat.

But the dog whimpered, and she couldn't leave without it. If she was terrified, she couldn't begin to imagine how the poor animal felt.

The corridor narrowed and veered to the left, leading her into a chamber. Damp walls gleamed under the haphazard glow of countless candles, some new and others mere stubs. In the center stood a stone altar.

A persistent whine split the air. She whirled around and gasped at the sight of Rocky, the terrier who was supposed to be recovering at the clinic. He was tied to an iron grate with a bowl of water next to him.

Daniel must have grabbed the little dog after he ran out. He had her keys, so he would have had no problem getting in the back door of the clinic where the kennels were.

She crouched down and unclipped the lead from the dog's collar then scooped him into her arms.

"Need some help?" Daniel Hartley stepped out from the shadows.

Harriet's heart lurched, and she took a step back. "Ethan," she managed to say, forcing herself to breathe. "What are you doing here? You were just at the clinic."

"Funny how fast you can go if you have an actual vehicle." He grinned as he dug into his pocket, drew out her keys, and dangled them in front of her. "And now you're where I want you." His voice shifted from buoyant and lighthearted to tight and hard within a single sentence.

"Why is Rocky down here?"

"I knew the amazing Dr. Harriet Bailey couldn't ignore the cries of a poor, defenseless animal."

She checked Rocky over. He seemed fine, at least physically, though he trembled in her arms. "You lured me here? Why?"

"I knew it was only a matter of time before you and Will figured it out. How did you like my latest verse? Will was my other ace in the hole for getting you here." He smirked. "By the way, you shouldn't leave your phone lying around the office. Someone might go through it."

A numbing terror washed over her. The phone call to the dean would be in her call log. There went any hope that he might not know she knew his true identity.

"You are amazing, Dr. Bailey, just like everyone in this ridiculous village believes."

Daniel reached into his large pocket and brought out the silver Christmas star.

She caught her breath. The star hadn't been sold to an anonymous buyer in Istanbul. It was here in White Church Bay and had been all along. She had heard that it was beautiful, but it was more than that. It was captivating, enchanting. No wonder Letty and Albie had seen the star as almost magical. The silver and sapphires caught the dim candlelight, scattering tiny reflections onto the bleak stone walls.

"But maybe if you were truly brilliant, Doc, you wouldn't be standing in a place where they bury people."

Harriet's heart thudded in her ears, its rhythm so erratic that it felt as though it might leap from her chest. "You'll never get away with this. Where is Will?"

"Let's just say Rocky isn't the only one tied up." He sneered and kicked a coil of rope across the floor.

She suddenly bent and released Rocky in the direction she'd come. Daniel screamed, but before he'd taken two steps, Rocky had scampered down the passage. Daniel raced after him but returned empty-handed. Harriet breathed a prayer of thanksgiving that she'd had the sense to prop the door open.

She did her best to mask the fear overwhelming her senses. "Where's Will?" she repeated.

Daniel leaned against the wall and clasped both hands over his heart with a smirk. “Why? You want to save him?”

She turned and made for the passageway. Suddenly, the toe of her boot caught on a protruding stone. She lurched forward, narrowly avoiding hitting her face on the floor.

Daniel yanked her to her feet then shoved her backward.

Her head slammed into the wall, and everything went black.

Consciousness crept back as a foggy haze, only to be replaced by a sharp surge of pain followed by a wash of terror as she remembered where she was—in an ancient, long-unused crypt. Rope bit into her wrists and ankles as she slumped against the wall. Her head pounded, and her hands throbbed where she’d caught herself on the unforgiving stone floor when she’d tripped.

Daniel sat on top of the stone altar, swinging his feet like a child on a park bench. “There you are.”

“Tying me up won’t change anything,” she croaked. “You’ll still get caught and face justice.”

“Keep telling yourself that,” he replied.

“What’s the game, Daniel?” She needed to engage him, to keep him occupied and talking. How long until someone realized she was missing? She had planned to attend the service with Aunt Jinny. Would her aunt become concerned if she didn’t show up? Or would she assume she was off on an emergency call on a distant farm? And who would think to search the crypt anyway, a place untouched for a hundred years?

Daniel towered over her, and she felt as if she were truly seeing him for the first time. His hair was unkempt, and dark circles underscored his wild eyes. This wasn't the man she recognized, the dedicated and skilled farrier whose praises were sung all over Yorkshire. No, before her stood Daniel Hartley—a notorious con artist, the thief of the Christmas star.

"You think I'll face justice? I'm carrying out my own justice," Daniel said, his voice hard.

"How so?" she asked, hoping she sounded genuinely interested. "Why are you doing this, Daniel? What do you want from me?"

"It's not about what I want from you. It's about what was taken from me. This village took everything—my dreams, my home, *everything*."

"How did it do that? What happened, Daniel, and how can I help make it right?"

"My dad died when I was ten, and this village did nothing to help us."

"How awful." She couldn't imagine the people of White Church Bay ignoring the plight of a family who had just lost their father and husband. "They did nothing?"

"Oh, for a while they loved helping us and bragging to one another about how good they were. But then my mother took us to London. I had to say goodbye to my pony, my dog, the moors."

"Why go to London?"

"She claimed she had a job there and that White Church Bay held nothing for her."

"Did she?" Harriet asked.

"That's not the point. The point is that I had to leave, and my life was never good again. This village should have given her a job. Not made her feel like she had to move."

"I'm sorry, but I don't see how stealing the star is justice."

"The star is the shining heart of this ridiculous little place. If they lose it, they'll be heartbroken. They'll suffer the way I suffered."

Unease skittered down Harriet's spine. He was clearly unstable, and what he was describing sounded more like revenge than justice. Misplaced revenge.

She chose her next words with care. "Daniel, please. Innocent people don't deserve to suffer."

"No, *I* didn't deserve to suffer," he snarled. Face twisting with rage, he lunged off the altar and charged toward her.

Before he reached her, two figures burst into the room and planted themselves between Daniel and Harriet. "Hold it right there, whatever your name is," Van ordered Daniel.

Will crouched beside her and untied her bonds. "Harriet, are you all right?"

"I will be." She tried to smile at him.

"Sorry it took so long," Will said as Rocky scampered into the chamber. "We wouldn't have made it at all if it weren't for the little dog there. He wouldn't stop barking until we followed him, but then he led us straight here."

She scooped up Rocky, who licked her face. "Good boy," she whispered in his ear. "Good boy."

Van was handcuffing Daniel. "You're under arrest for stealing the silver star ornament from the church, plus at least two counts of kidnapping, and I'm sure we'll find some other things as well."

"His name is Dan Hartley," Harriet told him.

Van peered at Daniel's face. "I remember now. You were the stable manager's son. Our mothers were friends. Last time I saw you, you were still in short pants."

Daniel smirked. "And I remember you. A mum's boy always sticking up for any blubbering kid in the schoolyard."

"And you were often the bully."

Harriet had never heard Van's voice so cold, but she wasn't surprised to hear he'd stood on the side of right even as a child.

"Maybe there's a chance to mend this, to make peace with your past," Will said to Daniel.

"Peace?" Daniel demanded. "With this place? There's no peace here. Not for me."

Van filled Daniel in on his rights then led him toward the entrance to the crypt.

Will helped Harriet to her feet, supporting her weight as the feeling came back to her limbs. "Never a dull moment with you, is there?" he asked.

"Hey, he got you first," she pointed out.

He laughed.

From the steeple above, the gentle chime of church bells drifted down, a soft reminder that it was almost Christmas.

CHAPTER THIRTY

Will led the way down a steep, narrow staircase. Sneaking into the church through a little-used rear entrance, they avoided the busy parish hall bustling with church members gathering early for the midnight service.

Van had taken the star to the police station, saying he wanted to photograph and log a report. He promised to return it to the church in time for the service. He would also return Rocky to the clinic using Harriet's keys, which he had retrieved from Daniel.

She spotted a small door at the base of the stairs. The floor near the door was made of flat square stones that resembled the crypt floor. "You're not taking me back into the crypt, are you?"

"No, of course not. But we need someplace to talk. If anybody sees us, they'll bombard me with questions that I don't have the brain space for at the moment. Like where this garland should go and whether there are enough tables set up for the reception. Whether it's okay to hang mistletoe over the pulpit. That kind of thing."

Harriet laughed. It felt good, as if she was breaking free of the tension and terror of the past few hours—longer if she was honest. "I can appreciate that. I need a moment to recover, and I'd rather do that in private."

"Well, this spot is as private as it gets in a church on Christmas Eve." Will pushed the door open and switched on the light, motioning for Harriet to step in.

As she passed him, she was finally able to see his face. His left eye was developing a bruise, and there was a cut across his forehead. She couldn't wait to hear his story, even as she felt a deep ache in her bones, and her hands throbbed. But they were in one piece. It was Christmas Eve. And the star was back. She had so much to be grateful for.

Finally focusing on the room, her eyes widened in astonishment.

In one corner, an old boiler hummed, radiating a warmth that Harriet found deeply comforting after the chill of the crypt. Nearby, a scarred wooden desk was cluttered with an array of papers and a coffee can holding nuts, bolts, and screws. Over the desk hung a wall calendar. A braided rug lay on the floor, flanked by two mismatched chairs angled toward each other, with a weathered wooden coffee table in between. A card table stood in a corner, topped with an electric kettle, a selection of tea bags, and a sugar jar.

"This is so cozy," she told Will.

"In all the churches where I've worked, the sexton turns the boiler room into a sort of retreat," he explained. "It's not quite as good as being in your own home, but I didn't know if you were up to that much moving around right now."

"This is perfect," she assured him. She unzipped her parka and hung it on a nearby hook, and Will followed suit. She sank into a chair, feeling the weight of fatigue settling in. She was content to stay in the warmth of the little sanctuary, enjoying its cozy atmosphere and Will's company.

He switched on the electric kettle then retrieved two mugs from an overhead shelf and dropped a tea bag into each one. The kettle whistled in no time, and he poured hot water over the tea bags. After adding sugar to each mug and stirring, Will set them on the coffee table then retrieved a tin from the same shelf that had held the mugs. He opened it to reveal cookies. "I was right. Amos does keep a stash of biscuits on hand."

"Will he mind us invading his haven like this?" Harriet asked. Amos Charlton was a good sort, and she didn't want to step on his toes.

"He's actually encouraged me to use it. He understands that sometimes I need more peace than I can get upstairs." Will settled into a chair and selected a biscuit. "So. We've had quite the evening, haven't we?"

"That's an understatement. I was terrified when I discovered that Ethan is actually Daniel Hartley." She chose two cookies from the tin. "It freaks me out that he's been posing as a man who's been dead for years."

"How did you even figure that out?" Will asked.

"Grandad, actually." Harriet grinned.

Will appraised her. "I might need a little more explanation than that."

Harriet took a bite and then sipped her tea, her body gradually warming up. She detailed the events of her afternoon, starting with the exploration of her grandfather's papers and ending with Daniel luring her to the crypt.

"I never would've seen that coming," he finally said.

"Me neither."

"Van was trying to locate you, by the way. He sent you two text messages and tried to call. Something about a surprise for Polly. When you didn't respond, he knew something was wrong. When he couldn't find you, he started searching for me."

"Where were you?"

"Daniel stopped at the rectory this afternoon asking for pastoral counseling. When I turned away to lead him to the kitchen for some tea, he tackled me. I hit my head on the edge of the stove." Will gestured to his injuries. "I blacked out for a bit. When I came to, he'd tied me up and gagged me with one of my own tea towels."

"That's awful," Harriet said. "I stopped by the rectory when I was trying to find you after Daniel's ugly note about losing a friend."

"I heard someone knock. It must have been you. I couldn't make enough noise to let you know I was in there and needed help. By the time I'd wriggled close enough to the door, you must have left. But then Van showed up—again, looking for you—and I was able to kick the door enough to let him know something was wrong. He was inside in no time."

"Sounds like we both owe Van extra-nice Christmas presents," Harriet observed.

"No kidding. As he freed me, Van explained that you were nowhere to be found. Then that little terrier appeared, yipping and barking. We tried to ignore him at first because we wanted to find you, but then he grabbed Van's pant leg and tugged, so we figured we'd better follow him, at least until we knew what he wanted. And you know the rest."

Harriet leaned back in her chair. "I don't get it. Daniel had the star. Why not run and sell it? Why attack us? We might never have caught him if he'd simply left."

Will nodded, his face set in a grave expression. "For Daniel, it's not about the star's monetary value. He's been holding a grudge against the village and the church for so long, it consumed him. He wanted to hurt the village the way he perceives that it hurt him, so he took the star for what it represents to us."

"But that's no reason to come after us personally."

"He had to make sure we didn't tell anyone he was behind the theft, and he must have realized we were close. I think he also wanted to demonstrate that he could outsmart us as another way of getting back at the entire village. It's twisted, but in his mind, it was how he could regain control and assert his power."

"I almost feel sorry for him," Harriet said.

"I hope he gets the help he clearly needs." Will leaned forward. "Now, enough of that ugliness. Tell me—are you truly okay?"

"I am. Especially now that I know I'm not spending Christmas Eve in that crypt." She grinned. "Although I think I'm going to skip singing in the choir tonight."

She eyed him nervously then plunged ahead. "It's been nice talking all of this over with you. I've missed that."

"I have too. And I feel I owe you an explanation," Will said. "I've probably ruined any chance of fixing our friendship after being so distant the past few days. I can only imagine how that must have made you feel."

"It hurt, but I understand. I didn't respond as well as I should have when you told me you wanted to stop looking for the star. I felt as if you didn't believe in me. I know you didn't mean that at all. You were thinking of your flock and my safety, as you always do. I'm sorry."

"I am too." He leaned forward and held her gaze, his eyes filled with regret. "If I could go back, I would handle things differently."

"Why did you withdraw? Did you need time to cool off?"

"Not at all. I much prefer to resolve disagreements before they have a chance to fester. But this was different. When you started receiving those threatening notes, I thought my being here was putting you in danger."

She gaped at him. "How?"

"Everyone knew we were working together on this. I thought that if I stepped back, if I could discourage you from continuing your search, perhaps you'd be safe." He shook his head. "But that was a mistake. If we'd continued to work together, Daniel might not have caught either of us alone."

"Why not tell me what you were thinking? I've been so worried," Harriet said.

"I was afraid you'd think I was foolish," he admitted. He peered into her eyes. "Afraid that you didn't feel the same connection to me that I've always felt with you."

"Connection?" She needed him to say it plainly. There was no chance she'd reveal her heart without knowing where he stood.

He paused then said, "Harriet, I don't want to make you uncomfortable, but I've always felt something more than friendship for you."

It took her a second to believe he'd actually said it. But when it sank in, she beamed at him. "And to think I was so unsure of how you felt about me."

He stared. "Unsure? I've been completely taken with you since you moved here. You couldn't tell?"

"I was afraid to hope you reciprocated my feelings," she told him, delighted to see his face light up.

He reached into his pocket and pulled out a small jewelry box. "Even though I didn't know if we'd ever be able to repair our relationship, I wanted to get you something special for Christmas. Something to show you how important you are to me. There's an artisan jewelry maker your aunt recommended, so I thought I'd check it out while I was in London. And she was right. I found the perfect thing." Will smiled that warm smile she loved so much and handed her the box. "Merry Christmas, Harriet."

Inside the box lay a silver necklace, its pendant a finely crafted star studded with tiny blue stones.

"It's gorgeous," she whispered, feeling a little breathless.

"I wanted to commemorate this adventure, whether we succeeded or not. After all the work you put into this search, I wanted to make sure you had at least one star to show for it." He stood, took the necklace from her, and carefully clasped it around her neck. "I hope we have many more adventures together."

"To adventures," she echoed, her voice soft. "And to discovering if camels really do fancy figgy pudding."

They both laughed then Will grimaced and touched his eye.

"How is your eye?"

"It's fine. Though I expect I'll have some explaining to do when I face the congregation."

She smiled as the sounds of preparations for the Christmas Eve service echoed from upstairs. She gently touched the silver star around her neck, and then she remembered. "Oh! I have a present for you too, Will." She smiled, thinking of what her gift would remind him of.

His phone chimed, and he checked it. "Van says he's brought back the star and placed it in its usual box. Now he's going to pick up Polly. I should head upstairs." He held out his hand and helped her up.

"You know what, Will?"

"What?"

She beamed. "We found the missing Christmas star."

He smiled at her. "We did, but I found something far more valuable."

She could only squeeze his hand in reply.

CHAPTER THIRTY-ONE

Upstairs, Will promised to find her after the service then let go of her hand with obvious reluctance and made his way to the sacristy. Her hand cold and her heart light, Harriet stepped into the sanctuary, resplendent with Christmas cheer and filled with joyful church members.

She paused for a moment, inhaling the fragrance of holly and soaking in the essence of Christmas. Her heart swelled with gratitude. As she scanned the crowded sanctuary for a seat, she spotted a young family standing together. The mother tenderly adjusted her daughter's hair ribbon while the father slipped the girl's coat off and folded it over his arm. The little girl gazed at the towering Christmas tree beside the altar, her eyes wide with wonder.

The sight transported Harriet back to her own childhood Christmases—warm embraces, the comforting readings of the Christmas story in Luke, and the familiar hymns sung standing next to her parents in the candlelit sanctuary. She could hear her mother's soft voice harmonizing with the choir, could feel her father's reassuring hand on her shoulder.

She slid into one of the back pews and watched as Keri Stone snapped photos from the pulpit then hopped down and snapped a few more as she navigated the aisle between the packed pews.

Aunt Jinny sat in the front with her son, Anthony, and Anthony's wife and twins. She was glad to see them and made a mental note to meet up with them after the service. She didn't want to draw attention to herself by making her way up the crowded aisle to them now.

At that moment, she felt her phone vibrate. Pulling it out, she saw a text from her parents. MERRY CHRISTMAS! WE LOVE YOU.

The message warmed her as she typed back, LOVE YOU TOO. ABOUT TO ENJOY MY FIRST MIDNIGHT CHRISTMAS EVE SERVICE AS A RESIDENT OF WHITE CHURCH BAY. MERRY CHRISTMAS! Then she powered off her phone and tucked it away.

Polly and Van, hands intertwined, stopped at the end of the pew, their cheeks pink from the cold. Polly, eyes sparkling, leaned in and asked, "Is this seat taken?"

Harriet grinned. "Yes, it's reserved for my best friend. That's you, by the way."

"Oh, lovely." She slid in next to Harriet and Van next to her. "Van told me everything. I can't believe it, and I'm so glad you're okay. And where did you get that gorgeous necklace?"

Feeling the heat creeping into her cheeks, Harriet said, "It was a Christmas present."

"From Will?" Polly guessed.

She nodded, knowing her face must be bright red.

Polly gave her a mischievous grin. "Obviously we have a lot to catch up on. Like Will upstaging my gift. I was thinking about giving you a camel pendant." Then her face grew serious. "I'm so glad you're safe."

"Me too, Polly," Harriet replied, gazing around the sanctuary with renewed appreciation. "Me too."

Conversation ceased as Will, resplendent in his clerical garments even with a black eye, took his place before the altar. "Good evening, my friends. As I'm sure you've all heard, we were all saddened by a theft a few weeks ago. However, thanks to the tireless efforts of those in our community, I'm happy to report that loss has now been rectified. In light of this, I thought we'd do things slightly out of order this evening, so that we all have more time to appreciate what we have."

He leaned down and opened the old wooden box that had held the star since Letty had found it on the moor in the hidden burrow. He carefully scooped the star from its resting place and held it aloft, where its surfaces caught and reflected the light from every candle.

The congregation gasped. Then a cacophony of joyful noise broke out as they cheered and applauded. Harriet applauded with them, understanding the true value of the star to this little church in Yorkshire. Everything she'd gone through—every false lead and dead end, every ounce of discouragement and fear, every moment tormented by Daniel—had been worth it to get the star back to the people who cherished it so.

The organ launched into "Brightest and Best," the hymn played every year for the star ceremony, and it seemed to Harriet that the congregation sang with extra fervor.

Brightest and best of the sons of the morning,
Dawn on our darkness and lend us thine aid.
Star of the East, the horizon adorning,
Guide where our infant Redeemer is laid.

As Will reverently placed the silver star at the top of the Christmas tree, a tear trickled down Harriet's cheek. The star gleamed, reflecting the candlelight, and casting its own soft glow across the church.

"For you, Great-Grandma Letty," Harriet whispered.

As if he'd heard her somehow, Will scanned the crowd and found her. Their eyes met, and she felt a surge of gratitude for their enduring friendship and the promise of something more. In that magical moment, Harriet realized that she wasn't homesick anymore. After all, home wasn't a place. It was where her heart had found true peace, and she certainly had that in White Church Bay.

CHAPTER THIRTY-TWO

White Church Bay
January 1954

The pot of stew simmered quietly on the stove as the back door's familiar creak announced Cecil's return from the barn. He stepped into the warmth of the kitchen, a fragile bundle of wool nestled against his chest.

"I found this little one out there all by himself," he told Letty. The lamb in his arms was a pitiful sight, damp and bedraggled, its eyes large and uncomprehending. "I think his mother rejected him. He's very cold."

Letty's heart clenched at the silent plea in the lamb's eyes. She set a jar of chutney on the table and crossed the room. "Poor little thing," she said softly.

Their six-year-old son, Harold, trotted into the room as Letty laid a soft blanket near the woodstove. "What's that, Dad?"

"It's a lamb, Harold," Cecil said. "Careful." He gently lowered the lamb onto the blanket. "He's the newest member of our little flock, but he's had a rough start."

Harold crouched near the lamb, murmuring to it. The boy might only be six, but it was clear to Letty that he was destined to follow in his father's footsteps. There was nothing Harold loved more than animals, and he soaked up Cecil's lessons about them like a sponge. He had a natural aptitude for them and their care.

After the war, Cecil had shed his military uniform in favor of his vet's scrubs and white lab coat. He and Letty now kept a few lambs and chickens on their dear Cobble Hill Farm at the edge of White Church Bay. Their veterinary clinic was thriving, and Letty's parents were within easy visiting distance.

Letty had been as surprised as anyone else when she'd become a mum in her late thirties at long last. Harold—born August 14, 1948, during the London Olympics—quickly became the center of their world, named after Cecil's father.

Now Harold asked, "What happened, Dad? Where's his mum?"

"Well, his mum couldn't care for him. It happens sometimes."

"Why?" Harold's brow furrowed as he gently stroked the lamb's wool.

"Sometimes the ewe will be too stressed or confused, or she might think there's something wrong with the lamb."

"That's sad. What should we do?" Harold's large, solemn eyes—eyes that reminded Letty so much of her beloved Albie—fixed on the lamb.

"Well, what do you think we should do?" Cecil asked him.

Harold considered for a moment. "Could we have another ewe adopt him?"

"That's a very good idea," Cecil said. "Unfortunately, we don't have any other ewes who can take him right now, because none of our other lambs have been born yet this year. Even if another ewe accepted him, she wouldn't be able to feed him. What else?"

Harold's expression became resolute. "Then I'll take care of him. We'll get him warm, and I'll bottle-feed him." Uncertainty crept into his tone. "But I've never done it before. What if I do it wrong and make him sick?"

Cecil smiled, laying a hand on Harold's shoulder. "We'll do it together, okay? He'll need all our help to get strong and healthy."

Harold's face lit up with determination. "I'll do it, Dad. I'll take care of him."

"That's my boy."

Together, they made a cozy nest beside the stove, the lamb's new sanctuary from the cold.

Letty guided Harold's small, eager hands, showing him how to mix the formula and feed their new charge. Letty couldn't help but feel this was a moment of significance, a shared duty that brought them closer, the quiet scene punctuated by Harold's soothing words to the lamb, who seemed to relax under his ministrations.

Later, Letty stepped outside for firewood and stood alone for a moment in the quiet of the Yorkshire evening, enjoying the cool air against her skin. The stars shone bright against the night sky. She looked up and spotted the blinking lights of a small plane. She listened to its rumble. It sounded like a Spitfire. There were a lot of small planes left over after the war, and she occasionally saw them in the skies. They seemed to Letty to be like old friends, almost waving as they flew by.

For a moment, she was back in the cockpit, the thrill of flight coursing through her veins. But the sound and the lights faded, and she was returned to the present, to the reality of her life on the ground. Occasionally, she still missed flying, but it was a pleasant ache. Someday, she would find her way back up there. But for now, she had important work to do right here, helping her son grow up to see the world as a place full of goodness and possibilities.

As she gazed up at the endless sky, Letty felt a deep sense of peace with where she was in life. The skies would be there when she was ready to return. Until then, she enjoyed a different kind of adventure—one of love and family. Together, she, Cecil, and little Harold would explore the vast horizons of life on the ground, just as she had once explored the skies.

And every Christmas Eve, she watched the pastor of White Church place Albie's silver star on top of the church's grand tree and she smiled a secret smile. As long as that star was part of White Church Bay, she and her beloved brother would be too.

FROM THE AUTHOR

Dear Reader,

As you turn these pages and immerse yourself in the world of Cobble Hill Farm, I want to share with you the spark of inspiration that I had for this story. At the heart of Harriet's adventures in this close-knit village lies a verse that has profoundly moved me: "In Him was life, and that life was the light of all mankind. The light shines in the darkness, and the darkness has not overcome it."

This verse served as a beacon as I wove this tale of Cobble Hill Farm, guiding me through the narrative like a lighthouse in a stormy sea. It reminded me that even in moments of uncertainty and challenge, there is a light that never dims—a light of hope, resilience, and unyielding spirit.

Writing this story was a journey of discovery, not just for the characters, but for myself as well. Harriet, with her unwavering dedication to animals and the community, taught me the importance of compassion and the impact one person can make. Will, with his quiet strength and wisdom, reminded me that leadership is not about wielding power, but about guiding others with humility and grace.

The mysteries at Cobble Hill Farm are always met with the light of community, friendship, and love. This, I believe, is the essence of the verse that inspired me—the acknowledgment that though we may face darkness, the light within us and among us prevails.

May this tale of Cobble Hill Farm remind you that even in the smallest acts of kindness, in the warmth of community, and in the courage to face the unknown, there lies a brilliant light capable of illuminating the darkest of nights.

Thank you for joining me in this adventure. I hope that you found inspiration, joy, and perhaps a bit of that enduring light within these pages.

With warmest regards,
Reverend Jane Willan

ABOUT THE AUTHOR

Reverend Jane Willan writes contemporary women's fiction, mystery novels, church newsletters, and a weekly sermon.

Jane loves to set her novels amid church life. She believes that ecclesiology, liturgy, and church lady drama make for twisty plots and quirky characters. When not working at the church or creating new adventures for her characters, Jane relaxes at her favorite local bookstore, enjoying coffee and a variety of carbohydrates with frosting. Otherwise, you might catch her binge-watching a streaming series or hiking through the Connecticut woods with her husband and rescue dog, Ollie.

Jane earned a Bachelor of Arts degree from Hiram College, majoring in Religion and History, a Master of Science degree from Boston University, and a Master of Divinity from Vanderbilt University.

TRUTH BEHIND THE FICTION

During World War II, the Air Transport Auxiliary, or ATA, emerged as a cornerstone in Britain's war machinery, tasked with the pivotal role of ferrying military aircraft from factories to airbases across the United Kingdom. This critical mission ensured that combat pilots were reserved for frontline engagements, maximizing the effectiveness of the Royal Air Force in the theater of war. Among the ranks of these heroes, a remarkable chapter unfolded that would redefine the boundaries of gender roles in wartime Britain—the integration of female pilots, affectionately dubbed "Attagirls."

The inclusion of women in the ATA was a radical departure from the conventional norms of the era. In a time when societal expectations largely confined women to the domestic sphere, the Attagirls shattered archaic limitations, taking to the skies to pilot an array of military aircraft. These women, drawn from all walks of life, embodied the spirit of progress and inclusivity. They were homemakers, shop assistants, factory workers, farmers, and city dwellers—each stepping into the cockpit with a shared purpose. Their backgrounds were as varied as their personalities, but they were united by a common endeavor: to serve their country in its hour of need.

The ATA's female pilots were tasked with navigating some of the most formidable aircraft of the time, including fighters and bombers, without the formal military training afforded to their male counterparts. This not only demonstrated their exceptional skill and determination, but also challenged the prevailing gender stereotypes that questioned women's capabilities in such demanding roles.

Beyond the mere transportation of aircraft, the ATA's responsibilities encompassed the delivery of critical parts and personnel, underscoring their indispensable role in maintaining the operational tempo of the Royal Air Force. Their contributions extended far beyond the physical relocation of machinery. They were a vital artery in the body of Britain's war effort, ensuring the continuous flow of resources essential for military operations.

The legacy of the ATA, particularly the pioneering women who soared through its ranks, is a testament to courage, change, and the dismantling of gender barriers. The war necessitated a reevaluation of women's roles in society and the workplace, propelling a movement toward greater equality and recognition of women's capabilities. The Attagirls not only contributed to the wartime victories but also paved the runway for future generations of women in aviation, the military, and beyond.

YORKSHIRE YUMMIES

Harriet's Holiday Cranberry Pie

Ingredients:

For the Crust:

2 cups all-purpose flour
1 teaspoon salt
⅔ cup shortening or butter
4–6 tablespoons ice water

For the Filling:

4 cups fresh cranberries
1 cup white sugar
1 tablespoon all-purpose flour
1 teaspoon grated orange zest (optional)
¼ cup orange juice

Directions:

Prepare the Crust:

Mix flour and salt in large bowl. Cut in shortening or butter until mixture resembles coarse crumbs.

Gradually add ice water, mixing until dough comes together. Divide into two portions, wrap in plastic, and chill for at least 30 minutes.

Prepare the Filling:

Combine cranberries, sugar, flour, orange zest, and orange juice in large bowl.

Bake the Pie:

Preheat oven to 375°F.

Roll out one portion of chilled dough and line 9-inch pie pan.

Pour cranberry filling into crust. Do not make a top for the pie. The cranberries are very festive, and you don't want to cover them up!

Bake in preheated oven for 45 to 50 minutes or until filling is bubbly.

If crust edges start to brown too quickly, cover them with foil.

Allow pie to cool before serving. This gives filling time to set.

Read on for a sneak peek of another exciting book in the Mysteries of Cobble Hill Farm *series!*

On the Right Track

BY SHAEN LAYLE

Harriet Bailey's day—a blustery Monday in January—took an unusual turn toward late afternoon.

"So, do you know what's wrong?" Teenage Oliver Hawthorne wrung his hands as he stood across from Harriet in an exam room. She normally didn't work at Cobble Hill Farm, the veterinary clinic she'd inherited from her grandfather, this late in the day, but she had heard the panic in the teen's voice when he'd asked for an emergency appointment. She could never refuse someone in distress over an animal.

Poor Oliver. One day into his first job pet-sitting, calamity had already found him.

Harriet placed a steadying hand on Signe Larsson's rabbit, Lilla. Then she back-combed Lilla's soft fur with her other hand so she could see the skin underneath. Nothing seemed amiss. She lifted Lilla's upper lip to see her teeth.

Harriet's thoughtful humming did nothing to soothe the worry on Oliver's face.

"What?" he asked. "What's wrong with her?"

"I'm not sure yet, to be honest."

Lilla was a juvenile English Angora rabbit, a breed known for their fluffy coats and bent ears. Lilla's vitals were normal, and she didn't show signs of infection, but her fur had scattered patches of slate-blue color. Most of it was in her undercoat, but that wasn't the only affected area. Harriet's original instinct had been to check for a bacterial skin condition called *Pseudomonas aeruginosa*, or "blue fur disease." It was frequently caused by damp bedding or excess weight, but Lilla didn't seem to suffer from either.

She addressed Oliver. "You're sure Lilla didn't get into anything?" Perhaps the rabbit had been lying on something, like a blanket, which caused dye transfer.

"No, I don't think so."

"She's been eating normally? No new foods?"

Oliver shook his head. "All I gave her was the food Mrs. Larsson left for her. Fresh vegetables and timothy hay. Plenty of fresh water."

Harriet ran through possible scenarios but couldn't latch onto any definitive cause for Lilla's blue fur. "And she's been acting all right otherwise? No unusual behavior?"

"No, she's totally fine. No issues other than turning blue."

Harriet lifted Lilla from the examination table and cradled her in her arms. Then she directed Oliver to the clinic lobby where Lilla's carrier waited. Harriet secured the rabbit in the crate before addressing Oliver again. "She appears healthy. I don't see cause for concern, but I'd like to keep her for observation overnight. I'm also going to give her a dose of antibiotics in case we're dealing with a bacterial infection. You can come pick her up tomorrow, providing she isn't showing signs of any complications."

At this, Oliver's face finally relaxed. "Aye, right then."

Harriet supposed he was relieved to have Lilla's welfare shifted onto someone else's shoulders for an evening. She didn't blame him. She was well-acquainted with Lilla's owner and knew for a fact that Signe would be none too pleased if something happened to her pet while she was off celebrating her wedding anniversary with her husband in Denmark. Signe's perfectionism made her the perfect owner for Lilla, as Angora rabbits required lots of specialized care and attention, but that also put extra stress on anyone who was in charge of Lilla in Signe's absence.

Harriet led Oliver across the room to the front desk, where her assistant, Polly Thatcher, waited. "You can finish up with Polly while I get Lilla settled. Then you can run back home and fetch some of her food. I don't want to alter her diet in case it would cause additional problems. Rabbits can be delicate, and Angoras even more so."

"I can manage that."

"Great. Thanks for coming in today, Oliver." Harriet patted the teen's shoulder as she passed him with the carrier. "And don't worry. Lilla is in good hands."

"Ta, Doc."

Harriet had picked up enough of the Yorkshire dialect by now to know Oliver was thanking her. "You're welcome. Be sure to tell Polly you'll be in tomorrow to fetch Lilla."

Harriet returned to the exam room and administered an antibiotic to Lilla. Then she transported her to the clinic's boarding and recovery area, where she transitioned her from her carrier to a larger crate.

Just as Harriet was wrapping up Lilla's file in her office, Polly peeked around the doorframe. "Call for you up front. It's your aunt."

"Oops. I haven't checked my cell phone lately."

Harriet's aunt Jinny lived close by in the property's adjacent dower cottage, where she also ran a medical clinic. She probably wanted to ask why Harriet was running late for tea. Tea was a tradition that Harriet enjoyed, but sometimes she had trouble setting work aside for it, especially on busy days like today.

Harriet hurried to the reception area and picked up the landline. "I'm so sorry I'm late, Aunt Jinny, but—"

"Hi, Harriet! It's me! I'm in England!" The voice on the other end of the line was friendly and familiar. But it wasn't Aunt Jinny.

Harriet gasped. "Ashley?"

Ashley Fiske had been one of Harriet's good friends in Connecticut, but they had fallen out of touch since Harriet's move to White Church Bay in Yorkshire, England. Other than a few scattered emails and text messages, Harriet's normally talkative friend had gone radio silent when Harriet had crossed the Atlantic.

"Bingo!" Ashley sounded triumphant. "Did I surprise you?"

"You certainly did. What are you doing in England?"

Ashley's cheerful tone sobered. "Oh, we needed to get away for a while. I had some flight miles saved up through work and figured we might as well use them. We're never promised tomorrow." Ashley worked in hospitality for a large hotel chain in Connecticut, a job that was a perfect match for her outgoing personality.

"We?" Harriet echoed. "Is Trevor with you?"

Trevor was Ashley's son. A pang shot through Harriet as she thought of the turmoil the boy must have been through in the last year. He had lost his father the previous spring. Jon's sudden passing due to a car accident still seemed surreal. Ashley hadn't even messaged Harriet about it. Harriet's parents had been the ones to break the news to her, and when Harriet tried to contact Ashley with her condolences, she had been met with an answering machine. It was as if their years of friendship dissolved overnight. Or maybe they'd never been as close as Harriet had thought.

Ashley's reply brought Harriet back to the present. "Yes, Trev is with me."

"Oh, wow. That's a big trip for a ten-year-old," Harriet said. "How's Trevor doing? And you?"

If Harriet thought a nicely timed pleasantry was going to get her friend to open up, though, she was wrong. Ashley neatly skirted the question and kept the conversation shallow. "We're doing great. Trev's grown a foot since you saw him last. What time do you get done with work?"

Maybe it would take some time for Ashley and Harriet to find solid footing in their friendship again. Harriet could be patient.

"Just finished a walk-in appointment, and I'm wrapping up for the day right now." Harriet covered the mouthpiece of the phone with one hand as she spied Polly putting on her coat.

"I've clapped Charlie and Maxwell in the cupboard. Need anything else?" Polly asked.

"In the cupboard?" Harriet was perplexed.

"Sorry, I mean they're secured for the night."

Harriet smiled. Another regionalism to add to her ever-growing list. It sounded like the clinic dog and cat were safely shut up in Harriet's house, which was conveniently connected to the clinic. She told Polly thanks and waved her out the door. Then she returned her attention to Ashley. "Where are you staying?"

"The Windmill Inn in Whitby."

Harriet knew the place. It was a charmingly rustic B and B a short distance from White Church Bay. Ashley and Trevor would no doubt be comfortable there.

Harriet had another idea though. "Why don't you stay with me? If you're able to cancel your reservations, that is."

"Oh, I don't know. I don't want to intrude."

She wouldn't be intruding. Though Harriet had family in White Church Bay, and she'd made friends since her move from the States, January created in her a particular brand of loneliness. With the hustle and bustle of Christmas packed away and the moors thrust into gray gloom, Harriet found herself longing for the welcome familiarity of Connecticut. There were plenty of gray days in Connecticut as well, but her parents were there. She could visit well-known restaurants and stores with a quick drive on the *right* side of the road. So many memories were woven into the tapestry of the place where she was raised.

Here, she still felt out of place on occasion. Moving to England had been wonderful in so many ways, but in quiet moments, she wondered if she'd made the right choice in uprooting her life.

Ashley was a welcome reminder of home. Besides, if she stayed with Harriet, they might be able to figure out where their friendship had gone wrong and mend the broken pieces together.

"Trust me," Harriet said, "you're not intruding at all, Ash. I'd love for you to stay with me. It would be like old times, rooming together at college."

"The reservation is fully refundable, and that does sound like fun."

Harriet didn't leave room for her to change her mind. "Good. It's settled then. I'll be at Aunt Jinny's in two shakes of a gimmer's tail."

"What?" Ashley sounded baffled.

At least someone was less acclimated than Harriet. She laughed. "It means I'll be right there."

"Oh. See you then."

Harriet hung up then pulled on her coat and braced herself against the wind as she stepped outside and locked the clinic door. It was quick work to make her way to the dower cottage.

She opened the door to her aunt's house to find a mess.

Aunt Jinny's normally cozy and tidy sitting room was cluttered with antique furniture. Her aunt was cleaning an armoire while Ashley flicked a feather duster at an old desk. Even Trevor was going through a drawer.

"Harriet, come on in. Mind your step." Aunt Jinny led Harriet through the maze of furniture to a clear space on the floor. "Sorry about the clutter. I pulled some old pieces out of a back room. New Year's cleaning and all that."

"And then Trevor and I showed up," Ashley added. "Of course, we wanted to help. When in White Church…" She shook her feather duster and sneezed.

"She's a real gem. Especially after traveling so far. She must be exhausted." Aunt Jinny squeezed an arm around Ashley's shoulders as if she'd known Harriet's friend for years.

That's Yorkshire hospitality for you, Harriet reflected with a grin.

Ashley shook her head. "I don't think the jet lag has kicked in yet. I feel like I've had a gallon of coffee."

"You're probably running on adrenaline. It'll hit you soon enough." Harriet swapped places with her aunt to hug her friend. It was so good to see a familiar face from back home. Although "home" wasn't quite the right word, because White Church Bay was starting to feel like "home" as well, with its own roster of familiar faces. Spunky Polly Thatcher. Generous Doreen Danby, who lived close by. Pastor Fitzwilliam "Will" Knight, whose serious, thoughtful gaze reminded Harriet of a hero from a Jane Austen novel.

"So, Ashley, why don't we get you set up at the house? It's a hop, skip, and a jump from here. I have some delicious gooseberry scones from my neighbor if you're hungry." Doreen was forever dropping off some baked good or other.

"Sounds good to me." Ashley picked up her feather duster again and ran it over the front of the desk. "Just let me finish up this piece before I grab our suitcases."

"Here's the drawer, Mom." Trevor picked up the empty desk drawer he had cleaned and positioned it to slide into the empty space in the desk.

But the day wasn't done yielding surprises yet.

A crunching sound could be heard as Trevor tried to push the drawer closed. "Hey, there's something in there." He pulled the drawer out again and peered into the recess.

Ashley set her feather duster down and bent to follow her son's gaze. "Oh, wow. You're right." She reached in and removed a thick stack of curled papers, which she handed to Harriet's aunt.

Harriet moved to look over Aunt Jinny's shoulder. "It's a manuscript. '*Tracking Lies: The Truth Behind the Great War's S&W Railway Crash* by Adelaide Evergreen.'"

Aunt Jinny pressed a hand to her mouth. "It can't be. There was a report on the crash?"

"What?" The significance was completely lost on Harriet, and from the blank expression on Ashley's and Trevor's faces, they felt the same way.

Aunt Jinny gently thumbed through the pages. "There was a railway crash here during World War I. I think your great-great-granduncle—his name was Rhys Bailey, and he was your great-great-grandfather Harold's younger brother—was involved in some way, but I'm not sure how. They said the accident happened because of damaged track. Loss of transportation set the war effort back a bit, and White Church Bay people were blamed. Blight of the Bay, as it were."

"And those papers tell the story of the crash?" Trevor asked, his eyes wide.

Aunt Jinny stared down at the yellowed manuscript in her hands. "Apparently, this tells the truth of it."

A NOTE FROM THE EDITORS

We hope you enjoyed another exciting volume in the Mysteries of Cobble Hill Farm series, published by Guideposts. For over seventy-five years, Guideposts, a nonprofit organization, has been driven by a vision of a world filled with hope. We aspire to be the voice of a trusted friend, a friend who makes you feel more hopeful and connected.

By making a purchase from Guideposts, you join our community in touching millions of lives, inspiring them to believe that all things are possible through faith, hope, and prayer. Your continued support allows us to provide uplifting resources to those in need. Whether through our communities, websites, apps, or publications, we inspire our audiences, bring them together, and comfort, uplift, entertain, and guide them. Visit us at guideposts.org to learn more.

We would love to hear from you. Write us at Guideposts, P.O. Box 5815, Harlan, Iowa 51593 or call us at (800) 932-2145. Did you love *The Christmas Camel Caper*? Leave a review for this product on guideposts.org/shop. Your feedback helps others in our community find relevant products.

SECRETS FROM GRANDMA'S ATTIC

Life is recorded not only in decades or years, but in events and memories that form the fabric of our being. Follow Tracy Doyle, Amy Allen, and Robin Davisson, the granddaughters of the recently deceased centenarian, Pearl Allen, as they explore the treasures found in the attic of Grandma Pearl's Victorian home, nestled near the banks of the Mississippi in Canton, Missouri. Not only do Pearl's descendants uncover a long-buried mystery at every attic exploration, they also discover their grandmother's legacy of deep, abiding faith, which has shaped and guided their family through the years. These uncovered Secrets from Grandma's Attic reveal stories of faith, redemption, and second chances that capture your heart long after you turn the last page.

History Lost and Found

The Art of Deception

Testament to a Patriot

Buttoned Up

MYSTERIES OF COBBLE HILL FARM

Pearl of Great Price

Hidden Riches

Movers and Shakers

The Eye of the Cat

Refined by Fire

The Prince and the Popper

Something Shady

Duel Threat

A Royal Tea

The Heart of a Hero

Fractured Beauty

A Shadowy Past

In Its Time

Nothing Gold Can Stay

The Cameo Clue

Veiled Intentions

Turn Back the Dial

A Marathon of Kindness

A Thief in the Night

Coming Home

SAVANNAH SECRETS

Welcome to Savannah, Georgia, a picture-perfect Southern city known for its manicured parks, moss-covered oaks, and antebellum architecture. Walk down one of the cobblestone streets, and you'll come upon Magnolia Investigations. It is here where two friends have joined forces to unravel some of Savannah's deepest secrets. Tag along as clues are exposed, red herrings discarded, and thrilling surprises revealed. Find inspiration in the special bond between Meredith Bellefontaine and Julia Foley. Cheer the friends on as they listen to their hearts and rely on their faith to solve each new case that comes their way.

The Hidden Gate
A Fallen Petal
Double Trouble
Whispering Bells
Where Time Stood Still
The Weight of Years
Willful Transgressions
Season's Meetings
Southern Fried Secrets
The Greatest of These
Patterns of Deception

MYSTERIES OF COBBLE HILL FARM

The Waving Girl

Beneath a Dragon Moon

Garden Variety Crimes

Meant for Good

A Bone to Pick

Honeybees & Legacies

True Grits

Sapphire Secret

Jingle Bell Heist

Buried Secrets

A Puzzle of Pearls

Facing the Facts

Resurrecting Trouble

Forever and a Day

Find more inspiring stories in these best-loved Guideposts fiction series!

Mysteries of Lancaster County

Follow the Classen sisters as they unravel clues and uncover hidden secrets in Mysteries of Lancaster County. As you get to know these women and their friends, you'll see how God brings each of them together for a fresh start in life.

Secrets of Wayfarers Inn

Retired schoolteachers find themselves owners of an old warehouse-turned-inn that is filled with hidden passages, buried secrets, and stunning surprises that will set them on a course to puzzling mysteries from the Underground Railroad.

Tearoom Mysteries Series

Mix one stately Victorian home, a charming lakeside town in Maine, and two adventurous cousins with a passion for tea and hospitality. Add a large scoop of intriguing mystery, and sprinkle generously with faith, family, and friends, and you have the recipe for *Tearoom Mysteries*.

Ordinary Women of the Bible

Richly imagined stories—based on facts from the Bible—have all the plot twists and suspense of a great mystery, while bringing you fascinating insights on what it was like to be a woman living in the ancient world.

To learn more about these books, visit Guideposts.org/Shop